Kill Maggie Bauer? Fine. I could do that. But he would pay for his request. He would pay, like they all did. I would leave Maggie dead with his letter on her body. That was my price. They paid with their freedom. They would never be able to forget what they had done, because no one else would forget. It would follow them all the days of their lives.

For a long time it had seemed so strange to me that they would keep coming when I incriminated them so obviously. It took me a while to realize why, exactly, they kept coming, but when I realized, it all made sense, and it made me a little proud. And a little sickened.

They all called on me because I was the best. I always got it right. And calling on me instead of someone else made them feel better about wishing for murder—there was an element of chance about it. Sometimes I killed, sometimes I didn't, and that uncertainty made people feel less responsible.

I held them captive.

KATHERINE EWELL

 KATHERINE TEGEN BOOKS
An Imprint of HarperCollins Publishers

Katherine Tegen Books is an imprint of HarperCollins Publishers.

Dear Killer
Copyright © 2014 by Katherine Ewell

Library of Congress Cataloging-in-Publication Data
Ewell, Katherine.
    Dear killer / Katherine Ewell. — First edition.
        pages   cm
    Summary: "Kit, a seventeen-year-old moral nihilist serial killer,
chooses who to kill based on anonymous letters left in a secret mailbox,
while simultaneously maintaining a close relationship with the young
detective in charge of the murder cases"—Provided by publisher.
    ISBN 978-0-06-225781-9
    [1. Serial murderers—Fiction. 2. Murder—Fiction. 3. Interpersonal
relations—Fiction. 4. Schools—Fiction. 5. Letters—Fiction. 6. London
(England)—Fiction. 7. England—Fiction.] I. Title.
PZ7.E94716De 2014   2013005072
[Fic]—dc23   CIP
                                                                   AC

Typography by Michelle Gengaro-Kokmen
15 16 17 18 19   PC/RRDH   10 9 8 7 6 5 4 3 2 1
❖
First paperback edition, 2015

For my parents,
who are nothing like the parents in this book

♦ ◊ ♦

Chapter 1

*R*ule one.

 Nothing is right, nothing is wrong.

That is the most important guideline, and the hardest one for most people to understand—but I have understood it my entire life, from the moment I laid my hands on that first victim's neck to this very moment as I think about the blood under my fingernails and the body I have so recently left behind. Nothing is right and nothing is wrong. For some people a thing may be right, and for others it may be wrong. There is no greater truth to morality—it is merely an opinion.

 I don't crave death. I've heard of serial killers who love it, who live for the moment when their victim stops breathing, who thrive on it. I am not like that. I kill as a matter of habit and as a consequence of the way I was raised. I could walk away from the killing and never look back.

But I won't walk away, not now. My faith in my way of life has been tested. I have doubted myself. But I have overcome my doubt.

My name is Kit, but most people know me as the Perfect Killer.

I kill on order. I am everyone's assassin. I belong to no one but the grim reaper herself.

◆ ◆ ◆

I checked my mail on a late-summer Sunday. School had just come back into session. It was afternoon, the cool kind of afternoon when it's too warm for a sweater and too cold for bare arms. The irritating kind of afternoon. But really, I didn't mind the weather too much. It's hard to mind something when you know you're going to get paid soon.

As I walked along the sidewalk, I imagined I was looking at myself from the outside, from the perspective of the strangers I was passing. They would see a girl of average to tall height, a girl who was teenaged, brown eyed, blond, fairly pretty but not memorable; they would see a girl dressed neatly and casually, with a pair of jeans that was wearing thin a bit at the knees, a silver Tiffany bracelet the sole indication of her family's modest wealth. They would see dark eyes under dark eyelashes, prominent collarbones, and a smattering of freckles dashed across a thin nose like Audrey Hepburn's, the only truly beautiful feature of a small pale face—would they see a seventeen-year-old murderer?

No. They wouldn't. No one would.

I didn't chv death, but I did love my secrecy. It made me feel like a superhero, sort of. A double life. One life average and easily passed over, the other famous. And I *was* famous. I was London's most famous killer since Jack the Ripper, had been for years, and I loved it.

I was suddenly called back into memory. Eight years before, when I was nine. I remembered it well, remembered his staring marble eyes and the bruises I left on his neck—

Before me, the mailbox had belonged to my mother. She had been the one to begin things. In her day, she hadn't been like me. She had longed for murder, needed it somehow, seen a dire need for her unique morality in the world, felt bloodlust. Murder had always been more of a job to me than a calling. But of course, like me, she wasn't stupid. She was sensible enough to not allow herself to be caught.

Eventually things had gotten too unsteady, she told me through offhand comments and casual snippets—she had gotten too close to being identified. She was never really suspected by anyone, though. Every time she told the story, she made a point of telling me that much; she had gotten close to being suspected, but not too close. She had stopped to keep herself safe.

She had settled down, started a family. Married a man who had been carefully chosen to be ignorant, busy, and emotionally distant. Carefully chosen, so he wouldn't realize what she was and what I would become. Because even after she stopped killing, even after the end, the longing for murder still itched at her—she still needed death, needed to know that someone was carrying out her work. So she trained me. She made me a murderer in her place; she lived through me. I have carried on her legacy.

In time, her mailbox became mine. When I was nine, we began to manage it together, and when I was twelve, she let me have it all for my own. I only killed four between the ages of nine and twelve, but when I took absolute possession of the mailbox, I set a quicker pace—about ten a year. Sometimes there were more, sometimes less, sometimes a few in the span of a few weeks and sometimes no kills for months—but that was my general guideline.

And like my mother, I found my trademark. She drew hearts in Sharpie on her victims' chests, though she was a much less prolific murderer than me. She had never achieved my fame. The Perfect Killer—there's not a person in London who doesn't know and fear that name nowadays.

And what a name, too! The media, who coined it, do love their sensationalism. I can't say that I dislike it, or that it's inaccurate. As far as monikers go, I think I've done pretty well for myself.

I'm not alone in my talent, though. I saw a picture of a murder of my mother's once, and even though she was never famous, I had to admire her prowess, her precision. The murder was exquisite. The picture I had seen had been of a young female, neck broken perfectly against the corner of a table, splayed out halfway on the floor, halfway on a chair, her shirt torn open and a cartoonish heart drawn neatly in black on her skin. My mother had pushed the pen down so hard that the skin was bruised blue and green around it.

It surprised me to know that she had once been so powerful.

My own trademark was probably the main reason for my fame. I left my mail behind.

I walked down King's Road, pretending to admire clothing in windows and ponder going into small cafés I passed without actually considering going in. I made my way slowly and calmly toward my destination, not drawing attention, blending into the scenery like a chameleon. I was invisible. No one would notice me.

I stopped and gazed through the window of a friendly-looking café called the Brass Feather. It was new. The building, of course, had been there for a long, long time, longer than most people knew, but the café had only recently come into business, after the one that had been there before went out of business. The new owners had totally redone the decor. But they had left the bathroom alone.

That was tradition—and superstition.

No matter how many times the shop was sold and bought, the women's bathroom stayed the same. The same and incredibly secret. Strangely few people knew about it, considering the fact that I was so famous. Not even the police knew about it. Or at least I assumed so, since they hadn't taken control of or searched it yet. And that was what the police *did* for these sorts of things. They were very crude in their customs.

I smiled and walked inside. The walls, painted in a pale brown color like sandy dirt, felt warm and comfortable. My boots clicked against the wooden floor. It was all very pleasant. People talked at nearby tables, chattering and laughing, or read the newspaper, or texted or talked or played games on their phones. Bland, generic music came quietly through the speakers. But a small note, written on printer paper, was hung in the back of the room, next to the bathroom door, looking out of place, reminding everyone always of the darkness that resided here. I knew what it said. I had been here before. I liked that note. It reminded people of the superstition surrounding the shop, in case they forgot. The dark superstition—the superstition that wasn't entirely false. Or even remotely false, really.

I headed for the counter, running my eyes over the selection of pastries in the glass case in front of me. The bored-looking teenage boy behind the counter stared at me insipidly as I considered, his green eyes flat and uninterested.

"What do you want?" he asked, as if I were insulting him personally in some way.

I ordered Earl Grey tea and carrot cake, and he gave them to me.

"Eleven sixty," he said. I handed the money over, he

gave me change, and I headed toward a table in the middle of the room. I sat down and started at my cake cheerfully, biding my time. I would check my mail after I was done, and then I would leave.

I watched the people entering and exiting the bathroom carefully, marking their entrances and exits in my mind, smelling the scent of sugar and coffee in the air; the smells were pleasant together, even though I had never much been one for coffee.

I would have to be the only one in the bathroom in order to do my work. I ate slowly, carefully, innocently. My senses were sharp. I waited. I would have to be clever about it.

I took a sip of my tea and realized I was done with it. My cake, too, was nearly gone. The woman who had been in the bathroom came out, dark hair swishing; it was empty now. Now was as good a time as any. I swallowed the rest of my cake, tasting the strange sweetness of carrots and cream cheese, and stood, strolling toward the bathroom, glancing at the sign next to the door as I came closer and could read it.

REQUESTS TAKEN INSIDE, it read in sharp, insistent letters with angles like blades. Not my own words. Someone else, a believer, had written that, but I appreciated it. Beneath the words was a sketch of a postcard, with scribbles where the writing should be. A generic postcard. As if anyone could fill in the blanks where the scribbles were and file their own request.

Well, that *was* generally how it worked.

I didn't have the time to grant them all, of course. I had school. And if I killed too often, I would inevitably call too much attention to myself. I was famous in London, but I didn't want to be a worldwide criminal—that would mean too many people on my tail, and too much danger, even for me. But I tried to fulfill as many requests as I could. My clients repaid me with money and with secrecy. None who had their requests filled, even those tracked down and interrogated by the police, ever confessed the location of my mailbox. The mailbox set a strange spell of silence over them. The police didn't know of that secret place, and I was glad of it.

As I had predicted, the bathroom was empty. The yellowed white tiles on the walls that cracked like spiderwebs at the edges, the ones that hadn't been changed since the forties, were covered in graffiti. Outside, in the restaurant, they might be able to mostly deny the legend that lived in their shop, but in the bathroom there were no secrets. I traced my fingers across the graffiti on the walls, satisfied, trailing them along the curls of the *G*s and the straightness of the *T*s.

"The devil lives here," one read. "Thank God for angels," read another. "He saved me." That irritated me a bit—everyone automatically assumed I was a man. This was the *women's* bathroom, wasn't it? "My wish was granted." "The killer didn't listen." "This place is a joke, nothing but a stupid urban legend." "Don't tell." "Death will come to the unworthy."

I slipped into the third stall and locked the door behind me. The large tile above the toilet was loose, like it always had been.

I didn't have to use gloves to check my mail, really, because there were so many fingerprints on the tiles that individual fingerprints were hard to identify, but I put them on anyway, the latex making my hands feel sticky. I pried the tile out of the wall and set it down across the toilet seat. I stared into the small compartment behind the tile that had been built into the wall so many years ago, and smiled.

I checked my mail only about once every two months. Since I had last come, a lot of people had made requests. Letters nearly filled the mailbox, at least thirty of them. They were stacked on top of one another, money paper-clipped to some and inside the envelopes of others. My fee. I opened my bag and, trying to be quiet, picked up a handful of letters and slid them inside, sandwiched between my wallet and a notebook. Then another handful, the paper rustling between my fingers with a sound like bird wings.

I heard the sound of clicking heels outside the bathroom door, moving toward me. I cursed under my breath and moved faster, trying not to drop any of my letters. Even though the door was locked, the sound of paper would be easily heard. I put handful after handful into my bag, tense and quiet, biting my lip hard until I almost drew blood and lightened my bite. The heels clicked into the bathroom.

I flushed the toilet to conceal the noise and stuffed the

last few letters into my bag, zipping it shut, wedged the tile back into place, and exited the stall as I slipped off my latex gloves and stuffed them neatly into my jeans pocket. I dipped my hands under a faucet, just for show, the coldness of the water surprising me. I left the bathroom quickly. That was too close. Of course, there was nothing I could have done about it. But it was too damn close. At least I had gotten away. I had good luck, I supposed. Always had. I walked through the café and toward the street, forcing myself to act casual. The boy at the counter looked at me vaguely.

After a few moments of walking down King's Road toward home, I relaxed. In the end, nothing had happened. I had my letters and my money, and no one had seen me. Like always. Things were always the same, and always would be.

I would read my letters tonight.

Chapter 2

The sun set over London. The glowing ball sank below the horizon in a stately and mature fashion, sending spangles of blazing red light through the streets. As the city descended into darkness, it called out to me. Wandering my way home, I watched the sunset with one eye.

I remembered my first kill in vivid detail. It was the sort of memory that came up sometimes and could not be ignored or thought about halfheartedly. It had occurred to me a few minutes ago and still occupied my mind, sticking to me like a burr.

I remembered my mother's shadow standing over me, watching me, teaching me and guiding me. I remembered that I had been only nine years old. I remembered the dead man—almost a boy—on the ground before me, the one she had to help me with because I wasn't quite strong enough to squeeze all the air out of his throat. It had been in an apartment, late in the afternoon. I remembered he had a red armchair and a small dog that we locked in the kitchen, and I remembered he had been cooking before we came so the whole apartment had smelled of oregano. And I remembered that I had asked my mother if we should use knives instead of hands because I wasn't strong enough, and she had shouted at me for that, because no, of course, knives were evidence and we couldn't leave any evidence, could we? Evidence was for amateurs. So we killed him with our bare hands, or rather *I* killed him, because even though she had to help me near the end, she made sure to let go just before the last bit of life drained out of his blue, blue eyes. That first time I didn't leave a letter, I just killed the man and left the apartment calmly, anticlimactically, without any sense of closure. I wasn't decided on my trademark then. I hadn't even *thought* of leaving the letters at that point. That thought would come a few days after, in a burst of morbid inspiration.

It had been an afternoon a bit like this one. Only the red sunset hadn't been quite as brilliant then. It seemed strange to me, remembering, how horribly I had hated it. Death. Death was natural. I had cried for that boy. God, I had been so young then.

◆ ◇ ◆

"Welcome home, sweetheart," my mom said, leaning her head out of the kitchen to watch me as I walked through the four-story town house's shiny black front door. Her blue eyes, the eyes I had not inherited, sparkled beneath long blond lashes; her hair, which I envied because my hair didn't dry the same way when it was cut as short as hers, bounced stylishly. She had a chin that looked like it had been cut out of marble. She fit with the house, somehow, our house of white bricks decorated with silver flower boxes and black shutters—they felt the same. Cool. Posh. Luxurious.

"Hi, Mom."

"Did you have a good time while you were out?"

"I went to check the mail," I said in reply. She laughed and put her head back in the kitchen, beckoning to me. I followed her into the neatly groomed room. It was decorated in civilized, carefully calculated, quietly expensive neutrals like the rest of the tall house, but right now was filled with steam and smoke that lent it an almost comically mysterious air. She was working over a pan on the stove, and the whole room smelled like food. The recessed lighting lit everything in a muted glow.

"So? Any interesting requests?" she asked, glancing back at me after a moment.

"I haven't read them yet," I reminded her. She knew that. Rule one was seeing no wrong and no right. Rule two was to be careful. And reading the letters at the mailbox was not being careful.

"Oh, that's right." She smiled, as if she didn't know, that familiar infuriating look of almost apathy settling on her features. "You should take them up to your room, then. I'm nearly done with dinner."

She stuck a spoon in the pan and moved it about. For a moment neither of us said anything. I saw her left hand twitching. I could see it there—her longing for cruel power, stuffed beneath a surface of cool glass, shoved away because she no longer had any use for it. Beneath her indifference something dangerous languished.

"All right." I paused. "Dad's not home?"

"No, of course not," she said without any unhappiness in her voice, or at least none that I could hear. I shrugged. I wasn't surprised.

"I'll be right back down, then."

I went out of the kitchen and up the three flights of stairs toward my room. The stairs were steep—usually, when I climbed stairs, I skipped steps and went quickly, but in my own home, I couldn't do that. It always took me a while to reach the top, and it was never quite as easy as I felt it should be after seven years of doing the same thing.

So I went up slowly. Like always, I looked around at the photographs on the walls as I rose through the house. We had a nice photography collection—my mother liked collections. So we had a collection of fine china, a collection of old records, a collection of photographs, and collections of a dozen other kinds of things. I liked the photographs best. They were expensive, naturally, and most of them quite old. A picture of the blurry sun over New York. A picture of cracking ice. A picture of a violinist with his eyes closed, enraptured. All of them were lined up neatly alongside the staircase, in perfect black frames, matted with white paper. They demanded attention, contrasted as they were with the pale tan uninspiring walls.

My room was the one farthest away from the front door.

I wasn't quite sure why I had chosen it when we had moved into the house seven years ago; climbing so many stairs so often was simply a pain, but what was done was done, and I wasn't about to move at this point. My mother had allowed me to decorate it however I wanted to, and it was too perfectly done for me to leave it now.

I walked in and closed the door behind me. It was the only room in the house not decorated in brown, tan, navy, white, gray, or black. It was decorated in cream and scarlet, with rich fabrics and an antique sort of elegance—thick, heavy curtains, crushed-velvet pillows like old paper, a towering four-poster bed with carvings that looked oddly like Monet's irises, heavy floral potpourri in a glass dish on top of my dresser. Everything was neat, in its place. I liked to keep things neat.

"Your room is like an old lady room," my mother had said to me once, sighing about the disparity between my room's decoration and the decoration in the rest of the house. I couldn't really deny it.

Somewhere, a dog barked.

I set the bag of letters down next to my bed and took the latex gloves out of my pocket. I wrapped them in a piece of printer paper, crumpled the paper to look like a discarded piece of scrap, and dropped the ball into the wastebasket next to my desk. I didn't need any curious eyes wondering why I had gloves in my wastebasket. We had maids who came three times a week to clean, because God forbid my mother should do any cleaning. She had her hands full with cooking, and that was about the extent of her domestic duties. The maids helped, and my mother was thankful for the fact that she never had to clean anything, but to be honest, their presence made me nervous. Of course I hid my unused letters—I never threw away a single letter; it felt inconsiderate, somehow—and other things as well, beneath false bottoms of drawers and in other such secret hiding places, but it wasn't much comfort. I wondered if the maids would be nervous too if they knew they were cleaning the house of murderers.

I waltzed back downstairs and found my mom in the dining room, laying out three place settings at the table, forks and knives and spoons positioned precisely on blue placemats. I looked at her curiously.

"I thought you said Dad wasn't home."

"He's not. Sorry, I've forgotten to tell you—we have company. What you're wearing is fine, so don't worry about changing."

"Company?" I asked, grinning. "What kind of company?"

Whenever my mom had company, it was interesting. Sometimes she had affairs her husband was too detached to notice, and invited the men in question over for dinner;

sometimes the people she invited were important people she felt would be advantageous to have as friends, and sometimes they were just interesting people she had met and taken a liking to.

She had a skill for making friends, and she spent much of her time doing just that. Aided by her businessman husband's earnings and nearly constant absence, she had gone into the business of entertaining and being entertained. Endless parties, elaborate adventures. Jaunts to Rome, Vienna, even New York on occasion. She often showed up in the front hallway in the mornings, a bag packed, about to run off on another adventure without warning. My father didn't know much about it, or at least didn't care enough to mention any of it, and I didn't resent it—she did what she had to in order to remain sane. She was no longer the woman she had once been; she couldn't be. I understood that. She moved to avoid the uncomfortable stillness that her lack of murder created.

She was perpetually surrounded by activity.

Surrounded, that was, until she came home in the evenings. The moment she came through the front door and we were alone, something always seemed to just *slip* from her. The smile faded, the high heels were removed, and she hung her white jacket by the door, entering into a place where she no longer needed to run wild in the same way to be content. At home, I was there. And as long as I was there, she had a piece of her justice to hold on to. Knowing that I killed in her way, I believed, was enough for her—she felt freedom through me. She was quietest and happiest at home, when we kept each other company.

Sometimes I got the fleeting feeling that it wasn't *quite* enough, though, that she was screaming silently from underneath her skin. But most of the time she was fine, when we were together and at peace.

But of course, company was nice too. It was variety. Something different. We enjoyed each other's company, but even we could get bored.

As I watched her set the table, I thought, not for the first time, about the fact that she had a sort of *pull* that I lacked. I wish I had it. She drew people in, made them trust her. If she hadn't been a murderer in her day, she would have made a good politician. As it stood, she had too many secrets that could be unearthed.

"He's a young policeman, very accomplished, well regarded at Scotland Yard," she said with a smile. I looked at her, even more confused than before.

"You're inviting the *police* to our *house*?"

"Don't sound so stunned. He's a nice man. He's—he's the man unofficially in charge of the Perfect Killer case."

I gaped.

"And you've just invited him over?"

"I went to a cocktail party the other day, since your dad couldn't make it. Went in his place, you know. He was there. We got to talking, and I figured that we should have him over for dinner."

"Are you sure that's a good idea?"

She looked up from the table and met my eyes pointedly. "Keep your friends close and your enemies closer, Kit." Such a cliché.

The doorbell rang, chiming like a music box.

"And that's him!" my mom exclaimed happily. "I'll get the door, you wait here. Actually, you can start serving the food. It's in the warmer. Relax, Kit. It'll be fine."

She bombed off toward the door as I looked blankly after her. I tensed. *Relax.* That was easy for her to say. Her days as a murderer were over, and she hadn't killed as much as me or been as famous as me.

I heard the door open and then muffled voices.

And now the man who was in charge of hunting me down was in my house.

I walked quietly over to the warmer and pulled out the steak and mashed potatoes my mom had made. I picked up a set of tongs. I put a steak on each of the three plates my mom had set out, and then ladled mashed potatoes onto each. Step by step, methodical. I listened to the voices in the hallway, trying to hear what they were saying. But I couldn't. The voices grew louder, and I strained to hear them even more, but still, no luck. I walked over to the mahogany table and put the dishes down crookedly; I was distracted now and couldn't be bothered to straighten them. I turned around.

And he was walking into the kitchen.

He was young. Younger than I had expected. Much younger, in fact. He couldn't have been older than twenty-five or thirty. I remembered that my mom had said he was only unofficially in charge of the investigation. He looked like the law, through and through. Order personified.

Tallish, with light-brown hair and hazel eyes that were cold and steely and a little bit angry, if a little young. But he was smiling. And also, strangely, he had a bit of a studious feel to him, as if he were a professor or some other scholar. Not in the eyes so much, but in the cut of his jaw, and in the way he held his shoulders. His posture was remarkably graceful. He was slim and wiry, but I could see quiet strength in the way he stood—he was vaguely catlike. He was wearing gray slacks and a white-collared shirt, as if he had just come out of a meeting and had taken off his tie and jacket, and his thumbs were hooked in his pants pockets.

He was attractive. Surprisingly so.

Not that it particularly mattered, I reminded myself. He was the enemy.

I felt uncomfortable. Not afraid, exactly, because I knew he wouldn't suspect me, but definitely very uncomfortable. As if I were standing beneath an air vent that was too cold or too hot. He and my mom stopped near the doorway to the kitchen.

I forced myself to smile pleasantly, trying to make myself look a little dull around the edges. No one suspected stupid people.

"Alex, this is my daughter," my mom said energetically, gesturing to me.

"Hello. I'm Kit," I chirped, adding a silly giggle to the end of my name. He looked in my direction and smiled patronizingly.

"I'm Alex. Nice to meet you," he said.

"I heard you're an inspector."

My mom's eyes narrowed with amusement. I suppose it was funny for her, seeing me wear this mask of innocence and stupidity.

"I'm still just a sergeant," he replied flatly.

"Oh, but aren't you, you know, in charge of investigating that murder? Or murders, whatever?"

And now my mom was stifling laughter, biting her lower lip until it hurt, trying to keep a straight face. Alex glanced down at the ground, and I took the opportunity to give her a halfway-serious warning look. She giggled silently and nodded, as if to say *I know, I know.* But she kept laughing; as she continued, I tried to restrain a smile as well. Even when silent, her laughter was somehow contagious.

"The Perfect Killer?" Alex asked uncertainly, looking up again.

"Yeah, that."

"I'm not officially in charge of that."

My mom was calming herself down now, taking deep breaths, settling into her role.

"But you're running the show, aren't you?" I regretted that comment. It sounded too intelligent, especially with the way I said it.

"Well . . . ," he said, voice trailing off. He didn't want to say anything that might be perceived as out of line. I was starting to see, a little bit, why my mom had invited him. It was a good idea to know my enemy.

"Stop embarrassing the poor man," my mom scolded me playfully, and gestured to the small table on the other side of the kitchen counter, where we always ate. The actual dining room was dark and stuffy—we ate there only on special occasions, when we felt that we had to. "Let's eat, shall we? I'm sorry I don't have any cocktails, Alex. As a rule, we don't keep alcohol in the house."

"No worries," he said, waving a hand. "I don't drink much anyway."

"You sit at the head of the table, 'cause Dad's not home," I said flippantly. He nodded awkwardly and walked around the counter to take his place at the end of the table. My mom and I followed.

As I sat down, I giggled once more for good measure. I really wanted him to believe I was an idiot. He seemed a bit uneasy with me, probably because I was acting like such a dimwit and people are usually a bit awkward with people they think are less intelligent than they are. That was good. He was easier to handle than I had expected.

"It's lovely to have you over," my mom purred.

"Thank you for inviting me," he said with a glance at me, as if he were regretting coming. He didn't quite know what to do with himself—he was so uncertain. I flashed him a smile, trying to make him feel better about things, and he returned it uncomfortably.

The poor man! Sitting at a table with two murderers, one of whom was a supposedly idiotic teenage girl. It was somehow comedic how clueless he was. He still made me nervous, but the humor of his situation didn't escape me. He was out of his depth, a small fish that had unknowingly swum out into water far too deep. And now, of course, he couldn't go back. We had found him, and we would make him ours.

I ate a few bites of my steak in silence. The policeman—what was his name, Alex?—stared off into space.

"You have a beautiful home," Alex said, gesturing around with his fork. My mother batted her eyelashes and put her fingers to her neck as if clutching at pearls.

"Oh, thank you!" she said aristocratically. I rolled my eyes. She saw me and glared.

For a moment more I looked down at my plate. Alex said something, my mother laughed, but I wasn't listening. There was another lull in the conversation.

After a moment I glanced at my mom and met her eyes. Alex was staring at his plate; he didn't see us. We shared a long look, and I smiled slightly. It was the smile of two people who shared a secret. And what a good secret it was.

◆ ◇ ◆

Alex left late. It was past ten o'clock now, and the crescent moon sat glowing like a painting in the sky. I usually went to bed late—sometime in the hours past midnight—and I liked to take time with my letters, a few hours at least, reading them, memorizing them, tasting the ghosts of the words on my tongue as I mouthed the messages to myself. But I did have school tomorrow, so I couldn't stay up too far into the morning. I had to be reasonable. And being reasonable left me less time for my letters. Sitting in my bedroom near ten o'clock watching the policeman's car drive away, I felt a small surge of irritation, directed pointedly at his retreating rear bumper as it faded into the darkness.

I sat on my bed with my bag in front of me. I didn't dump out all the letters, though I wanted to. I wanted to dump them and let them spill out of the bedspread and watch them fall wherever they pleased. I wanted them to spread out and I wanted to truly see how many of them there were, see how many people wanted my expertise and my individual, incredible instinct.

But no. They would be too hard to clean up if someone inconvenient decided to come into the room without much notice. Not that I was expecting anyone to, but it was always best to be prepared for anything.

I was wearing my usual latex gloves, stretched too tight over my hands, so I wouldn't leave fingerprints on the letters. The last box of gloves I had bought was a size too small for me, and they were really bothering me, but I didn't want to buy gloves any more often than I needed to lest I begin to look suspicious.

Dad was still out, and Mom was getting into bed. My light was the only light in the house still on. It glowed out of the house's top window over the empty black street. I plucked the first letter out and opened the envelope. Inside was a thoughtfully written note and seven hundred pounds. Not a bad amount. I scanned the letter.

Dear Killer,

I hate my fiancée, but she's blackmailing me into staying.

A couple of months ago, I was driving. And okay, maybe I had had too much to drink, maybe I shouldn't have been driving, but I didn't mean anything bad. I was just going home. But there was this red light and I didn't really know what I was doing, and I drove through it—and there was this other car that swerved to avoid me, and it crashed and someone died.

I just kept driving. I didn't know what had happened—I realized it only when they were talking about it on the news the next day. They didn't know who had done it, and they were asking for information. But I couldn't go tell the police it was my fault—I couldn't. They'd charge me with a felony. Being charged with something like that would ruin me.

I felt really bad about it, so I told my fiancée about the whole thing. But then things got bad between us, and I told her that I wanted to leave. She's crazy. Legitimately. I can't stay with her. But she's told me that if I leave, she'll tell the police about what I've done. I could go to prison. No one would ever hire me again. All I've worked for, gone.

I can't let my fiancée ruin my life like this.

Kill her. Her name is Lily Kensington, and she lives at 28 Lark Place, in Chelsea. She gets home every night at nine.

The letter writers, like this one, always did their desperate best to prove their point, convince me that their request was the most worthwhile one. They could do that without much danger. When the letters were found, their contents weren't released to the general public, for legal reasons, though it was revealed to the public that there *was* a letter; and the police couldn't actually prove who had written them—I made sure of that. Before I left the letters, I cleaned them of fingerprints by spraying them with oil-based cooking spray; it was the oil in fingerprints that allowed them to be lifted, so covering the pages entirely in oil confused and thwarted any test that the police might want to use. It was a simple and clever solution.

My mother had come up with it when told her I wanted to leave the letters as my calling card, so many years ago.

I never left any proof at all that the letters were real. No fingerprints or DNA from the writers, nothing. I had to be careful. If I made a single mistake, I knew they would stop coming to me, and then I would be nowhere.

Because of my meticulousness, the writers couldn't be convicted, only questioned; they could say whatever they wanted in their letters without fear of legal punishment, and they always did. They would be branded socially, of course. Any given person had only so many people who could honestly want them dead—usually one or two, at most. More often than not, people who knew the deceased could guess the writer without seeing the letter. The writers' friends would always suspect them of hiring a murderer, and occasionally, in cases like this, the police might suspect them of other crimes in addition to murder. Of course, though, due to questions about the letters' authenticity, the police could do nothing about those suspicions. All that, in the end, was a small price to pay for what the writers wanted.

Outside, a faint breeze rustled the leaves of trees planted in small squares at the edge of the sidewalk.

Like the vast majority of letters I received, this one was unsigned. But it was obviously this woman's fiancé who had written it. Of course, someone might be framing said fiancé. That was always a possibility. I might be killing people not because they deserved to die, but because someone else wanted to frame someone for conspiracy to commit murder. I consoled myself with the fact that for some reason or other, by someone's standards, the people I killed probably deserved to die.

Rule one, I reminded myself. There is no right or wrong.

Chelsea—28 Lark Place. The girl was close, then. That might be a good one. And the money was good, too. The sender had been generous. The generous requests got highest priority. I set the letter aside to look at again later and put the money in a different place, starting my pile. By the end of the night, I could have over twenty thousand pounds, all in cash. That wasn't too uncommon. One time I pulled in forty-six thousand in a night. I had a higher salary than many adults. And if I spent it cautiously, no one would ever know.

I went through the letters slowly, reading each one with care, weighing the difficulty and generosity of each request against the risk. Risk didn't factor into my decisions too much, though, to be honest. Perhaps it should factor in more, but I had never paid much attention to "should." There were a few authors of letters who were liberal with their money and a few who were obviously being stingy. There was no set price, but I had no sympathy for the stingy ones. Ten letters, twenty letters, twenty-five letters, twenty-six.

Letter number twenty-seven honestly shocked me.

It wasn't because I was unused to teenagers being brutal. I had received and fulfilled requests from teenagers before. And besides, I was a teenager, and I was famous worldwide for the horrors I had committed. I was the most brutal of them all. That wasn't why I was surprised. I had to read the letter twice, to make sure I was seeing it correctly.

I was seeing it correctly.

I was shocked because it was so close. I had never encountered a request that involved people I knew. But this—this was incredible. This was heartless. This was intriguing.

Could I get away with it?

I didn't relish murder. I didn't treat it as a game. But

I was confident in my abilities, and even though I knew I should follow rule number two—be careful—sometimes my ego got the better of me. The writer of this letter had unknowingly issued me a challenge.

I grinned.

It was a challenge I would take.

Chapter 3

The London morning air tasted like steel, in a vaguely unpleasant way, but that's London for you. The streets of Chelsea were quiet as I wound my way through them, watching the last pieces of the sunrise disappear from the sky. I liked the streets in the morning. They calmed me, and they even managed to make me feel alone.

It's hard to feel alone when you're me, sometimes. Sometimes even the houses crowd me in. I can imagine the people in them, still sleeping, or making breakfast, or dressing for work. It's hard to feel alone when you're me, when you can imagine the throbbing of blood through each of them and you know the way each of them breaks, like dolls lined up on a shelf.

Such intricate knowledge of what it means to be human can never be forgotten. So I see nearly all of them acutely, and those I don't see I imagine, and it is hard to feel alone.

◆ ◇ ◆

Ivy High School was quiet, vicious, and beautiful. In many ways, it was a lot like me.

Thinking about it, I realized it was probably strange that I hadn't gotten a request from a student there before. Everyone had some stupid grudge against someone else. And everyone always had too much of a stick up his or her arse to do anything about those grudges themselves. Most of the time people just sulked about it, simmering, glaring at each other ludicrously across classrooms and talking about people behind their backs as importantly as if they were discussing matters of international importance. But this time—this time someone had actually decided to do something. It felt almost like a breath of fresh air.

The grudge was based on a wonderfully juvenile issue.

Dressed in my neat navy-and-white school uniform with the skirt that just brushed the tops of my knees, I walked through the gates of Ivy High School. I was in a good mood.

I looked at the crowds of teenagers moving down the oak-lined front walkway toward the overlarge school doors. They chatted, leaned their heads on each other's shoulders, chortled rudely. Cruel little bastards, all of them. I laughed inwardly, finding it funny. The gray stone school rose up before me in a pretentious sort of way. It was a newly built campus, actually, less than ten years old, but it had been designed to look like it had been there for hundreds, with turrets and gray stone and even a stone statue of an angel standing high overhead, arms outstretched, on the highest point of the tallest building of the school. We weren't a religious school. I don't even know why the statue was there, except for effect. Young green vines wound part of the way up the outside walls, stretching cautious tendrils in between the bricks. Eventually, they would make the buildings look old and wise. Now they made them look half-baked and silly.

As I walked through the plain white plaster hallways, up flights of stairs, and toward my classroom, I managed to avoid anyone who might want to talk to me. I liked people, I really did. But at the moment, I didn't trust myself enough to talk to them like a normal teenager instead of a serial killer.

I made it to morning homeroom and made myself smile normally, smile like a silly teenage girl, smile like the version of Kit they all knew.

I walked in grinning.

"Hello," I said. The ten or so people in the room looked up at me halfheartedly and gave me slight unenthusiastic smiles. We had been in the same class for three years already, and because there were only eighty-three people in our grade, everyone knew each other. It was a sort of running joke among us all, or at least a well-known piece of information, that I was irritatingly cheerful in the early mornings. I felt obliged to comply with their expectations.

"What, no happy replies?" I laughed, walking to the center of the room and sitting down next to Maggie Bauer. Dark-haired, rosy-cheeked, looking positively exhausted, she yawned and put her head down on the desk. She was wearing a red ribbon in her hair that bobbed childishly as she moved, and the collar of her uniform shirt stuck up sideways, lopsided, giving her an off-kilter, not-entirely-there feeling. I felt bad about thinking of her so judgmentally, but whenever I looked at Maggie Bauer, I imagined that she was going to end up as a crazy cat lady or with a house full of garden gnomes or something equally strange.

She had been sick all last week, so today was her first time being in school this year. I had hoped she'd be in school today.

I had good luck, just like always.

"Oh, come on, mornings aren't that bad. Welcome to school, by the way," I said, nudging her in the shoulder with my elbow. She grumbled and turned her head away from me. She laughed quietly to let me know that she was being more joking than flat-out rude, and I laughed back.

I had always been on good terms with Maggie Bauer, but I made it a point to never have actual friends; I had far too many secrets to hide for that. It was easy to talk to her, since she never really said much. Or rather, it was easy to sort of talk *at* her.

"How much coffee have you *had* this morning?" Michael, tall and pale, grumbled back toward me from where he sat at the front of the classroom. I waved my hand playfully at him.

"Enough," I said. I didn't want to say any more to him than I needed to. He gave me the heebie-jeebies, just a little bit. And that was saying something, considering who I was.

Next to me, Maggie yawned, sat up, and pulled a crumpled sheet of paper out of her bag. She stared at it for a few seconds. I leaned over her shoulder.

"Your schedule?" I said, looking over the paper. She nodded.

"That's a bitch of a schedule," I said honestly, grimacing at it.

"I'm good at math," she replied blearily.

"So it seems." I adjusted my skirt. "I like that, it's cute," I said, pointing vaguely to the red velvet ribbon tied in Maggie's hair. It took her a moment to realize what I was talking about.

"Oh, yes. It's a tradition. I always wear a ribbon on the first day of school. Well, I guess this isn't really the first day of school, but it's close enough."

"You do?" I replied, trying not to sound too disbelieving. I'd never noticed it before.

"Yeah."

"How did that start?"

She hesitated, then shrugged.

"Can't remember."

"Well, we're glad to have you here, glad you're better, anyway." I smiled, reaching out to touch the soft end of the ribbon thoughtfully; she didn't react. It was a deep charismatic red, almost dark enough to be black.

Maggie laughed uncomfortably.

"And aren't you glad to be back?" I prompted, knowing full well what the answer was. It was no, of course. No, she wasn't glad to be back. Not at all. I let go of the ribbon and leaned casually away from her.

"Of course I'm glad," she replied uneasily.

At the end of last year Maggie had had a falling-out with her friends. I didn't know the details, but I had heard that it was somehow her fault—her friends had thought she was being antisocial or a prat or something. I didn't know if she was actually being one or not. Either way, at the start of this new school year, she was friendless. Which, of course, made things all too easy for me.

The bell rang, signaling the end of homeroom. I stood, stretched, and patted her on the back again, like I would pat a small dog.

"I'll see you at lunch."

Seeing her grateful smile, I felt a little guilt. But not too much guilt. Not enough guilt to make me doubt myself.

The first three classes were calculus, biology, and French. Nothing very interesting, and I was smart enough to learn nearly everything on my own, so I mostly didn't listen. But fourth period was philosophy. A class I very much liked in general, though some others found it boring. In every other class I sat in the back. In that class I sat nearly all the way in the front and leaned forward over my desk.

We talked about moral nihilism as an introduction to unusual ways of interpreting morality. And, of course, moral nihilism was a subject I knew something about.

"Can anyone tell me what moral nihilism is?" Dr. Marcell said slowly as soon as class began. She had on this draped, toga-like dress patterned with green bamboo; it didn't suit her figure, and it bothered me, but she was one of my favorite teachers despite her odd dressing habits. I'd had her a few years ago for an English class. She taught English when she wasn't teaching philosophy, and I liked her and how she spoke. Her short black hair was no-nonsense, no-frills. She didn't talk too fast. She took her time with things, and sometimes I even believed that she might understand me and why I killed. But I would never tell her, of course. She was legally obligated, as a teacher, to tell the police.

I raised my hand. Slowly, so no one suspected anything or thought I was too eager. No one else raised their hand, even though they were supposed to have learned this much in the reading assigned over the weekend. After a moment of looking aimlessly around the room, her eyes settled on me, and she nodded, signaling that I should speak.

"It's the belief that nothing is wrong and nothing is right," I said, making myself sound a little uncertain, even though I knew exactly what I was talking about.

"Correct. Though it's a bit more than that. It is the belief that"—she turned and began to write what she was saying on the whiteboard—"nothing is inherently wrong and nothing is inherently right, because morality is only a set of rules created by society and not based on any greater truth."

I nodded. That was exactly right.

"For example, a moral nihilist might say that killing a person is neither wrong nor right."

Yes. Exactly.

"That's sick," Michael, the pale boy from my home-room, said with disgust, loudly. There were murmurs of agreement from the eleven other students in the class. Michael. He was interesting to me. I disliked him, for one—and also, he was a factor of Maggie's life, which now made him a factor of mine by extension. I focused on him just a bit more than usual. He had been friends with Maggie last year, before his little clique had kicked her out. He had been something of a ringleader to that group, until he too had left them after Maggie's departure. Michael was a drifter, a destructive one. He had a talent for making friends and he was even good at keeping them; he was easy to talk to, and he had a smile as charming as the Cheshire cat's. But he never seemed to *like* keeping friends. He would be friends with a group for a few months or so, and then, for seem-ingly no reason at all, he would move on to something new. Right now he was floating between old groups, undecided about who he would be friends with this new school year. The uncertainty didn't seem to bother him.

He looked innocent for the moment, with his high, attractive cheekbones, fluffy brown hair, and shiny brown eyes that always sort of made him look like he was going to cry because someone had kicked him in the shin or something. He looked almost pitiful. But I knew better. I made it my business to know better. Sometimes, in flashes, for some reason or another, you could see it. Something in his eyes, his face, even something in the way he held his body changed. It was hard to explain. He never actually did anything, but looking at him, you could just *tell*.

I frowned, ever so slightly. Dr. Marcell saw it.

"You disagree, Kit?" she asked curiously.

I winced and closed my eyes as everyone turned to look at me.

"Well . . . ," I said hesitantly, feeling everyone's eyes on me. Dr. Marcell looked at me with waiting eyes. "Well . . . ," I said again.

I didn't want to say anything. I really, really didn't. But now I had to, didn't I?

"Well, throughout history, in different cultures, there were different social standards based on different morals, right?" I said tentatively. Dr. Marcell nodded faintly. I gained a bit of confidence and went on. "So if you look at that, morality is just . . . a social construct. There's no greater truth to it. It's just . . . you know, what people of the time think is right."

"You're onto something there. See, that is exactly what moral nihilists through the ages have seen and thought about. Is there a greater moral truth? Or are our morals just a product of our society? I think it is an inarguable truth that our society does have morals that we have to adhere to. But do those morals hold any truth, or are they just rules that have been superficially created?" Dr. Marcell asked. No one responded. Everyone in the class looked faintly skeptical.

"Anyone?" Dr. Marcell said encouragingly. Still silence. She glanced at me. Our eyes met. I could see it—she wanted me to say something. It was only the second week, but I was obviously her most enthusiastic student, and she knew it. I spoke up when there was silence and guided class conversations back on track when they went in odd directions. She knew I had something more to add and looked at me pleadingly, her eyes asking me to say it.

But I didn't.

After class, as everyone filed out of the classroom, she tapped my arm and gestured for me to come to her desk. I glanced toward the students walking out into the hallway, then uncertainly back to her, then back to my classmates. But I couldn't just blatantly disobey her. So I went with small steps to stand nervously before her desk in the front of the classroom. She had been walking around during class, but somehow, now that she was sitting, books piled up before her, a nameplate centered in front of her chest on the edge of the desk, hands folded, she seemed more imposing. More official. I looked at her expression, and I couldn't tell whether she was irritated or just disappointed.

"Yes?" I asked doubtfully, looking at her face, which was turned up toward me.

She met my eyes without blinking.

"You had more to say today. You were holding back," she said bluntly.

"No, I didn't have anything else to say," I protested.

"I saw it in your eyes. You weren't done talking. You shut yourself up."

"No, I–"

"There's no use in lying, Kit. I consider myself a good judge of character. I can see what kind of person you are. Intelligent, thoughtful–but timid. You seem very outgoing, very individual, but you're scared of not fitting in. At the risk of sounding clichéd, you're better than that. You're a good student, and you have a good interest in philosophy. I want to urge you to speak out more and be yourself. Don't be afraid to say what you mean, if you have something good to add to the conversation."

I looked at her hesitantly.

She was a bit like a caricature of a person, I thought. Exaggerated. Like something out of a children's cartoon, or a bad movie. The thought was funny to me, and I resisted the urge to laugh.

"Okay, Dr. Marcell," I said. I didn't mean it.

She sighed.

"I mean it, Kit. You're more intelligent than this."

She had no idea.

"I'll keep your suggestions in mind." I smiled blandly. She stared at me for another few moments, sighed again, gave me a slight, unenthusiastic smile, and waved her hand to let me know I could leave.

I nodded and left the classroom.

It was lunch. I wandered through the hallways, following the crowd toward the cafeteria, deep in thought. It was conversations like the one with Dr. Marcell that made me feel like an outsider. Unless I was actually in the midst of murder, I usually could make myself feel normal. I could think of murder as a hobby, as an extracurricular. In the same way some girls did gymnastics or watercolors, I killed.

But when I had to make excuses for myself or pretend, like I had to pretend in philosophy, and especially when I was called out on it, I couldn't feel normal. And I liked to feel normal. At least sometimes.

I woke myself up out of my thoughts as I wandered into the cafeteria. I had a job to do, I reminded myself. I had responsibilities. I couldn't just drift off into my own thoughts.

I looked across the sea of white plastic tables and clean food counters, searching for Maggie. The roar of conversation was deafening, and everything smelled like antiseptic; the school administration was anal about cleaning. After a few seconds, I saw her in the far left corner of the room. She was staring at the scratched plastic table beneath her folded fingers. I began to make my way through the maze of people and chairs and tables, heading toward her. I bumped past other students, muttering halfhearted apologies, until I finally made it to her.

"Hello." I smiled, putting my hands down on the plastic just in front of hers. She looked up at me, surprised, and strangely enough, almost scared, like a deer stuck in head-lights.

"Oh, Kit. You scared me," she said, with relief clear in her voice. I sat down across from her and noticed she wasn't eating anything.

"You're not going to eat?" I asked. She shook her head morosely.

"No." She offered no explanation.

"Why not?"

"Don't feel like it," she muttered.

"I know the feeling. They make me feel a bit sick, too," I said, waving in the direction of the other kids in the cafeteria. She gaped, looking as surprised as if I had just told her I was a time traveler or an alien.

"You don't say that *out loud*," she whispered furtively, absurdly, looking around to see if anyone had heard. No one had, of course. No one was paying attention to the two of us in the slightest.

"Why not? None of them like you anymore, anyway. And I don't care if they like me."

She winced a bit, then looked at me curiously. "You look like such a goody-two-shoes."

I laughed. "What does that have to do with anything?"

"Well . . . you talk like such a rebel. But you look stuck-up and . . . prissy."

"Do I?" I asked, dismayed. "Sorry."

She shrugged blandly and went back to staring at the table.

Out of the corner of my eye, I saw someone staring at us from across the room. I looked away from Maggie momentarily, focusing in on that someone. It was Michael. Quiet, still, eyes narrowed. That was interesting.

I smiled my most infuriating smile in his direction, and my attention went back to Maggie. He wasn't my concern at the moment.

"So, since we're apparently both stuck-up and unlikable, we should be friends," I said jauntily. "We have something in common."

"What?"

"Well, you need a friend, and I don't particularly care if I have friends, but I'll seem like a complete arse without any. So we should stick together—what do you say?"

She looked a bit overwhelmed.

"You're sure? Everyone hates me; you're right. No one really thinks you're stuck-up, even though you look like it. Everyone's sort of fine with you."

I looked up, pretending to think.

"Why exactly do they hate you? I know your friends all sort of abandoned you. Sorry, that's harsh. But why exactly did that happen?" I asked with an apologetic grimace. I did want to know her side of the story.

She hesitated and looked at me tiredly. "I rejected Michael when he asked me out," she admitted quietly. She looked uncomfortable, as if that simplistic explanation didn't quite cover everything, as if that were just the neatest answer and the one she had grown accustomed to giving, even if it wasn't quite true. I raised my eyebrows.

"Why did you say no? He's cute," I said.

"He's dangerous," she muttered bitterly, as if she were remembering something she couldn't explain. "He's pretty, yeah, but he's a bastard. I swear."

"What happened between you two? It sounds like there's some history there."

She hesitated.

"He hurt me once," she murmured, so quietly that I could barely hear her.

That was interesting.

"Want to talk about it?" I asked, with perhaps a bit too much cheer.

She shook her head. "No."

I shrugged. I didn't really need to hear it from her to imagine what had happened. He'd probably hit her–there were rumors he'd beaten up at least three people from various schools across London, though there was no way of definitively knowing which, if any, of those rumors were true. They'd all gotten blown up to a point where it was impossible to distinguish fiction from fact.

Strangely enough, people didn't really seem to mind all that. Michael was charming, so everyone continued to like him; mostly, people just ignored the rumors or dismissed them as fiction. He did have a bit of a crazy reputation, though, depending on who you talked to, and of course, I had never liked him myself.

"Fair enough. We're friends, then?"

She smiled a soft smile, ever so slightly.

"Yeah. Friends."

My stomach churned a bit.

No, I reminded myself. I could do this. There was no morality. I could not doubt that, or doubt myself. No good would come of it. No good at all.

• ◆ •

As the end-of-day bells rang and the students left the building, I stood in a bathroom stall on the third floor and looked thoughtfully down at the letter in my hand, scrawled in hasty, angry letters on lined paper ripped out of a notebook. I read it, considering the words.

Dear Killer,

Kill Maggie Bauer.

We used to be friends—we were friends for a long time. I thought she was different from the rest. I thought I saw something in her—something beautiful. She was everything to me. I depended on her. I thought we were the same, or at least we could be the same. I thought she saw the world like I saw it, and could understand what I meant if I chose to talk about it with her. I thought she saw the way that nothing has hope, the way everything in the world is dark, and the way that you must understand that to have any hold on reality at all.

You understand what I'm talking about, don't you? You must. Considering what you do.

But she refused me. She let me down. When I needed her, she went away. One day she was there, the next day she had vanished from me. I've realized that she's just like the rest. Just vapid and useless. Just absolutely nothing. She can't understand anything you want to tell her—she pretends to understand, but when you really need her to understand, she just runs away like nobody matters but her.

I still want her to understand. I still want her to be with me, I still want her love, her everything, but—it can't be, can it? No. You must understand. I can no longer go on, so long as she's alive to taunt me with her existence.

I've realized that she's a superficial idiot. She's disgusting. I am so alone. I hate her.

She broke my heart, and she deserves to die.

I didn't know exactly what to make of the letter.

The writer had to be Michael. That was interesting. It was all interesting, actually.

Kill Maggie Bauer? Fine. I could do that. But he would pay for his request. He would pay, like they all did. I would leave Maggie dead with his letter on her body. That was my price. They paid with their freedom. They would never be able to forget what they had done, because no one else would forget. It would follow them all the days of their lives.

For a long time it had seemed so strange to me that they would keep coming when I incriminated them so obviously.

It took me a while to realize why, exactly, they kept coming, but when I realized, it all made sense, and it made me
a little proud. And a little sickened.

They all called on me because I was the best. I always
got it right. And calling on me instead of someone else
made them feel better about wishing for murder—there was
an element of chance about it. Sometimes I killed, sometimes I didn't, and that uncertainty made people feel less
responsible.

I held them captive.

They were tied to me; their letters tied them to me.
If I was ever caught, arrested, I could incriminate them,
explain everything to the police, prove that they had all in
fact hired a murderer. I kept a silent hold on them, always.

I was sure that fact, more than anything, bothered them
the most.

I folded up the letter and put it away. I had to get going
if I wanted to make it back to Chelsea in time to make a
quick social call.

Chapter 4

L ondon was unusually hot that afternoon. As I walked through the streets, I felt heat bearing down on my back and remembered another heat, a long time ago. The train of thought that had occupied me after I went to pick up my letters was still lingering.

I remembered being in a never-used guest bedroom on the second floor of our old town house, converted by my mother and me into something all our own—small and stuffy, because we had to keep the curtains drawn and the door locked. The air-conditioning had been turned on, but it had only wheezed through the vent and hadn't really cooled anything down. Gymnastics mats carpeted the floor. I remembered what we wore more vividly than anything else, though; I had been in gym shorts that hung down nearly past my knees, a tank top, and tennis shoes with laces that were too long. Ragged black hand wraps had been twisted around my hands like a second skin. My mother, across the room, stylishly dressed as usual, had stood silently in white jeans and a gray shirt, cool and quiet and joyous and beautiful, with eyes like glass.

There were many of these days, but as I wandered through the streets that afternoon, I remembered one in particular. A day that had meant something.

I remembered gray skies, muggy air, darkness fading over everything. I had crouched down in the corner, near the brass hinges of the door. Panting. Eight years old. Sweat. Exhaustion. My mother standing over me, determined, pale hair swept back into a high ponytail, weight balanced evenly on both legs.

She had been so dazzling then! Back in the days when she had held a more secure role in my killings. It was only when I reached back into the past that I realized how much she had lost. Today, she was still partially the woman she had been in that room—but the measured cleverness in her eyes, the fight in her stance, her clipped tones had faded away into quiet stillness as I pulled away from her and became my own force. A force she could touch but could no longer guide or hold like she wanted to.

"I'm tired," I had said that day. "Can I be done for today?"

At that point we had been training for the past year or

so. Martial arts, strategy, acting, anything that could ever be useful. We sparred, did drills, played dangerous games, and both of us sustained more bruises than we could count. We hid them all beneath scarves and jackets and gloves; once, I accidentally gave my mother a long gash down her cheek by shoving her into the windowsill. She had congratulated me for the move that did it, and told all her friends that she had fallen against the edge of a sharp picture frame.

The injuries we sustained there were good injuries. They bespoke hard work.

Both of us knew that room was *our* place. When I came home from school, I always changed and went there for hours on end, not eating until we stopped late in the evening so I wouldn't be training when and if my father returned home. Every night I trained until every muscle in my body ached.

I had been her dutiful student, never questioning. I suppose others might have said that it was a cruel way to treat such a small child—but it had never seemed cruel to me. It was a necessity in my eyes. I had grown up knowing I would be a killer. My mother, perched on the edge of my bed before I went to sleep each night, my blue-eyed guardian, had told me stories. She had told me of what it felt like to kill. She had told me that it was my duty. She had told me that there was no right and no wrong, and that I shouldn't believe anyone who said there was. I had never known anything else.

Hearing my question that day, she had hesitated strangely.

"No," she said eventually, drawing one hand across her cheekbone, tucking a stray piece of blond hair behind her ear.

Shivering in the corner, I clenched my teeth. She was being unreasonable. I was physically incapable of obeying her. Usually when I told her I was done, she listened—I had never been the type to exaggerate my tiredness.

"Tomorrow. I can't do any more today. I'm going to fall."

We had been practicing boxing all afternoon, and I was still on my feet only because I was leaning against the wall.

She looked down at me expressionlessly.

"Again," she said, inviting me to punch the mitt she held in her right hand.

Struggling to stand—wavering—crumpling back against the wall, breaths short and aching.

"Not today," I pleaded. The air felt like I was standing in the center of the sun, and it bore down on me, crushing—

I felt fuzzy. In that room, in that moment, I felt sick, and dizzy, and not entirely present, as if I were watching things from the outside.

"No," she said.

"Please—"

She held up the mitt.

"Again."

Again I tried to stand on my own, and again I failed. This time the attempt unbalanced me enough that I could no longer even lean against the wall. I crumpled to my knees.

"Please."

"No. Get up. Again."

It was cruel! What was she doing, how could she be doing this—she wasn't usually this cruel, what was wrong, why was she so cruel today?

"I can't," I moaned, collapsing into tired sobs.

She watched me in silence. I imagined looking up into her eyes, seeing for myself the dissatisfaction there. I couldn't even muster the energy to look up, though. I just stared impassively at the blue mat between my knees and cried.

And eventually my tears stopped, faded away, and I was just left in silence.

"Again," my mother said quietly.

And then something snapped. Head jerking upward, I spoke sharply, each word biting angrily through the air.

"We are *done* for today," I barked. "And I don't care what you want."

As soon as the words left my mouth, I winced and anticipated her anger.

My mother was momentarily expressionless.

Then—

"Okay," she said.

And slowly, slowly, she smiled and walked over to me.

She knelt on the sweaty mats; and then she wrapped her arms around my shoulders and held me tight. And my anger was suddenly gone.

"Good girl. I'm sorry," she whispered.

"What?"

"You learned it."

"What?" I said again, dumbly.

"What I was trying to teach you. It's not something I can just tell you. You have to learn through experience. You have to see for yourself. Some things are like that. The important things."

"I don't think I've learned anything," I protested limply.

"Challenge everything," she breathed. "Challenge everything, even me. If you don't, you'll get pushed around. Take what you want. Don't take no for an answer. It's important."

"Oh."

And I had a moment when it rushed through me, her lesson, every part of it, and I realized that everything she did, she did with purpose.

And with that she swept me tenderly up in her arms and unlocked the door, climbed the stairs, and brought me to my bedroom, where she peeled back the sheets and gingerly set me down in my bed.

I fell asleep almost instantly. But in those brief moments before sleep came, I felt my mother sitting beside me, stroking my hair with warm, gentle, familiar hands.

Beneath those hands, I felt safe, and grateful, and home.

She was softly singing a nursery rhyme.

"Three blind mice, three blind mice . . ."

◆ ◇ ◆

I walked into the Chelsea Police Station bearing pastries and a smile.

It was a heavy-looking redbrick building, very official, with no hint of humor within its thick walls. There was a small stone statue of a dog outside the front door, a dog sitting with its mouth gleefully open and one paw raised as if it wanted to break free from the stone and play. It fascinated me for a moment. But then I moved on.

I was thinking I would have to *ask* for Alex, which could have been awkward, but luck was on my side. As I walked in, he was walking out. He saw me and froze for half a second, before giving me an uncomfortable smile. He stood with most of his weight on one foot, graceful and tall, but he wasn't relaxed. His deep eyes, murky beneath long lashes, studied me carefully. For a moment, I was frozen in his gaze. Then he blinked, and I remembered to breathe.

I lifted the bag of pastries in my hand, waving them, smelling suddenly the wafting scent of sugar. I gave him a sweet, almost saccharine smile.

"Hello," I said.

"Ah . . . hello."

"I've brought pastries. They're quite good. They're from a café a ways down King's Road."

"That's . . . nice."

I noticed a few police officers looking at me, the girl in the school uniform, and looking at him. I pretended not to notice.

"What are you doing here, Kit?"

"Well, I thought it was a nice thing to do, stopping by and all," I said, looking innocent. He sighed.

"Let's go talk somewhere else," he muttered, and ushered me out the door.

We walked about half a block until we found a bench and sat down. He sat as far away from me as possible and looked me suspiciously. As ingenuously as I could, I held the bag of pastries out toward him. Not taking his eyes off me, he reached inside and took out a lemon scone.

"Those are good. Good choice," I told him. He glared.

"What exactly do you *want* from me?" he asked after a moment.

"What?"

"You're a kid. Why are you following me to work? You want something, I can tell, but I don't know what that is. Last night, too, I saw it. . . ."

"Ah . . . well . . ." I laughed nervously.

He really was born to be an inspector. His instinct was fantastic. I was a good actress, but he saw right through me. Time to change tactics. Innocent and stupid weren't working on him.

Despite my attempts to keep my face blank and unreadable, a very faint smile tinged the edge of my lips. Alex was more interesting than I had given him credit for at first.

"Fine," I said, putting the bag down on the bench between us. My eyes sharpened. I let myself look clever, dropped my bovine facade, showed him my slyness. "You're right. I want something."

He looked at me, waiting, a faint satisfied smile lighting up his face in a way that made me distracted for a moment.

I sighed.

"I want to know about the Perfect Killer."

He chuckled. "That's not kid stuff."

"I'm not a kid."

"Yes, you are."

"You're barely older than me," I said accusingly. "And I'm smart."

"Smart has nothing to do with it. Murder is brutal, horrible—too much for you to handle."

I resisted the urge to laugh.

"I can deal with it," I scoffed stubbornly.

"Your mom invited me over because you're nosy, didn't she?" he said, shaking his head, looking vaguely amused.

I laughed quietly. "Yes, something like that."

"Sorry. I can't help you. It's against the rules, anyway."

He stood up, pushing the bag back toward me. He took a bite of the scone.

"It's good." He smiled. "Sorry I couldn't give you what you wanted. You should forget about this. Although it looks like you've got a good head on your shoulders, so maybe I shouldn't worry too much about you, eh?"

"I like to think so," I said.

He waved slightly to me and took a few steps backward.

"If you ever want to work for the police when you're older, give me a call."

"I don't have your number," I pointed out petulantly.

"Oh." He paused, sighed like an indulgent older brother, and walked back toward me. Digging out a piece of paper and a pen from the black bag hanging at his side, he scrawled down his number and handed over the paper.

"Give me a call in a few years or so," he said with a lukewarm smile. He didn't really mean it.

I frowned at the paper. This was something, but it wasn't good enough. I had to keep him close. I was beginning to see. I couldn't just know my enemy. I had to be closer than that.

I had to control my enemy.

"It was nice meeting you, Kit."

He waved politely to me and turned his back, walking away down the sidewalk.

I had to take a risk if I wanted to gain his trust. I stood and took a deep breath.

"The Perfect Killer is based in Chelsea and is a student," I said loudly.

My heart beat quickly. I had to do it. I was afraid. But I had to make him trust me. My mind whirled, my thoughts anxious and out of order. But I had to do it.

He stopped and turned to face me again.

"What?" he said quietly.

"Based in Chelsea and a student."

Slowly, he walked back over to me.

"How do you know that?"

"The—the reports. In the papers. It was easy enough to figure out."

"What do you mean?" he said, a bit louder than before, his eyes a little too wide—

"You . . . didn't know that," I realized with a touch of despair. I had said too much. I had assumed I was just giving him facts that the public wasn't supposed to know but the police had figured out through logic—the necessary information was staring them in the face, anyway. I only wanted to prove my cleverness to him, seemingly using information that was public property. But instead I had given him new clues that could lead to me. I had overestimated the police's intelligence.

Shit.

"I know the killer is based in Chelsea. The murders are widespread, but a larger-than-normal portion of the murders take place in Chelsea," he said. "But how did you know he—or she, I suppose—is a student?"

"The . . . times of death."

"What was that? I couldn't hear."

"The—ah—times of death. In the newspapers, they always say the times of death of the victims. All the weekday murders happened in the late afternoon or night, except for two that happened on school holidays at around midday."

Those two kills had been mistakes. Too much of a clue.

I had been younger then. I had assumed the police had made those connections by now. But I suppose not.

He looked at me, shock in his eyes, staring.

I grinned slyly.

Oh well. I had sacrificed a clue for an advantage. Now I had his trust. That, I thought, could be helpful later. Perhaps even necessary.

"Alex," I said amusedly.

"You *are* smart," he murmured. His eyes softened, just a bit, just enough.

I smiled and turned away. I walked away from him without another word, sauntering down the sidewalk. Once I was about ten feet away, I laughed and looked back over my shoulder toward him.

"I'll see you tomorrow, Alex," I called.

"Yeah," he agreed very slowly, with the hint of a smile; of course he was wondering, *Why tomorrow?* but to be honest I didn't even know why I had said that myself. Maybe it was a promise. Maybe I was assuring him, yes, we would be friends, and we would see each other soon, and he shouldn't doubt me.

"I'll see you tomorrow," he replied.

Chapter 5

I stood in front of 28 Lark Place, in Chelsea.

The street was quiet, and everyone's curtains were drawn. It was late. This was a neighborhood with many children, and the families were sleeping. There weren't any surveillance cameras around to watch me—this place was too far from the city center for that. This would be an easier murder than most—but it had to be quiet.

It was 11:52, eleven degrees Celsius. Cool, for late summer. I had to wear a jacket. Black, of course, so the stains wouldn't show. My gloved hands were shoved deep down in my pockets.

It was a clean-looking house, white with blue shutters. A pot of blooming purple petunias was set on each of the three steps leading up to the front door. I stood across the street in the shade of a small thorny tree, blending into the shadows. I wore a scarf to cover most of my face and a knit black hat to cover my hair, lest anyone see me and try to identify me later. But I didn't think they would see me. I was too quiet, too easy to pass over, and too good at what I did.

I walked across the street, hands in my pockets, and rang the doorbell.

The simple way in was always the best. People might remember me if I was looking through the window, trying to lift the shutter, for example. If they glimpsed me that way, I wouldn't be forgotten. And there was no way to get into the house except through the front. No one suspected or even remembered someone who just waltzed up to the front door and rang the doorbell like they were being expected.

For a moment there was silence, and darkness. I rang again.

A light went on inside.

I heard footsteps down stairs and then on flat wooden floor—and the door swung open to reveal Lily Kensington in a rose-pink bathrobe, tired-eyed and yawning. She was a pretty thing, much taller than me, with black curly hair and deep hazel eyes like wood and water.

"Lily Kensington." I smiled benignly. "It's such a plea-sure to finally meet you."

She looked at me, confused.

"What?"

"After all this time, it's nice to finally meet you."

"I think you have the wrong person."

"You are Lily Kensington, aren't you?"

"Well, yes."

I smiled wider.

"Then I don't have the wrong person."

She paused, searching my face for something, looking completely baffled.

"Who *are* you?"

"My name is Diana," I said. It was the name I always gave to my victims, if they asked. I liked that name. I had taken it from Roman mythology a long time ago. Diana was the goddess of the hunt, wild animals, and the moon, and it had seemed appropriate—also, I just liked the sound of it. *Diana.*

"Who?"

"Diana. Didn't . . . didn't your fiancé tell you about me?"

Her eyes widened a bit.

"My fiancé?"

"Yes. I'm a friend of his. I've heard so much about you. He said he thought you'd be home now. I'm sorry the visit is so late."

"Yeah."

I looked around, biting my lip. I needed to get in. Usually by this point in the conversation I was already inside. People didn't usually like standing in cold doorways at night and didn't usually even feel uncomfortable about asking a slim little teenage girl like me inside. She was tough. Now, what should I do?

"Actually, I have to talk to you about something," I murmured.

"Yeah, well, whatever you want to talk to me about, we can talk right here," she said, leaning against the doorway imposingly, making it clear that she was taller and stronger than me. Her expression was distinctly unfriendly.

"It's . . . well . . . I don't want to," I said childishly, petulantly. She looked at me with a skeptical expression.

"Yeah, well, that's too bad, isn't it?"

This was taking too long. Far too long. Long conversations were suspicious, and suspicion was not something I wanted to gather.

"I'm pregnant with your fiancé's baby," I snapped. Crude, but I imagined it would be effective.

It did the trick.

She gaped. She looked shocked, stunned, betrayed, and stepped away from the door just long enough for me to sneak inside and close the door behind me. With a click, it settled into the doorframe. She reached a hand out and weakly put it on my shoulder.

"You're lying," she whispered hopefully. I shook my head and led her slowly into the next room, facing her as I walked backward.

"I'm not lying," I said, feigning shame. Inside, I was darkly satisfied. This room was perfect. Thick, dark curtains so no one could see shadows through the window.

A large space in the middle of the carpet between the sofa and the TV.

She collapsed down on her caramel leather sofa and put her head in her hands. She breathed deeply. In, out, in, out. I hoped she was savoring those breaths.

I stood by the flat-screen hung high on the wall and prepared myself. She was small, low to the ground, as she sat hunched with her head in her hands, staring at the floor.

I liked this part. I left things to chance most of the time. It might be foolish, but I was well trained and well practiced in my art. I knew which ways of killing were the most effective and which made the least noise.

I remembered the rules my mother had taught me over dinner, making me recite them night after night until I not only remembered them, but lived them, and had them printed into my very existence. One—nothing is right, nothing is wrong. Two—be careful. Three—fight using your legs whenever possible, because they're the strongest part of your body. Your arms are the weakest. Four—hit to kill. Don't waste time. The first blow should be the last, if at all possible. Five—the letters are the law.

And I remembered the breathless heat of many days, one after the other after the other, sparring, sweating, bruising, learning to kill by hand. . . .

Other, more silent and sure ways of killing, like poisons or knives, left a paper trail or permanent evidence. I might leave a lot to chance by killing with bare hands, but at least I would make myself untraceable.

"I'm sorry," I said sincerely. She leaned down to hug her knees, shuddering, her head hanging limply toward the floor.

"But—is that why he wanted to leave? You? Why does he want to leave, he can't leave—"

She started to move away from her knees to look up at me; she wanted to look me in the eyes. But this was already taking too long.

I stepped forward and swung my knee upward into her nose before she had a chance to see my face. She really was a pretty thing. All elegance and sharp beauty.

I heard and felt the bone splinter against my lower thigh. She opened her mouth to scream, but I kept driving upward with my leg and the shattered bone plunged upward into her brain and she was dead.

She fell forward onto the black carpet, her pink fluffy bathrobe making her look like some sort of grotesque flower. Quick and silent and simple. I crouched down and turned her over. Wet blood, the color of cherry cough medicine, dripped from her mutilated face. Her eyes were open. I left them that way and made sure not to get any blood on myself. Bloodstains were hard to wash out, and I already had one on my knee. I would have to get rid of these jeans.

Carefully, making sure not to touch anything else, I slid one hand out of my glove and checked her pulse and breathing. Both were gone. I slid my hand back into the glove, pulled a damp sponge out of my coat pocket, and carefully scrubbed away the print from her neck. I put the sponge back in my pocket.

I reached into my jeans pocket and pulled out the letter.

I stood up and looked down at her. Looked at her ruined face and bloodshot eyes and that pretty hair.

"Sorry," I said coldly.

I dropped the letter on her chest and walked away as blood began to soak through the corners of the paper.

I thought about the clockwork of it all as I walked back out onto the street, the night air biting into my skin. The precision, the order. The fact that no one was there to tell me that I was wrong, or disgusting.

Do you remember what I said about not enjoying murder?

That was a lie.

Chapter 6

My father, as he did most days, had left the house before dawn. The sound of the front door opening and closing downstairs had woken me up; I was a light sleeper, and the door was loud. After he left, I couldn't fall asleep again. I stared at the ceiling for an hour, dazed, unmoving, before my alarm rang to tell me I had to get up to go to school.

I slipped downstairs in a bathrobe and slippers at half past six; I needed something to drink. I found my mother sitting at the bottom of the stairs, leaning against the railing. As I approached, she stood and turned to look at me.

"You're up early," I remarked, descending the last few stairs. Her blue eyes glistened softly in my direction, wide and watery.

"Am I?"

I raised my eyebrows slightly. She looked tired.

"Couldn't sleep?"

She shrugged. "I guess not."

"Nightmares again?"

"Yes."

I felt sorry—I knew how bad the nightmares got sometimes, how upset they made her. She never told me much about those dreams, but I knew that they were rife with blood and terror and ghosts of the past.

"You're all right?"

"Yes, of course." She looked absently around the front hallway. "You were out late last night," she remarked. She wanted to change the subject, and I would let her.

I walked past her into the kitchen. As I passed, I shrugged and said, "I killed."

"Who was it?"

"Her name was Lily Kensington."

"Why did she die?"

"Her boyfriend said she was blackmailing him. She seemed nice enough, though."

I emerged from the kitchen with two glasses of orange juice. I took a sip from one and handed the other to my mother, who nodded a brief thank-you.

"Well, you never know with people."

I shook my head and grinned drily. I thought about us in our gray-walled, elegant hallway, the two slender blondes on the edge of an expensive rug, pale-skinned and frail-looking, pausing beneath famous photographs, drinking orange juice from designer glasses.

"No, you never know," I laughed.

She got the joke and laughed too. Softly, she sighed and smiled.

I nodded and returned her smile as tenderly as I could.

"You should go finish getting ready for school," she said.

"Okay."

I turned away from her wordlessly and went upstairs. She didn't move. She was lost in thought. The morning wrapped her in a blanket of light.

◆ ◆ ◆

"Hey, Maggie," I said, leaning over her with a smile.

She looked up at me, morose.

"Hey."

I frowned. "What is it?" I asked.

"What's what?"

"Why do you look like someone just shot your puppy?"

"Nothing—nothing, just Michael being . . . Michael."

I sat down on the table in front of her, resting my feet on a chair. We were in our painting classroom next to a row of easels, basking in midafternoon sunshine—it was the only class we had together. She wasn't very good at it. Admittedly, neither was I, but her painting skills were almost beyond pathetic. The vase of flowers she had attempted to paint had ended up looking more like a bouquet of turquoise butterflies, which was oddly pretty, I supposed, but definitely not accurate.

School was over—the bell had just rung. Michael was in that class too. While I was putting away my paints, he had been talking to Maggie, and now he was gone.

"Ignore him." I laughed spitefully, glancing at the door to the classroom. "He's an arsehole."

"He's just . . . sharp," she said, somehow defensive. Just the day before, she had called him a bastard. But that bitterness was suddenly gone, vanished. It was a bit frustrating.

"No. Trust me. He's *definitely* an arsehole," I said knowingly, and continued in a whisper, "He *hurt* you, didn't he?"

She frowned again and stood, picking up her purse from the ground next to her chair.

"Maybe." She smiled weakly.

"Maybe? How about definitely. Come on, be a bit more confident."

"I don't want to stir up trouble," she said.

"Why ever not?" She didn't reply to that. I shrugged and changed the subject. "So—I'm visiting a friend of mine now. Want to come?"

She looked around, as if something in the classroom would answer whatever question she had.

"Now?"

"Yeah, now. I'm walking over to where he works. He works for Scotland Yard, so he's not suspicious or anything, so you can tell your parents that if they want to know. It's about twenty minutes away, walking, and fifteen minutes more to my house. Actually, do you want to come over for dinner afterward? Or maybe even sleep over? I know for a fact that you're already done with your homework for tomorrow."

She looked at me, faintly surprised.

I remembered Lily Kensington's surprise and for a moment felt cold.

The moment passed quickly.

"But I do have homework," Maggie protested pathetically.

I scoffed. "No, you don't. Come on."

Maggie shrugged and followed me out the door.

After walking to the station and being reluctantly informed by an easily intimidated secretary that Alex was at the scene of a murder at 28 Lark Place, in Chelsea, Maggie and I headed in that direction. I looked up where it was on my phone and pretended to follow the directions, even though I knew exactly where it was. Maggie didn't realize. She just gave me a misty sort of smile the whole way along as I chattered at her about Alex, and about my mom's habit of inviting people over for dinner, and about how I wondered if the house was a Perfect Killer crime scene. I don't think she was listening half the time.

When we got to the crime scene, there was crime-scene tape everywhere and a near army of reporters. Maggie and I wound our way through the throngs of onlookers and cameras, glancing at the people who lived in the neighborhood as they stood wide-eyed near the outskirts of the scene.

I did my best to keep them from seeing my face, given the fact that they were possible witnesses. Of course, I was subtle about it.

Maggie followed me as I went toward the blue-shuttered house. She was quiet but didn't look particularly disturbed or nervous. She did look a little blank, though, as if she were ignoring things that were going on around her, shutting them out, simply pretending that they didn't exist and hoping they would go away.

We got to the tape line in front of the steps and stood looking up at the house. All around us were police officers and reporters. The reporters stood aimlessly, waiting to film, or talked at the camera in calm, slow voices. The officers were silent and steely faced. I stood on tiptoe and tried to see inside the door, which hung slightly ajar.

Maggie tugged on the hem of my shirt.

"Yeah?" I said hazily.

"Are you sure we're supposed to be here?" she asked.

"Yeah, sure. Why not? The street is public property, yeah?"

"Yeah, but . . . this is . . . murder. . . ."

"I told you, I know one of the inspectors. No, wait, sorry, he's not an inspector yet. But he's sort of important."

Maggie looked uncertain. I laughed at her.

"Calm down, all right?" I entreated her.

"Yeah," she murmured.

Alex walked out the front door, talking to an older

man. He was in strict uniform today, his hair swept messily away from his face and black-rimmed glasses sitting on his nose, pushed close to his focused eyes.

"Alex!" I called, standing on tiptoe and waving to him. The police officers in the vicinity turned to look at me with a bit of confusion. Alex paused, taking a moment from his conversation with the man to look in my direction. When he saw me, he smiled grimly and said something to the man. I suddenly found myself smiling too—it was nice to be recognized, especially by him. I felt like something was beginning to bind us together, and I rather liked it.

The man nodded and glanced at me, and both of them began to walk in my direction. They came down the steps and stopped on the other side of the tape. The older man stuck a hand out toward me sharply. The nearby police officers held back enthusiastic reporters as they homed in on him like hungry dogs.

"Oh," I said, a bit startled, and took the proffered hand with raised eyebrows. He shook my hand and gave me a quick nod. He was tall but thickset, with heavy silver eyebrows and sharp blue eyes.

"Chief Superintendent Davies," he said, introducing himself gruffly. Alex stood off to one side, expressionless.

"Oh," I said again, shaking his hand. "Well. It's nice to meet you. Sir. I'm Kit Ward."

Maggie, I saw out of the corner of my eye, looked suddenly nauseous.

I felt a little bit the same way. I wasn't entirely

comfortable with the police to begin with, and someone as highly ranked as a chief superintendent made me a little more than uncomfortable.

"I heard you added an interesting insight to the case yesterday," he said.

"Ah—well—yes, I suppose," I said uncertainly.

"It was a clever thought."

"Thank you, sir."

Superintendent Davies turned back toward Alex and nodded at him.

"I'll leave you in his capable hands," the superintendent said. "I have things I have to attend to, so he's really the one running the investigation, even though it's officially my responsibility. Smart boy, he is," he said, as if I didn't already know.

"Thank you, sir," I said awkwardly as he slid under the caution tape and walked away through the crowd without another word.

Alex stepped toward me, brushing slightly against my arm, making me shiver, though the air wasn't unusually cold. He gestured after the superintendent's retreating back.

"He's bit pompous, but he's good at what he does. And no, that something isn't investigating murderers. He's too important to do the grunt work. He's administration, mostly," Alex said to me, friendly, as if I were a pet or a new toy. "I was hoping you'd come. We need a new eye here. It's the same deal as before—an untraceable murder. It's frustrating."

I grinned, despite the fact that I knew I shouldn't, despite the fact that I knew people didn't smile at murder scenes.

"You're beginning to trust me," I said cheerfully. I raised my eyebrows as if to say, *I promised! I told you I would see you tomorrow and I did!*

"You're smart. You've already proven that." He shrugged. "And honestly, at this point, I'm willing to try anything."

He lifted up the tape and gave me a *what the hell* look. I smiled wryly and walked underneath. Then I remembered Maggie. I turned back to her to say something, mouth open, but she beat me to it.

"I'll wait here, if you don't mind," she murmured. I nodded.

"I'll be back in a bit. I won't be long," I told her.

"I'll wait on the far curb. It's less crowded there."

"All right. I'll see you in a few, then."

"Right."

Alex let the tape fall, and shoulder to shoulder, we walked inside. Police officers passed by me, looking very official, making me feel like a child. Once we got into the front hallway, where Lily Kensington had put her hand on my shoulder, he gestured to the room to our left, where I had killed her. I let him guide me.

They had moved the body. On the black carpet, white tape outlined where Lily had been, crumpled up like a doll. Other than that, the room was untouched. The bloodstains weren't even visible on the carpet.

"Perfect," I whispered under my breath. It just slipped out before I noticed it had left my lips.

Alex heard me.

"It is, isn't it?" he said resentfully.

I bit my lip and reminded myself to be careful before I said something really incriminating.

"It's so . . . clean. No signs of struggle at all."

"The *couch pillows* are still in place," he said angrily. "No DNA, no fingerprints, no witnesses, no broken windows or picked locks, nothing. Nothing but the body."

"What did the body look like?" I asked. He was silent for a moment, as if wondering whether he should tell me, and then he sighed.

"She was by the couch, on her back, with her face smashed in. The shards of her nasal bone just went up into her brain and killed her, as far as I can tell, though don't quote me on that, that's not confirmed."

"On her back?' I said, feigning confusion.

"Yes," he replied, biting his thumb, concentrating, trying to figure it out.

This was why I wanted him to consider me an idiot. Idiots weren't called on to solve their own murders. Idiots didn't have to wonder about how much information was too much information, or how much they could say in order to gain the trust of the police without giving themselves away as the murderer.

Idiots had it easy.

"Hmm," I said quietly, thoughtfully.

"Any ideas?"

"Well . . . I don't know . . ." I hoped my act was convincing. "What kind of smashed-in face was it? Wow, that's a morbid question, but you know, it could help."

"Eh . . . well . . . I don't know, just smashed in."

"Like . . . was the whole thing smashed in, or was just the nose smashed in, or . . . you know . . ."

"Just the nose, I think," he said, his voice a bit lighter.

"And she was faceup by the couch?" I asked, eyeing the white lines.

"Yes."

I pretended to think about this.

"It looks almost like . . . because her center of gravity would be really down . . ."

"What?"

"She would have been sitting on the couch. If someone came up behind her . . . no, the front of her face is smashed in," I muttered discontentedly. "You're sure no windows were broken?"

"Yeah. No picked locks either. And the neighbors didn't hear anything. And there wasn't any surveillance video either."

I backed up and leaned against the wall near the TV, where I had leaned just the night before.

"Shit," I said.

I'm good, I thought.

"You don't see anything I don't?" he asked.

I shook my head. He sighed and ran his fingers tiredly through his hair.

"Normally, I'd say that the murderer was a friend, since there were no picked locks or anything, but since this is a serial killer, I guess we can rule that out," he said, thinking aloud. "It's the same every time. A perfect murder, simple and clean, with no clues and no witnesses. And every time, a letter."

"You're never going to solve it," I muttered.

"What?"

"It's nothing."

"But it's interesting. He's a strange serial killer. Most serial killers have a way of doing things, a way they murder all their victims. But the Perfect Killer's modus operandi is different every time. The only similarities the murders have are their perfection and the letters."

"But they're all too perfect to be a series of copycats."

"Exactly."

I was silent for a moment. I couldn't tell him the answer to his very legitimate question. I wished I could. I knew I couldn't make him understand, but it might be interesting to try. It was because I wasn't psychotic or bloodthirsty, didn't depend on a consistent modus operandi to keep my sanity. It was because I treated murder as a job.

"What did the letter say?" I asked curiously.

"Something about blackmail and her fiancé hating her. I haven't read the whole thing, I haven't had a chance yet."

"Poor girl," I said. "And poor bastard who wrote it."

Alex tilted his head and sighed.

"Most of the time I find the Perfect Killer disgusting," he said, and continued in a breathy voice that he let only me hear, though the room was swarming with police officers. "But other times I wonder why we aren't congratulating him."

Chapter 7

Maggie and I walked into my house to the smell of something cooking in the kitchen.

"Hey, Mom," I said, closing the door behind us. "I've brought company."

From the kitchen, my mom laughed cheerfully. No trace of the morning's tired melancholy was left in her voice; she was bright and beautiful now, just like usual, having had a day's rest.

"Finally. You're beginning to be like me," she chirped.

"Hello," Maggie replied meekly.

Maggie and I walked to the kitchen door and looked inside to see her surrounded in smoke that billowed around her head as she cooked something on the grill part of the stove.

"Mom, this is Maggie. Maggie, this is my mom."

My mom stepped away from the stove and held out a hand to shake, which Maggie took lamely.

"Hello, Maggie."

"Nice to meet you, Mrs. Ward."

"Lovely to meet you as well. I'm glad you've become friends with Kit. She doesn't often bring people over."

"Ah . . . thank you."

Maggie stood gawkily for a moment before I realized that I should take charge of the situation again.

"Oh." I laughed. "Maggie, let's go to my room. It's way up on the top floor. Don't know why I picked it, but I like it."

"Okay," Maggie said with an agreeable smile.

The two of us started out of the room toward the stairs, Maggie going first.

"Kit, can I talk to you alone for a moment?" my mom called after me. I stopped and walked back into the kitchen as Maggie waited, looking rather lost, sinking deep into the Turkish rug at the bottom of the stairs. My mom beckoned to me, telling me to come closer, closer, closer, until our faces were only about a foot away and I could see the tiny, near-invisible flecks of brown in her intensely blue eyes.

"Are you going to kill her?" she asked, expression utterly cold and unfeeling.

I paused.

"Yes," I said.

She looked at me carefully, warningly. *Be careful,* she was saying silently.

"Don't get too close," she whispered.

"I know." I smiled.

"Kit, I mean it. I–" She paused and continued in an even quieter voice, barely loud enough for me to hear. "Why is she here?"

"It's good to know what you're up against, right?"

"I . . ." She hesitated.

She was so concerned. Her eyes glistened sharply out of the smoke, and her slender fingers quivered. The sharp curve of her jawline was a strangely angled shadow.

"It's fine. I'll be fine–you don't have to worry," I said to her comfortingly, and she was uncertain for a moment, but then she softened. She remembered my precision, my carefulness, my fastidious organization.

She smiled back, reassured that I knew what I was doing and hadn't forgotten how to keep myself safe. She tossed her arms around my shoulders quickly, her breath wafting across my neck.

"Just be careful," she sighed tenderly. She let me go.

Before I went back to Maggie, I flashed my mother a cocky, vibrant grin. She really didn't have to worry about me.

She returned the smile with a motherly, reassuring, thoughtful, vaguely uncertain nod of the head.

◆ ◇ ◆

Maggie and I lay on our backs on the floor in a pile of pillows, looking at the pale cream ceiling.

We were tired—since it was a school day that day and a school day the next as well, we should probably already be asleep. But we were teenage girls. And teenage girls never go to bed on time. We kept ourselves awake by talking. Our voices sounded sleepy.

"I can't believe you know policemen. Like, actually know them, are actually friends with them. That's crazy. You just went into a crime scene, no big deal." Maggie yawned. She was more talkative when she was tired, apparently. My mother was that way as well.

I giggled. "I have my mom to thank for that. She invited him over for dinner. I told you she's got a habit of inviting random people over. And, you know, we became friends."

"Oh, so *that's* what she meant earlier about inviting people over."

"Yeah, yeah."

"That's cool. I'd like that. You know, if my family did that. You've got a nice house. You're right to invite people to such a nice house."

"Your family doesn't do company much?"

"Nah. We don't do much of anything . . . much. My immediate family, at least. My extended family's the only exciting part. They're nice," Maggie said softly.

The room went quiet.

"Nothing at all? That must be boring," I said, laughing, trying to lighten the mood.

"Nothing, really. My parents are . . . I don't know, quiet, don't bother me much. They're out of town a lot. And I'm an only child, so home is just boring."

"Look at the bright side. Freedom, right?"

"Freedom is just another word for no one cares," she said, and laughed breathily.

I didn't know what to say to that. But I had to say something, so—

"I don't think so."

"You don't?"

"Freedom is freedom, right? For whatever reason, you can do what you want, right?"

"I suppose."

"If you've got freedom and no one cares, you should be having more fun," I said jauntily.

"Like what?"

"Strike out. Do something crazy. Dye your hair pink or something, at least."

"That's against uniform regulations at school."

"Who *cares*?"

"I care."

"Why? It's not like you want to be a Nobel Prize winner or anything. You can take all those hard classes and stuff, but you can't fool me. You're a little rebel on the inside, just like me."

"I'm not," she said flatly. "I'm good. I stick to the status quo. And how do you know I don't want to win a Nobel Prize?"

"Because I can see right through you, that's how. Beneath that timid exterior is a . . . I don't know. A tiger or something. Waiting to break free. And Jesus, what's so good about the status quo?"

"You say that. But you stick to it too. You wear preppy clothes and don't cause trouble. You're just an upper-middle-class kid with her own agenda and a few nice pairs of shoes like the rest of us."

I grinned, still tired, but behind that wooziness, my heart was beating quickly.

"I stick to the status quo because what I like *is* the status quo."

Well, not entirely true. Murder wasn't the status quo. But true enough. There was enough truth in it so I didn't feel like I was lying. One-half of me was the status quo, at least—the half of me that went to school and went to cafés and ate lunch in the cafeteria. The half of me that murdered was absolutely separate from all that, another being entirely.

"And hey, befriending you wasn't the status quo, was it? You were a friendless loser and I befriended you. That's not what normal people do," I added.

"You say that, but in the end, you're just like everyone else, including me. You'd ditch that rebellious attitude the moment it endangered your social status."

I stood up suddenly, smiling a wild, wicked grin.

"You sure about that?"

"Yes," Maggie said, undaunted.

I walked across the room to the window and flung it open. The night air hit my face like a cold sheet, washing over me. Outside, I heard the soft call of London, the swish of cars passing in the distance down King's Road.

I put one foot on the low windowsill.

"Jumping out of windows isn't the status quo," I said loudly.

She gasped and shot up into a sitting position, eyes wide, mouth gaping like a fish.

"Don't do it, Kit!"

I laughed heavily, the sound coming from deep within my stomach.

"Don't worry. I've done this before, when I was younger. Accidentally, then, but I figure the same sort of thing would happen if I did it again. There's some nice bushes at the bottom that stop my fall. I'd come to school with scratches on Monday and I'd have to answer the questions, wouldn't I? Don't you think word would get around that I jumped out a window? Wouldn't that be breaking the status quo? Should I do it to prove a point?" I put my other foot on the windowsill, so I was crouching in the window frame, holding the bottom of it with both hands, the drop looming below me.

"Don't do it—I get it already, I get it!"

I smiled. I stepped backward out of the window frame.

"I won't do it," I said, looking back over my shoulder toward her. "Don't worry."

She sighed but kept staring anxiously at me.

"The point is," I said, "don't stick to the status quo. Live wildly. You've got your freedom—now do something with it, for God's sake."

"You're crazy," she said.

"I know."

"But you're the most honest friend I've had in a long time."

I hesitated. I bit my tongue gently.

"Thanks," I said.

"Thank you," she said.

"No problem."

◆ ◇ ◆

A few days passed innocently like that, with no change in Maggie's behavior or mine. I began to plot my next murder—a young lawyer who apparently cheated a divorcing couple out of their money—and I did well in school, especially in philosophy, where I excelled. I tried to take to heart Dr. Marcell's suggestion of sharing more of my thoughts, but it really was quite hard when most of my thoughts were of murder.

I began to gather strange, hostile glances from Michael. Beginning on Wednesday, in the early morning, in homeroom, he was silent in my presence. I caught him sneaking glances over his shoulder at me when he thought I wasn't looking, his eyes almost accusing, somehow, as if he knew my secrets. He made me sick.

And then, in philosophy, the only class we shared, he made a point of antagonizing me during discussion. Dr. Marcell praised him for arguing, of course, saying it was adding to the conversation. It wasn't. But I bit my lip and said nothing. I left the classroom quickly after the bell rang. And then in hallways, between classes and after school, I saw him lurking, watching me. I was sure he was watching Maggie too. This continued throughout the week, and I wondered what his problem was. I really wondered.

As the week went on, my vague curiosity turned sharper and sharper—and on Thursday, it reached a breaking point.

I hadn't planned on following him home after school. I did it on a whim.

It was fairly stupid. But it wasn't doing any harm, was it? If I got caught, I could just laugh it off, say I was walking toward the Thames and only happened to be walking just behind him—that was where he lived, just on the other side of the Thames, across Waterloo Bridge. It was about a twenty-minute walk. I'm not really sure what I was trying to accomplish. But whatever my reasoning, in the end, I did end up following him home on Thursday afternoon.

It wasn't too hard to escape notice. He took busy streets; it was easy to hide myself behind mothers with strollers and sickeningly sweet couples and other members of the scenery as I lingered about twenty feet behind him. I kept my eyes on his head as it bobbed along. His hair did this silly little bouncing thing with every step.

Strangely enough, I felt almost horrible about following him, now that I was doing it.

I knew I shouldn't feel bad. I knew moral nihilism—nothing right, nothing wrong. Though it didn't feel *wrong* to follow him so much as it just felt *uncomfortable*; so perhaps moral nihilism didn't exactly apply. As I followed him through the crowd, as cars drove past and people nearby sold newspapers and went into shops to buy earrings and groceries and whatever else, I felt somehow as if I were violating him. Robbing him. Watching with purpose, I supposed, might not have been so bad, but I was watching him for no reason. Senselessly. Invading.

He was just going about his business. He pushed past a group of women and looked absently into a store window, and he didn't know I was there. Someone had spilled their soda—he jumped to avoid it. I watched him. I kept following. As I kept following, I almost began to feel sorry for doing it. But not quite sorry enough to turn away.

After a while my mind and eyes began to wander, though I still kept him in the corner of my vision. The Thames and the Waterloo Bridge were discernible in the distance now. The sky was blue; there were birds winging over the rooftops, unconcerned with anything below; my hair was in my eyes, and I brushed it away, and it flopped back down again. I smelled oranges.

And then, suddenly, there was a crashing sound about twenty feet ahead.

I jumped, startled. I hadn't seen what happened. It took me a few moments to process the details. A bicycle had somehow fallen in the middle of the sidewalk, taking three people down with it: its rider—a red-faced and apologetic brunette kid in a yellow dress—a stately looking housewife type, and Michael.

I almost laughed. There they were. They looked ridiculous, the three of them tangled up in the middle of the sidewalk. It seemed like something out of a comedy sketch. The brunette girl's dress was ripped up the side—why was she wearing a dress on a bicycle anyway? The housewife had lost both of her pink kitten heels. One was in the gutter, and the other had gotten wedged between the spokes of the bicycle's front wheel. And Michael—

Michael.

Michael was *glaring*.

Or maybe not glaring, exactly, because glaring implies that you're looking angrily at one thing in particular. Michael wasn't looking at anything. He was staring out into space. His eyes were unfocused and narrowed—he was looking indistinctly in the direction of the bright sky, and he couldn't keep them open all the way.

And, oh, the anger in those eyes.

The scene wasn't funny any longer.

I didn't understand. This was a bicycle crash. Maybe a few scrapes, but no real harm done. Why was there so much anger? Sure, the housewife was yelling and irritated, but she was already on her feet, and a few other people were helping the girl in yellow disentangle herself from the handlebars. No one helped Michael. They all saw the same thing I did, and they were afraid. As they should be.

Because I was afraid too. And I was a serial killer. I was not often afraid.

There was something in those eyes. An empty hatred,

hatred with nowhere to go, nothing to be directed at. Hatred that let him blend in with the world for the most part, except when it grew too large for him to hold it in all the way. Hatred that bubbled to the surface but didn't quite overflow. Hatred that led him to wish for his former friend's death but wouldn't let him kill her himself.

He stood and wiped the dust from the pavement off his uniform and walked on. I pushed my hair away from my face, and this time it stayed.

I kept following him toward Waterloo Bridge. I no longer felt sorry for following him. How could I? He didn't deserve my pity. He didn't need it. I stepped delicately over the back wheel of the bike, nudging by the girl in yellow with a few murmured words of apology.

I followed him all the way down to the river, and there I left him. I stood in the shade of bright green trees and looked at the boats bobbing along the water. I didn't need to go any farther; I had seen enough. I would stop here. I stood at the edge of the bridge. The Thames was sparkling in the sun. It didn't sparkle like that very often, because the sky was so often cloudy; I liked to see it like that. I sometimes forgot that London was beautiful. The glittering Thames always reminded me.

As Michael walked away down the bridge, I kept watching him. He was a retreating shape now, one pedestrian among many. It was funny how things like that worked. A human can carry worlds of emotion, but the farther away you get, the smaller they seem, no matter how big they are on the inside.

And then, unexpectedly, Michael turned around.

He was too far away to see my face, and I was standing behind enough people to obscure the fact that I was wearing his school's uniform, but it still made me uneasy. It was a casual gesture. He wasn't suspicious or anything. He was just turning around for the sake of it. But still it set me on edge, just like everything else about him. He was looking back, but he was still walking. I saw the outline of his face from far away. Shadows for eyes, a thin line for a mouth. It was almost demonic.

He turned back around quickly.

Once he crossed the bridge, I left to go home. My skin was still prickling. I was disturbed. It was incredible to me that someone could hold so much anger within themselves and manage not to go insane.

But, I thought reasonably, I had no reason to be afraid. I was a killer, and he was just a teenage boy with issues. I was stronger than him, faster, more adept, better.

So slowly I reasoned my fear away. I had no use for fear. Even anger was better than fear.

◆ ◇ ◆

My father was home.

It was honestly a shock to see him there, sitting at the kitchen table, on a Thursday night, no less. He usually worked late into the night during the week doing something that involved stocks—like so many other things about him, the details of his work were sketchy to me. He was only ever home at a reasonable time on the weekends, and even that was seldom.

He was reading the newspaper as if his being home at six o'clock on a Thursday were the most common thing in the world. I walked into the kitchen to get something to drink—the afternoon's activity had left me parched and tired. I'd walked for nearly an hour and a half to get home. I'd dawdled. It was such a nice day, I felt as if I should enjoy the sun.

And I walked into the kitchen and there he was.

He was reading the morning's newspaper, and there was a cup of coffee on the table in front of him, steam still rising over the rim. His gray hair, brushed away from sharp blue eyes, was short and spiky at the back, where it had gotten messed up during the day. He was still wearing his suit, but he had taken off his yellow tie and draped it over the back of a nearby chair.

Where was my mother? I looked around. She must be here somewhere. He wouldn't make coffee for himself—he never did. I wasn't even sure he knew how to use the coffeemaker. My mother always made it. Despite his incompetence, he was always drinking coffee. It was something that defined him. It was one of very few defining characteristics, really. If he didn't drink coffee, I didn't know quite how I would remember him.

I didn't see my mother. I walked toward the table. He didn't notice me, or at least, if he did, he didn't let on. He turned the page in his tall newspaper; I set my book bag down, leaning against the leg of the table. I made sure that it hit the ground loudly, but he still didn't look at me.

"Where's Mom?" I asked at full volume.

He jumped, the newspaper rustling as he jerked it away from his face.

"Kit, you scared me!" he exclaimed, his voice melting into a cordial laugh. I tilted my head and replied with a similarly formal smile.

"Sorry. Where's Mom?"

"You're not going to even ask how I am?" he asked. I dragged my hands through my hair. He didn't care whether I asked him. He was just being difficult.

"I could ask you, if you like."

He laughed again, tightly, and didn't push the issue.

"So where's Mom?"

"She went out."

I nodded and went over to the kitchen cabinets, taking down a tall glass. I filled it with ice and tap water, and I listened to the ice crackle; I kept looking at my father, who had gone calmly back to his newspaper.

Newspaper. That was another thing that defined him, wasn't it, now that I thought about it. Newspapers grabbed off the kitchen table in the mornings as he went off to work, newspapers read as he went up the stairs at night. Spread out so I couldn't see his face.

Glass in one hand, I went back over to the kitchen table. I looked down at my bag and considered picking it up and going up to my room like I had been planning to in the first place. But instead I took a coaster off the kitchen counter and sat down at the end of the table opposite my father. I kicked off my shoes. I took a long sip of my water and set it down, watching as the bottom of my glass made a ring on the leather coaster. I stared at him. I waited for him to notice.

It had been such a long time since I had heard him talk, I realized as I stared at the newspaper–I couldn't stare at his face, because it was hidden behind the front-page headline. Perhaps weeks. He was usually so silent when he was home. He was like a ghost in his own house, drifting through, barely speaking, nearly invisible. Which was strange, because he was in business, and I knew that basically meant that he talked for a living. He was good at making friends. But he had no friends in his own home.

I set my head in my hands and remembered the Christmas so long ago that my mother always talked about when she was tired. She never really opened up except for when she was deathly tired. It happened more often than one would think. She had nightmares, after all, and sometimes I would come down to the kitchen in the middle of the night for a glass of water, or an extra blanket from the hall cupboard, and she would hear my footsteps and come out and hang over the banister and talk to me. She didn't drink, but when she really wanted to sleep, she slurred her speech and wobbled like she had just drunk a half bottle of rum. And she talked, and talked and talked. And usually she told the same story.

I was young then–too young to know my fate yet, too young to know much of anything. Older than one and less than three, the story went. I don't remember it myself.

It was Christmas Day, and Dad was home. Christmas was one of the few times a year that he was obligated to spend time with us—or at least, I suppose, he was obligated once. Now he had faded away even from that, appearing only on Christmas Eve, for example, or only for a few hours on Christmas Day.

Every Christmas during that time in my life, he bought my mother and me unsuitable presents—clothes in the wrong size, for example, or toys of the sort I had grown too old for—and helped to set the table; he pretended he was one of us. Every Christmas, my mother made him coffee, and he stood by the kitchen table and said nothing. What did they have to talk about?

Once they had been young, vibrant. My mother told me sometimes about how he had been able to dance, when they first met, and how he had been so charming then, with a crooked smile, a wicked sense of humor, and a casual way of speaking—she had seduced him, as well, with her own charms; once, he had loved her.

She had been different then too. Sometimes, with almost sadness, she told me about her past self. She had loved jazz and the kind of instrumental music where the trumpets seemed to belong to a different time—she had known the steps to every dance worth knowing, the name of every book worth reading. She had run through London at midnight, remembering the blood she was responsible for; she had worn bright colors and too much jewelry. My father, somehow and strangely, had once shared her vibrancy. For a while, they had danced through life hand in hand.

Until they had both changed.

It was just the way life went, I supposed.

Of course, she had never had any illusions about his true character. She had seen his inevitable change from the very beginning. He had always put career first, and respectability just behind. Career and respectability before everything, before family, before connection. That was why he had been so perfect—she had needed someone who would lose interest in her and drift away, no matter her allure, but would remain married to her in order to provide an illusion of respectable normality. We needed people to gloss over us, to not think about us too hard, and he gave us that essential veneer of the ordinary.

My mother had always called marrying him "logical." To me, it has only ever seemed lonely.

That particular Christmas, my mother had sent him out to buy something early in the morning. He had come back at around eleven. Two presents had been opened for me so I would have something to occupy myself with until he returned and we could open the rest together, as a family, as was tradition. When he came back in, my mother was in the kitchen making pumpkin pie, and the nanny was upstairs in the second-floor living room with me, watching me as I played with my new toys and discarded wrapping paper.

My mother smiled and went to him and hugged him around the neck, and he returned the smile very faintly. He said absolutely nothing. *Not a word,* my mother always said, *not a word, not a word.*

She led him upstairs to me, letting the half-made pie sit alone on the kitchen counter and letting the refrigerator stand open. I hadn't seen him the night before—I had been asleep—and I hadn't seen him for weeks before that either. He had been away on business.

She led him to the small Christmas tree and dismantled presents. She swept me out of the nanny's arms and—this was her favorite part—she held me up to my father, and he held his arms out to me, and I began to cry.

I didn't know him. I didn't recognize his face. He wasn't around enough for me to know him. To my approximately two-year-old mind, he was a strange man who wanted to hold me, perhaps take me away, perhaps worse. I was afraid.

He took his arms away and my mother held me close to her chest, soothing me, trying to calm my tears. But I kept crying, and crying.

So my father left. He just walked down the stairs, saying nothing, and went out and didn't come back for about a week, and even when he did come back, he didn't acknowledge the fact that his own daughter didn't know him. He just went on. And he was still going on. And that's just how he was, and there was nothing I could do, I didn't think.

Nothing any of us could do.

He was so still—so immovable. I wondered what went on beneath his surface. Was there pain there, or regret? If there was, was he facing it or running from it?

That possibility made me think for a minute. Running was possible. Maybe his fault was never that he cared too little, but that he cared too much. Maybe his fault was that he had only accidentally drifted too far from his family, and when he realized that he had floated so far, he also realized that there was no turning back. And so maybe his distance was always a way to protect himself. He never came home because he didn't want to confront a problem that made him hurt so much.

But that was probably just wishful thinking.

I stared at the man across the table from me, hiding behind his newspaper. He wouldn't notice me. There was no use in waiting, I realized.

I stood irritably up from the table and stretched, and then I picked up the coaster, the water glass, and my book bag all at once. I slung the bag over my shoulder, doing my best not to spill any water. I left my shoes behind. I kept looking at where his face should be behind the paper. Through my annoyance, I almost had to be amused. He really was precisely what he needed to be. He didn't pay attention to anything he didn't need to pay attention to, and he let things slip. He was so perfect it was almost scary.

I walked barefoot across the thick Turkish rug toward the stairs, and then, to my surprise, I heard my mother's footsteps coming down. I paused. She walked onto the landing above me and saw me watching her with curiosity, and she stopped as well.

"Why the puzzled expression?" she asked, drawing her

hands over her white wool skirt as if to smooth out imaginary creases. Her blue eyes looked at me, softly, I supposed. It was hard for her to seem truly soft; it wasn't her fault. She had a sharp face, and sharp eyes especially.

"I thought you were out."

"Why?"

"Dad said . . . ," I began, but my voice trailed off as I realized that yet again my father hadn't seen anything. Had just been an island. He hadn't really known where she was; he had just been saying something for the sake of saying something.

She laughed faintly.

"He sounded like he knew what he was saying," I excused myself lamely. My mother came down the stairs, and I shrugged and went up, meeting her eyes briefly, and I found something quiet simmering there.

Too quiet. She wouldn't do a thing. Not anymore.

I realized why, suddenly.

While stubbornly resisting her murderous impulses, she had forced herself so far into passiveness that it was beginning to become her true nature.

◆ ◆ ◆

That night I dreamed of a memory.

A dark midnight street, residential, lined with black-windowed houses.

I was eleven years old. I exited a redbrick house on a corner, stepping carefully out into the street, trying to close the door behind me without noise.

I walked three blocks to a more central area, where I met up with my mother. She was standing tensely outside a convenience store, a bottle of water and a silvery bag of half-eaten chips in her hands. She was waiting for me, making sure I got out of the murder unscathed.

As I approached, she looked anxiously around, pale skin glowing ethereally in the lights of streetlamps, as if she were afraid something catastrophic was about to happen. A few people were inside the convenience store, but it was late and they were tired and no one was paying any attention. There were no cameras around. I put my hands in my jacket pockets and was slightly amused by her anxious nervousness.

"Is she dead?" she murmured to me, making sure that no one could hear.

"Of course." I shrugged.

"No evidence?"

I looked at her and laughed. "You don't need to be so worried, you know. I'm fine on my own. She was short and thin and no one else was home. No evidence, no traces."

She looked faintly embarrassed.

"I'm sorry . . . I just worry. It was your first solo kill, after all."

I hugged her around her waist, and she tucked her arms around my shoulders and closed her eyes.

"I'm fine," I said.

"I know," she replied, with the air of a mother.

Then she let me go and held me out at arm's length and grinned wildly, proud of me, of what I had so professionally done, of what I was becoming for her sake.

I wasn't done with all my training at that point. I was still taking lessons in our converted bedroom, but it was in that moment, as I watched her joy and realized that it was all inspired by my actions, that she had no direct, violent part in creating it, that I had done it on my own, that the realization first bloomed within me—

I was self-sufficient.

It was an odd feeling, and right then, I remember feeling distinctly uncomfortable with it, because I hadn't known precisely what it meant.

And then the moment dissolved and I saw other flashes of memory float past me, winding senselessly about as memories in dreams often do—my mother teaching me to ice-skate—my mother laughing joyously across the table from me, crouched in a chair with a sheet around her shoulders, eating a bowl of strawberry ice cream—my mother sitting on the living room floor, drinking homemade lemonade—my mother teaching me how to shove my hands up beneath the chin of a tall opponent to snap the head back and break the neck—my mother, lean and athletic, kissing a strange man on the porch—

And again and again the memory of a photograph, that photograph, the photograph of the dead woman with a heart drawn violently in black on her chest.

Chapter 8

On Friday, as Maggie and I ate lunch in our corner of the cafeteria, Michael came over to visit.

It was unexpected. Maggie and I were talking about something fairly innocuous. One moment he wasn't there and the next he was, hovering over us, hands on the table, glaring at us each in turn with a wicked smile on his attractive face. It made him look ugly.

I sighed. What an idiot. Problems in this school were solved quietly, without anyone noticing. He was being too obvious. When you were in Rome, you did as the Romans did.

"Look at you two," he sneered. "How cute."

For a moment I just looked at him, not exactly sure

what to say to that. Across from me, Maggie sank down lower in her chair, becoming small, shivering. I glanced at her, then at him, then back to her, and then I set my face in a sarcastic smile.

Fine. If he wanted to play, then I would play his way.

"Almost as cute as your psychotic anger management issues," I sneered right back.

He was silent, biting his lip angrily. Then he sat down next to me and turned his attention to Maggie, shoving his elbow into my personal space. I frowned at him and nudged at it with my hand—he ignored me.

"I bet you're regretting leaving us now," Michael snapped.

"You kicked her out," I retorted quietly. He ignored me.

Maggie shivered, and for a strange moment I wondered whether that was the truth. Had she been the one to leave them after Michael hurt her, instead of the other way around, as I had always assumed? I didn't think she had the backbone for that—but maybe she did after all.

"Only one friend? That's sad, don't you think?" Michael smirked.

I whacked his elbow with my fist. He ignored me. Maggie, quiet as stone, shrank even further, turned her eyes toward her feet.

"Especially when that friend is a whore like this girl—"

I clenched my fist and hit him in the eye.

He fell to the floor, sprawled out on the linoleum.

I stood over him and looked down at him patronizingly.

I shook out my fist. That had hurt. He gasped, staring at the floor, breath heaving, and, when he had collected himself, glared in surprise up at me. He would have a bruise later. I could almost see it, the skin blossoming purple—

Suddenly my eyes narrowed, and I tasted blood in the air, and I realized that I could kill him easily, so easily.

I shook myself out of it. No. No. I couldn't kill him. Not here, not now. I just stared at him, made my murderous instincts fade away.

His eyes were still angry.

That interested me.

Most people, when I hit them, were upset. They cried, or yelped, or ran, if they weren't dead by the time they hit the floor. But he didn't run. He just looked up at me and glared. There was anger in those eyes, like I had seen before, so much anger, and something else. . . .

I sighed. "Look," I said. "This may seem selfish, but here's the deal. You say bad stuff about my friends, I'll be mad. You'll piss me off. But you say bad stuff about me, I get really mad. Really pissed. That sort of thing doesn't fly with me. You insult me, you end up on the floor like this."

I glanced up and realized that the cafeteria in my vicinity had gone silent. People were staring. People were looking.

I felt itchy, uncomfortable. I didn't regret hitting him. He deserved it. But I didn't want their attention.

I heard Maggie's gasping breaths behind me, thick with an emotion close to horror.

"Bitch, I'll get you," he spat, and pushed himself into a sitting position.

I quickly crouched, knelt on his chest, and pushed him back to the ground. Around me, I heard a collective gasp. He gasped too, but for a different reason, because the movement had pushed all the air out of his lungs. I grabbed his collar, forced his head up so my mouth was next to his ear. He made a gargling sound.

"Michael Vernon," I whispered venomously. "Let me make you understand. You won't get me. No one gets *me*. I get other people. And I'll get you, just like I get the rest. You mess with me again, Michael, and I'll kill you, I swear."

I let go of his collar. His head fell backward and hit the floor again with a dull *thwack*, and this time there was surprise in his eyes. Surprise, but still no fear.

"Hit him again!" someone exclaimed nearby. I breathed in sharply, angrily, staring at Michael.

I stood up and walked away from him, toward the door out of the cafeteria and into the hall. The crowds parted to let me through. By now the whole room was silent and tense. As I walked through, people watched me with stunned surprise and almost terror.

They hadn't been expecting that from me. Actually, I hadn't been expecting that from me. That was reckless. Too reckless. I needed to blend in, not gather attention or suspicion. As soon as I walked away and the anger and adrenaline faded, I was mad at myself.

That was stupid.

Stupid.

The hallway was empty. I stalked down it, not really knowing where I was going. And then, footsteps in the hallway.

"Kit."

I turned to see Maggie. Her eyes were wide and her mouth was open. I was beginning to think that she had only a limited number of facial expressions.

I didn't say anything, just looked at her expressionlessly.

"That was crazy." She gaped.

"Yeah, well, I'm crazy, aren't I?"

"Yeah. You are," she said admiringly. I laughed, feeling all my muscles tense, trying to relax.

"You like that about me?"

"Well, I've never been friends with anyone crazy before. It's kind of exciting."

I looked at her darkly.

"Be careful. Crazy can be dangerous," I muttered.

I heard footsteps from the opposite direction. Dr. Marcell was running down the hallway, a young freshman girl at her heels.

"I heard there was a disturbance in the cafeteria," Dr. Marcell said urgently, looking from Maggie to me and back again, looking for more information. Her dark hair bobbed, and the hem of her unflattering dress flipped up at the hem.

I raised my hand, inspecting it, shaking it out again. It felt almost like I had broken something. That could be inconvenient. But no, it was okay, the pain was receding now. My hand would be fine. I met Dr. Marcell's eyes.

"That was me," I said, nearly whispering. "Sorry."

She was surprised. Why? She knew that I believed in moral nihilism and other ethically controversial philosophies. Moral nihilists didn't usually punch people, I supposed. But she *must* have suspected at some point that I was a bit off-kilter.

"Really, Kit?" she asked. It was an honest question.

I shrugged. "Really."

"Oh, Kit," she sighed.

She stared into my eyes, no doubt looking for some kind of regret. She wouldn't find any. I had never been good at faking regret.

She saw my empty eyes, and suddenly I saw a spark, the tiniest sliver of suspicion, kindle in her mind. A traitorous spark, a dangerous ember. She was too smart for her own good.

Chapter 9

I met Alex for lunch on Saturday at a small bistro near the Brass Feather. I dressed in a smart blue dress and a pair of brown heels that were just a bit too big and made my toes slide down into the front of them and crunch painfully. I had forgotten that they didn't fit when I put them on, had just remembered that they made my legs look nice, and I was wincing as I walked into the bistro. I was trying to look nice for Alex—oh well. Beauty was pain.

He was already there when I arrived. As I walked through the door, he waved to me from a table near the back of the green-and-blue restaurant. When I saw him, something flared up unexpectedly in my chest, a feeling that could best be described, to my chagrin, as "butterflies";

I quickly forced the feeling away as best I could, though it still lingered. It was useless, and I didn't have time for it. Wiping away my grimace and replacing it with my nicest smile, I made my way over to him. He was looking at me with his head slightly tilted, resting on interlaced fingers. I felt his gaze on me intensely.

The people in the restaurant were mostly elderly, with a few odd smatterings of younger people—a couple at the window and a man with dark hair and glasses reading in the back, and of course, Alex. The walls were covered in faded wallpaper patterned with small birds, and the tables were made of fraying wicker. He had chosen it. He had told me that the decorating was awful, but the food was incredible. It really did look quite unimpressive, but I trusted him.

"My mom couldn't make it," I said as I sat down across from him. "Sorry. I asked her, but she said she had other lunch plans."

"Oh. Oh well." He shrugged.

I grinned at him. He was in street clothes today, a black T-shirt and jeans, with a gray sweatshirt draped over the back of his chair. He looked nice like this, less angry, younger. He was wearing glasses, the ones I had seen him in on Tuesday. Through them, I could see his hazel eyes—deep and dreaming, with flecks of blue I hadn't noticed before.

I gestured to the glasses.

"I like glasses on you. They make you look intelligent."

"I didn't look intelligent before?"

"You looked . . . sharp before. Now you look bookish." I hesitated, then shrugged. "It suits you."

"Thanks, I suppose."

"It's a compliment."

"Then thanks."

"Any action from the Perfect Killer? I haven't seen anything in the papers or anything, and the murders aren't usually that close together, but . . ."

He shook his head. "No news since that flawless murder you saw on Tuesday."

"That's good, then."

"Yes, but no clues isn't good. Your idea that the murderer is a student was very clever, but we can't find any leads to help us investigate that path. Or any path, really."

No clues is good for me, I thought wryly.

"I'm sure you'll find something soon," I said encouragingly. He shrugged.

"How's life?" he asked casually, leaning toward me. He didn't really expect an honest answer.

He absently brushed long fingers across the silverware on the table, straightening the knife and spoon. As I spoke I watched those movements—graceful, captivating. Mesmerizing . . .

For a moment, I felt as if I were being drawn in, as if we were the only two people in the room. I suddenly noticed the lack of distance between us, realized that the tip of my shoe was resting against his left foot, that there were only inches between our hands. His eyes were now looking softly, yet insistently, into mine. After a few seconds, I had to look away.

Alex was unnervingly easy to like. Unnervingly enthralling.

Eventually, I managed to answer his question.

"Fine. Not much is happening. School, home. Not terribly exciting. Your life is more interesting than mine."

He smiled in a half thank-you—how else exactly could you respond to a statement like that?—then remembered something.

"You've been bad!" he exclaimed.

"What?"

"I heard from your mom. You got in trouble at school."

"Heh. Yeah," I replied sheepishly.

"You *hit* someone."

"Yeah."

"Why? That was a stupid thing to do. If you ever want to become a cop, that's going to be a bad mark on your record."

I looked at him and raised my eyebrows.

"A cop?"

He raised his eyebrows too.

"Don't you want to become a cop? I mean, you spend so much time thinking about the Perfect Killer case and all."

"Well, I suppose . . . yeah, I might like that."

"But anyway, why did you hit him?"

"I don't know! He just was being awful."

Alex looked at me carefully. I felt a sudden need to defend myself.

"Calling my friend names and such, being nearly psychotic. I swear to God, I didn't just punch some innocent bystander or anything."

"Did he deserve it?"

"What?"

"Did he deserve it?"

"Yes . . . yes he did."

Alex leaned back in his chair and exhaled defeatedly. He looked at the ceiling.

"That's good, then."

"What?"

"If you're going to hit someone, it better be for a good reason."

I giggled and felt oddly satisfied with him. "You're funny, you know that? You look like such a straightforward person, but you're really not that way at all."

"Yeah, well, I can say the same thing for you."

"You think so?"

He looked at me strangely. "Obviously."

I didn't know quite what to make of this comment and spent the next few seconds mulling over it.

A waitress wandered over to our table, a young girl with short brown hair.

"Do you want anything to drink?" she asked.

"I'll have ice water, thanks," I said.

"Pepsi for me."

"Right." She nodded. "I'll be right back with that."

I unfolded the menu that was on my placemat and looked over my choices of paninis, light pastas, breads, and pastries.

"You're right, this all looks wonderful," I said to Alex. But he wasn't listening. I looked over to see him deep in thought.

"Alex?"

He looked at me and breathed deeply.

"If I say something, will you keep quiet about it?"

I closed my menu and looked at him judiciously.

"Yes," I said slowly.

He looked down and rested his forehead in his palms, brushing his hair smoothly back to rest in faint waves that curled away from his face. Then he breathed deeply again, put his hands in his lap, leaned back in his chair, and looked at me.

"I'm afraid," he murmured.

And he was. I could see it. In his eyes, in his posture, in his slightly quivering voice.

"I can't tell it to anyone else. Everyone else I know is from the Yard. They'd stop trusting me. I'm rising in the ranks. I'm basically in charge of this investigation. I can't show fear, or weakness."

"But you're afraid," I clarified uncertainly.

"I'm so afraid. So afraid."

"Why?" I murmured.

"I don't want to be next. This murderer . . . these

murders . . . they're terrifying. So many . . . perfect murders, perfectly untraceable. London's first real, famous serial killer since Jack the Ripper. But the murders aren't even confined to one area of London, like the Whitechapel murders. They're everywhere and anywhere. And the letters . . . I don't know where the murderer gets them. I don't know who writes them and where they're delivered to."

So he didn't know about the mailbox. The neighborhood myth really hadn't found its way to Scotland Yard yet. That was good. I wouldn't enlighten him.

"And I'm in charge of the investigation. I'm just afraid, so, so afraid that one day a letter is going to show up with my name on it."

"Have you done anything wrong?" I asked.

"I'm with the Yard, Kit. Think of all the people I've made angry, put in jail. . . ."

It was a decent point. Still . . .

"I don't think you have to worry so much," I said gently.

"Why not?"

"Because . . ." I searched for an explanation, one that I could reasonably give to him to make him feel better. After a moment of thought, I realized I could simply tell him the truth.

"Because I think the murderer has a code of ethics."

"What part of murder is ethical?"

"Think about it," I said. "By your reasoning, the murderer must get a lot of requests for the deaths of police officers, right? But not one's been killed yet."

He looked up.

"That's right," he realized. "But I'm different. . . . I'm in charge. What if he gets a letter for me and discards his ethics because I'm in his way?"

"But you're *not* in his way," I pointed out.

"What?"

"You are so far away from solving the murder. You are nowhere near being in his way," I said apologetically. "I'm sorry. But it's the truth."

"That's right," he said again. "I'm *not* in his way."

He looked blankly at me for a moment, trying to digest that, to make himself believe that. He sighed and gave up after a few seconds, leaning over the table and scratching the back of his head.

"Thanks," he said halfheartedly.

"You won't die," I told him.

He looked me in the eyes and smiled.

"Thanks."

"I mean it," I said, trying to make him understand that that was the truth. I wouldn't kill him. Not if I got a letter, not ever. He believed in justice, fought for it. I didn't kill people like him.

"Here's your drinks," the perky waitress said, setting them down on the table in front of us. I smiled at her, and Alex forced himself to nod kindly. She smiled at him and walked away.

"You won't die," I said one more time. Alex nodded again, at me this time. I smiled slightly, inwardly *begging* him to absorb what I was saying, to truly understand. I thought I saw his eyes warming, his uncertainty fading—but I wasn't sure. I hoped I saw it. His fear was unnecessary, and it made me feel guilty.

◆ ◆ ◆

I arrived home later that night with a pair of bloody latex gloves in my front jeans pocket. It was past midnight. The lawyer was dead. I figured that I should probably visit Alex sometime in the next few days, so he didn't get too anxious over yet another murder. Besides, he was good company, wasn't he? Just because he was the enemy, it didn't mean I couldn't have a little fun. I entered the house quietly, figuring that my mom would already be asleep, and my dad too if he was home. But when I walked inside, a light was on and my mom was sitting at the bottom of the stairs.

As soon as I came through the door, I saw her waiting figure—hair fashionably mussed, a black shawl draped heavily about her shoulders, pearls circling her neck. There was the scent of perfume as well, flowery and thick. Where had she been today—with another man, another affair with someone she would control and discard for the thrill of it? Another party with crystal glasses and gold-plated silverware?

I didn't know. I didn't say a word. I didn't want to know why she was waiting for me, but I was afraid I knew.

I hadn't seen her yesterday. I had called her about the fiasco in the cafeteria, just to let her know. I had left her a message when she didn't pick up. She had been out to dinner that night and had come back after I was asleep. I had left before her in the morning. I had managed to escape her until now. But I couldn't escape any longer.

"Kit," she said, standing up.

"Hi, Mom," I murmured, looking at my feet.

"Kit, you *idiot*," she spat, and stalked toward me. I flinched as she came closer. She swung her arm out and grabbed the nape of my neck tightly, almost suffocatingly. She forced my head up, forced me to look in her eyes. I tried to escape her. But it did no good.

"What were you even *thinking*?" she hissed. I looked helplessly into her eyes, like a trapped animal. She looked unusually disheveled. She was tired. I could see that. Because of me, she probably hadn't slept much last night. Her eyes were angry, afraid—and they were selfish.

I saw that she was worried about me—she was my mother, after all, that was natural—but the years had weakened her, and at least a significant part of her was now worried about herself. All that traveling, all those parties and affairs—they were something, but they weren't quite enough for her, and she was losing pieces of herself. Becoming less.

Still, this anger—this was a pure, unrepressed, vital anger, and something about it had echoes of the woman she had once been.

"Mom, let go. It hurts," I whimpered.

She gritted her teeth, spat, and let me go. She walked backward a few steps, eyeing me with something resembling disgust.

"You *fool*. You complete, utter *idiot*. What were you *thinking*? Getting into a fight—you're a murderer. You're well trained. Why in the world would you draw attention to yourself? Look, they might even call both me and your father in for a meeting with the school! We can't afford that! We can't afford him being even the least bit worried about you, or else he might start *noticing*!"

"I'm—I'm sorry," I stammered. I shrank back toward the door. I could feel the tears building. I didn't want her to hate me. God, no, I didn't want her to hate me. . . .

"Don't you realize? Your murders aren't just your problem. If they find you, they find me. I go to jail. I was a murderer too. Be more damn careful, Kit."

"I'm sorry," I sobbed.

Her eyes were fevered and bold.

"I don't care! I don't give a shit about being *sorry*. Be careful, not sorry. You're getting careless, befriending your victims, fighting in school—this isn't what I taught you! You know why we kill. We kill because there is no justice. And without us, the world is lost—"

And then her voice vanished as she realized, broken, that the correct word was not "we" but "you."

"I'm sorry, I'm sorry," I whined. Hysterical tears dripped down and spilled over my black jacket.

"I don't care," she snapped, and walked away, up the stairs, her steps thundering, her silence weighing on me.

"I'm sorry," I whispered, sliding down to the base of the door, burying my head in my knees, crying. I sat there until I fell asleep, wrecked and tired.

I had dreams of Diana.

Diana, not the Roman goddess of hunting and moon-light, but Diana the harbinger of death, my own personal goddess of the underworld and of letters. Diana, surrounded by bloodstained paper, laughing, beautiful, terrible.

My dreams of Diana were nightmares.

Chapter 10

On Sunday morning I went running.

I wasn't a runner, I never ran–but on Sunday morning I went running. Somehow I felt like I needed to do it or I would itch myself out of my skin. I was restless. I needed to run, to get whatever was in me out–so I ran.

I wore those ugly tennis shoes my dad bought me last Christmas and a pair of completely unsuitable denim shorts because I didn't have anything else. I ran through Chelsea and down to the Thames, and then alongside the Thames for a little bit, feeling the pounding of the cement against my feet, just running, running, running.

I needed to run or I felt like I was going to explode.

The morning air bit into me, and I felt the cold running

up and down my skin. I ran until my breath ran out and I was gasping for air and my legs felt like lead. And then I kept running, because I couldn't stop, not yet. The burning, aching, ripping pain in my tired thighs and the sting of the air on my cheeks somehow relaxed me, soothed me, felt good. I let it all wash over me and wash everything away.

I ran. I ran. I ran.

I ran until I was so tired that I simply collapsed to my knees on the sidewalk, unable to run a second longer. I forced myself to stretch so I wouldn't be sore the next day—or at least I wouldn't be too sore—and then I hailed a cab to take me back home as the sun rose in the sky and everything else came awake.

◆ ◇ ◆

School on Monday was terrible—and yet, somehow, exhilarating.

The moment I walked into school, I couldn't escape the gazes of the other students. Their eyes followed me in the hallways, glanced at me in class when their minds wandered. They were all interested. Of course, I felt awful about it. I had drawn attention to myself. I was a delinquent. That was dangerous. So very dangerous. But somehow, despite that, the touch of their eyes and their whispering mouths excited me. So this was what Maggie felt. I couldn't understand how she hated it so, how she could not feel this same exhilaration. It was wonderful, having them watch me.

I walked into homeroom to find Maggie missing. Michael sat in the front of the classroom. He turned to meet my eyes as I walked in. He was smiling.

"Good morning, Kit," he said with fake kindness in his voice.

"Good morning, Michael," I replied cordially, and ignored him. He was trying to provoke me again. I wouldn't let him. I looked around the room once more—but I was right. Maggie wasn't there. I looked at Michael and put my hands on my hips. He just smiled.

"Where's Maggie?"

"Why should I know?"

"Because you're a bastard, and you're harassing her, that's why."

He laughed. "I don't have a clue, honestly."

"Stop playing games," I hissed.

Yet again, everyone was listening. They had stopped what they were doing and they were all listening to us, wondering if we would deteriorate into physical violence again.

"I really don't know where she is," he said lightly.

"Look, you have no excuse to be psychotic, even if she did dump your sorry arse," I said, making sure I was loud enough for everyone to hear me clearly. There was a collective, gossipy, giggling gasp from the room, and chattering broke out as I smiled arrogantly at Michael.

"Hit him again," someone whispered, goading me on, like the person in the cafeteria before. And honestly, I wanted to. But I couldn't.

So I just smiled at him. He smiled back.

"She won't be coming to school today, I don't think," he said. And for a moment, the mask he seemed to be wearing slipped—he looked almost upset, but the turmoil was mixed disturbingly with fury—and he looked as if he wanted to kill me. Honestly and truly. But then he smiled again, forcing the expression away.

The end-of-homeroom bell rang. Everyone jumped. I narrowed my eyes. Smiling benignly, Michael headed toward the door, brushing past me.

I couldn't resist.

Venom in my voice, I whispered to him.

"I warned you."

◆ ◇ ◆

I was in the girls' bathroom, on my cell phone, trying in vain to call Maggie. She wasn't responding. I had already tried five times and left three messages. It was morning break, right between my second and third classes, and there wasn't the faintest trace of her.

Once again I got her voice mail and hung up.

"Shit," I muttered.

He had threatened her, I was sure of that. But I wanted to know if he had actually followed through on that threat, or whether she was just too afraid to come to school. I hoped she was just afraid. She belonged to me. She was not his to take.

I leaned back against the tiled wall and realized that I had two options.

One. The safest path. I could do nothing. I could ignore

Michael, let him carry on being a bastard and have nothing to do with him. I could go on with my life and kill Maggie when the time was right. Her death was my responsibility, and it still had to occur, of course. I had decided to play this game, and I would play it to the end. Once I chose a victim, I never gave up or flaked out, even if my opinions about the writer changed. Nothing was right, nothing was wrong—that was the rule. That was who I was, and without my conviction I was nothing. But that didn't mean that I couldn't protect her in the meantime.

Two. I could kill Michael.

I knew that my mother would choose option one—but I was not my mother. I didn't play it safe like her. I killed more freely.

But I was already in danger. I couldn't kill now; it truly wasn't safe for me.

But he was so irritating—

But I didn't have a letter for him—

My thoughts were a mess. I didn't know what to do. I breathed in and held the breath for a long while before letting it slowly slip away through my lips.

In my hand, my phone began to ring.

Sharply, I lifted it up and looked to see who was calling—it was Maggie.

I answered quickly.

"Maggie," I said. There was a short silence.

"Kit." She sounded as if she hadn't slept for a while, and also as if she didn't know precisely why she was calling me.

"Maggie, are you all right?"

"What?"

"Michael threatened you again, didn't he?"

Another silence.

"Yes."

"What? Maggie, when?" I asked urgently.

"Saturday. Saturday night."

"You told me before that you changed your phone number. How did he get your new one?"

"He didn't."

"What?"

"He came to my house."

I pushed off the wall and nearly toppled over forward. I spread my feet apart and shouted into the phone, indignant and stunned.

"What?"

"He just showed up on Saturday, and my parents weren't home, so he just came to my house . . . he threatened to hurt me if I came back to school and didn't agree to . . . be with him."

"Maggie, did he hurt you?"

Silence.

"Maggie, *did he hurt you?*"

"No, no, he didn't touch me."

"Maggie, is that the truth?"

"Yes, it's the truth," she said softly.

Perhaps he actually hadn't touched her this time—but if that was the case, she was hiding something else. She had always been hiding something. I had always felt it.

I wanted to understand. I needed to. I realized that now.

"Is this the only time you've been this afraid of him?" I asked, feeling somehow that this was the right question to ask.

Suddenly, unexpectedly, on the other end of the phone, Maggie burst into tears.

I stood dumbly next to the wall like a limp marionette. I didn't have anything to say. What could I do? Should I tell her not to cry—should I tell her that it would be all right? It occurred to me that I had never seen anyone but my mother cry before. I suddenly felt like a child.

"Um," I muttered helplessly as she sobbed into the phone, "what's wrong?"

"He really didn't touch me this time, I swear, but before, at the end of the last school year, it was different."

"Yes?" I prompted faintly, as her voice petered out into choked sobbing.

"He used to be so *nice*," she said through the tears. I heard her hand brush against the phone as she wiped water away from her eyes, and she went on unbidden, as if she had to get the words out to purge the emotions that went along with them. I listened without saying a word. She spoke in a tumbling stream, like a rock rolling down a hill.

"He used to be so wonderful. So bright. He used to laugh, we used to really be friends, and it was *all* wonderful. But then as time went on I began to see things about him. At first I thought I could fix them. He's so alone, Kit. He's so lonely. I thought that if I could just stay with him I could make it better. But then—" She paused here for a moment, as her tears momentarily thickened. "As time went on, I started to realize that his darkness went a lot deeper than I thought at first. He was dangerous. It was just in little ways, weird ways that I saw it at first—he used to mess with spiders, torturing them until he killed them—that sort of thing. You know. But then this one day he told me—he told me that the world was made out of dust, and that the world was so heavy and pointless—and he *meant* it, Kit. The fact that he truly meant it was the scary part."

"Maggie," I breathed sadly. "Maggie, Maggie."

"I went home right after he said that. I just left him. Ran. I couldn't stay with him any longer. I realized then— he's literally psychotic, Kit. Literally. Detached from reality. I didn't want anything to do with him. But I guess that he must have followed me home, because when I got home and went inside, he knocked on the door; and when I came to answer it, he just forced his way in. And my parents weren't there, I was alone. He was so angry—I was terrified." Her tears were fading now, turning into steely resignation, acceptance of an unfortunate fate.

"He pushed me against a wall. He broke a vase. Roses all over the hallway. He told me—he said I was disgusting for just going home and leaving him. He gave me bruises on my wrist, shoved his knee into my stomach. He told me that I was part of the darkness he hated. He told me that there was no lightness in the world at all, and that I didn't deserve the life that was in my bones, and that the only real thing in the world was pain. He asked me to love him, to understand—I kept saying no, no, but he wouldn't listen. He left eventually, but . . . it was like something had broken within him. You can see it, can't you, sometimes, when you look at him? That sort of on-the-edge feeling . . ."

Maggie took a deep breath.

"And after all that I had to leave my friends, of course. Michael was their ringleader, and I couldn't be around them as long as he was there."

"Oh God, Maggie . . . ," I said, not sure what else there was to say. She didn't really hear me, she just kept going on—and the words just kept coming, like she had no way of stopping herself now that she had begun.

"When he came to my house this Saturday, I didn't let him in. He snapped in the same way as the first time. He just stood at the front door and kept slamming himself against it and shouting at me, telling me to love him, like he was going to break—break the door down. And I kept telling him to go, and my parents weren't home again, and he wouldn't listen, he never listens . . . I didn't let him hurt me this time, but I'm so scared."

"Maggie, Maggie."

"And before you ask, because I know you'll want to ask, I haven't told anyone about this except for you. I can't. I'm so afraid. What if he hears about it and comes to hurt me again, even madder than before? There's no way out. I'm stuck. Please don't tell anyone, please." She paused. "I'm fine," she murmured, as if she were trying to convince herself, the last remnants of tears disappearing from her voice. "You don't have to worry."

"You . . . do you . . . do you think he'd really hurt you if you came back to school?"

Darkness sank over me.

The silence hung in the air—I realized that this answer could change everything. It could change me. It could turn me into something I never planned to be. A murderer who decides her own justice, who kills without letters. But I would do it to protect my prey.

"Yes, I think so," she gasped softly.

"Maggie," I murmured. "Oh, Maggie."

"Don't worry about me. I'll be fine."

"Not like this."

"I'll . . . be fine."

"Not like this. You can't come to school like this."

"I'll be fine."

I paused, clenching the phone to my ear, biting my lip until it bled, eyes narrowed and chest hollow.

"Not like this," I whispered, and hung up.

◆ ◇ ◆

After the phone call and before my next class, I went to the empty philosophy room and put a note inside Michael's desk to wait for him. After that I went out and wandered the empty hallways until the bell rang. I couldn't make myself stay still.

When we went to philosophy, I was restless. Gone was

the early morning's excitement. The gazes that I had earlier enjoyed now felt dirty and cruel. I tapped my foot against the floor, and I watched Michael.

I had positioned the note on the inside of his desk so that he would quickly see it as soon as he sat down. And he did see it. As Dr. Marcell began to speak, to say things I wasn't paying attention to, I watched Michael reach into his desk and quietly unfold his note.

I couldn't see his face, but I could imagine it. The tight lips, the twitching left eyebrow, the manicured fury in his pretty eyes.

I stared at the back of his head too long. Dr. Marcell noticed. She didn't say anything, but I felt her eyes on me, staring. She kept talking, but somehow I felt her words were angled at me. There was something strange in them. A curiosity, perhaps? Not suspicion, not yet.

I looked up at her and smiled. She smiled back, uncertain, and her eyes moved on.

The class passed more slowly than usual. I didn't speak. Not that day. That day I was too jumpy to speak. And I was not jumpy often. I was usually calm and collected, even in the worst situations. But the thought of my impending betrayal of my own morals left me edgy.

I didn't have a choice. He was in my way. No one was allowed to hurt my victims except me, and Michael was far too violent toward Maggie for comfort.

When class was over and we left the room, everything was silence. Neither Michael nor Dr. Marcell said anything to me, even though I knew both of them had things to say. Everyone kept their eyes down and moved quickly, even the uninvolved, as if even they could taste something nervous in the air. The only sound, until we got out into the hallway, was our own footsteps.

Once I got out of the classroom I stopped. I watched Michael's retreating back as it wove between the people in the hallway. He looked so quiet and unassuming, when he was seen like this, from a distance. Almost forgettable.

I smiled a sharp smile, a smile with many emotions in it. Anger. Fear. Sadness.

They would all remember him soon enough.

Chapter 11

After school the hallways were quiet.

I spent two and a half hours in the library, and then I walked through them, meandering toward my destination. Lazily wandering up stairs, hands trailing along the banisters, making my way up to the third floor, where he waited.

I knew he would be there.

Waiting inside the third-floor girls' bathroom, looking uncomfortable, arms crossed—oh, I could just picture it. Despite my anxiety, the image made me smile.

I walked along the third-floor hallway. My steps echoed. The fabric of my skirt whispered, my hair silently bounced around my shoulders. The sun came through the window and cast a shadow against the wall beside me. My shadow and I walked together toward the end of the hall.

I would be corrupted. My rules—gone. My way of life—deserted. And somehow I was ready.

Yes, after so long, I was ready.

The door to the bathroom hung slightly ajar. Within, it was quiet. I paused outside. My canvas backpack was slung over one shoulder. Casually, I swung it around so I could get into it. From a zipped side pocket I quietly took a pair of latex gloves. I always had some with me, just in case. Lucky that I did.

The teachers had gone home. It was nearly six o'clock now. I had made up an excuse for myself—I was sure Michael had one too, though I wasn't sure what it was or how he was spending his time before the main event. I had a large project due tomorrow for which I had to use the library. I hadn't done it in school, during my free period, like I had planned to—and so I had to stay after school. It was just Michael and me now, and the headmaster in the far corner of the school, where he couldn't hear.

It was the perfect stage.

The actors were in place, the scene ready to be played—the red curtain opened.

I put the gloves on and walked into the bathroom. I looked around, across the green tiles and into the open metal stalls. He wasn't there.

My breath quickened, and I became wary. He had to be there. I knew he would be there. I *knew* it.

But the bathroom was empty—where was he?

My eyes flickered around the room, watching, waiting, my murderer's senses on edge. I listened to the air-conditioning and the quieter sounds. The sound of my breathing, the sound of the breeze outside the window.

And then footsteps.

Behind me, quick, quiet, urgent.

I started to turn, inhaling sharply, heart pounding. But I was too slow. Before I could whirl to face him, his arm was wrapped around my neck and crushing my windpipe. I gasped for air, clawing at his arm, but he didn't let go. He must have been hiding—in a nearby classroom, perhaps, or maybe just in shadow.

"Let go," I choked out, as if that would do any good. He laughed. It was Michael's laugh, of course.

"For someone so cocky, you're careless," he said into my ear as I struggled against him. I had to get away. If I didn't, his arm would leave bruises around my neck, and the fact that we'd been fighting would become obvious. I didn't want that. I wanted no traces of my fight left behind.

I didn't have time for this shit.

I swung my arm down and slammed it into his groin.

He moaned and let go of me, sinking to the ground weakly like the slime he was. He rocked back and forth, pained, in a ball on the floor. I looked down at him with disgust. His hair flopped into his face, obscuring his sight— he was so vulnerable. I could kill him so easily, with just a knee to the face or a punch to the back of his exposed neck.

But I wanted him to know why he died. I didn't want it to be unexpected. I wanted him to see it coming and be afraid.

I walked past him and closed the bathroom door, locking it quietly.

"Michael," I said.

He muttered obscenities and stayed where he was, curled up on the floor in pain. His back was to me, his eyes downturned, staring at the floor of the third-floor girls' bathroom.

"Michael," I said again, louder this time.

"What do you *want*?" he spat at me, finally looking up to meet my eyes. Usually when people met my eyes as they were about to die, they looked afraid, or at least uncertain. I don't think he understood yet. Even with my note, he didn't understand yet.

I knelt down to his eye level, reached out, and grabbed his hair, forcing his head upward so he could not look away from my eyes. I held it there, eyes like iron, neither one of us giving way.

"You look pretty, but you're just a little bitch," he breathed.

I smiled.

"That's right," I hissed in reply.

"But you don't mean it. You talk big and you even hit hard, but in the end you got nothing. You're not like me. You're afraid. You won't do anything."

I stared at him.

"Michael," I said calmly, "what did my note say?"

"It was a bunch of bullshit."

I grabbed his hair tighter, fingernails scraping against his scalp, and smiled grimly as he winced.

"*What* did my *note* say?" I asked once more. This time he would give me an answer.

He clenched his teeth and looked for a moment like he wouldn't reply—but then he did, angrily and resentfully.

"It said to come here, now, so we could settle the score."

I sighed and stood with a little smile.

"Yes, that's right. And I'm not stupid, Michael. I know that there can be no more talking between us. That will solve nothing. Neither of us are rational people, Michael. We can no longer pretend to be civilized, or even mildly humane. The score will be settled now. You have violated what is mine. You have threatened Maggie. You have gone too far, Michael. And you're going to regret it."

He knelt, looking up at me.

"You're all bullshit and no action," he said without a trace of doubt in his voice.

"No," I said, "I'm not."

"You think you're all fancy, with your prissy little hair-cut and—and—your smug little voice. Maggie's yours? Are you psycho? She's *mine*. She'll always be mine. I bet you never even punched anyone before you hit me."

I laughed instantly. He was so naive.

For the first time, he looked surprised—and then doubtful.

I tapped my foot a few times and then aimlessly wandered to the other side of the bathroom. There was a small window there, thin and high, letting in a wavering sliver of early-evening sunset that lit up a rectangle of light between Michael and me.

I looked out the window. From where I stood, I could see the school's stone statue of an angel standing silhouetted against the sun, wings outstretched triumphantly and a peaceful smile on its androgynous face.

"Michael, what's my name?" I asked quietly.

"Kit."

"Wrong," I breathed.

I turned to him.

And like every time before, I met his eyes and readied myself and something changed within me. Like a clock striking midnight. Something darker filled the air—something dangerous, something wild, something strong and beautiful. Like lust, or arrogance. I breathed it in, and I became someone new, someone I liked better than Kit, someone truly amazing.

"My name is Diana," I said.

"No, it's not," Michael said accusingly. "Your name is Kit, it's not Diana."

I shook my head. "It's Diana now. You see . . . it's tradition."

Slowly, I began to walk toward him. Step by step, echoing over the tiles.

"I think you've got me wrong, Michael."

Step. His eyes were angry, determined.

"You think I'm all bullshit and no action. You think I'm normal, when it really comes down to it."

Step. He bit his tongue.

"That's just a mask I wear."

Step. He bit so hard that he drew blood.

"I hit you. I assumed you had seen it then. I suppose not."

Step. His eyes wavered.

"You still don't understand. Silly boy."

I stopped in front of him and knelt again.

"You see," I murmured, "I'm the Perfect Killer."

He was at last afraid.

I smiled a terrible, exquisite smile, lifted one hand up toward my forehead like Scarlett O'Hara, made a fist, and swung it down toward his temple. I felt my knuckle crack against the artery–

And Michael fell to the floor like a broken plate, the blood vessel shattering, his eyes wide open and afraid. He hadn't even had time to consider running.

He would harass Maggie no longer. He deserved death. That was my judgment. Nothing is right and nothing is wrong, but there are some things that need to be done. He would have had an unhappy life, had he lived. Tormented, plagued by insanity. His death was mercy, almost.

Almost.

"Was it worth it?" I whispered to the empty body.

A cloud passed over the sun, and the rectangle of light

faded away into shadow.

I took off my gloves and checked his pulse—it was gone, of course. I wiped away my fingerprint with my sponge, hid it inside my bag again within a secret pocket, and began to search his body. In one of his pockets I found the note I had left him, the note that could incriminate me. I took that and flushed it down the nearest toilet. This murder had been a bloodless one, save for the blood that was now seeping out of Michael's mouth because of the trauma to his skull and his bitten tongue. I was clean. There was no evidence to pin me to the death.

Another perfect murder.

I backed away a few steps, took off my gloves, and hid them carefully inside the waistband of my jeans. They were the most dangerous piece of evidence against me. They had to be hidden where no one would look.

I positioned myself by the door, took a deep breath, and screamed.

Chapter 12

*A*lex cradled me in his arms, and I pretended to cry.

I had no actual tears to cry, but I had to put on a good show or else I would be immediately suspected. Though there was no physical evidence against me, all the circumstantial evidence pointed toward me. Though, of course, I was a teenage girl. People were much more likely to pin murders on tall men than on teenage girls.

This murder was not being treated as a Perfect Killer murder. Of course—there had been no letter. I could have figured that out myself, had I thought about it. But it still felt strange to have committed a murder that was not grouped with the rest.

It was a bit dangerous. My serial murders had gotten

to a point where all but a few had given up even trying to solve them. This individual murder would be approached with more enthusiasm. I was sure I had left no trace of myself behind. But I was still unusually nervous.

There were other feelings stirring too, other than fear. But I didn't allow myself to think about those, not yet. I had other things to deal with first.

Alex let me pretend to cry into his chest. I felt the movement of his breathing, the comfortable warmth of his hands; I clenched myself closer to him than he was holding me and realized that he smelled like peppermint. He whispered things into my ear that I couldn't hear over the sound of my own wailing. The hallway was crawling with police officers, and he was the only one sitting still.

And here, in the hallway, despite the darkness of the situation, emotions began to float up in my chest again, accentuated and amplified by the physical closeness between Alex and me, and again I pushed them back. No, no, no, I told myself once more. There's no use in that. Those feelings can't lead to anything. I'm a murderer, and he's hunting me. There's no use at all.

And yet I felt my heartbeat quicken.

"Shh," he whispered as he rocked me back and forth. "Shh, it's all right, it'll be all right."

"It's not all right. It's not—he's dead—I hit him, I hit him, but I never wanted this, no, never, oh God—" I moaned. "Oh God, he's dead, he's dead. . . ."

"Kit, it's all right. Your mom is coming, she'll be here

soon, we'll get you away, it'll be okay," he said. I cried louder, clenching his shirt desperately between my fingers.

"He's dead," I yowled, the sound momentarily filling the hallway, making everyone pause. The police officers were unsettled. I could feel it. Good. I was convincing.

"Shh," Alex said forcefully, as kindly as he could. I let my screams slowly fade away into anguished sobs, shuddering. I closed my eyes. I sat there, very still, for a few minutes, occasionally crying, as if I were close to falling into restless sleep against him.

I barely knew him, but something about him made me feel safer, bit by bit, though paranoia and emotional turmoil still gripped me tight. I think it might have been his demeanor that helped me feel this growing safety—his chin-up, stubborn everything-must-be-just-fine attitude. I was grateful for it.

It was late. After I had screamed and the headmaster had found me, I had kept up this act for hours on end. It was nearly ten o'clock now. I actually was tired.

I tried to keep my mind blank. I tried so hard. But even as I struggled to keep myself from thinking, every time I lost a shred of concentration, the same question appeared in my mind, filling me up and making me feel cold.

Why had I done it?

Nothing was right, nothing was wrong, so why had I passed judgment on him? I wasn't God. I wasn't supposed to have my opinions. I was an assassin. I followed the will of others, not my own. I worked the way my mother had taught me, according to her rules. Our moral nihilism had kept us sane. And now I had broken that tradition, stepped into something dangerous and new.

I had judged for myself who was right and who was wrong.

At some point I realized I actually was crying. Slowly, quietly, tears falling down my face and soaking through Alex's shirt. Out of the corner of my eye, I could see that he looked uncomfortable. He didn't know what to do with me.

That made two of us.

Eight o'clock, nine o'clock, ten—my mom hadn't come. She wouldn't come until the last possible hour. Someone would have called her, of course—but she would have come up with a clever excuse as to why she couldn't come immediately. She was a coward. She would have realized, of course, that the murder was mine. And she would have realized as well that I had taken a risk. And she would be afraid to associate herself with me, though she had no choice.

I fell asleep as the police officers worked and Alex held me and the metallic scent of blood spread insidiously through the air.

Some time later Alex shook me awake. I opened my eyes regretfully and yawned. I felt spent. It was midnight, according to a clock across the hall. Absently, I looked at Alex and studied the flecks of blue in his eyes.

"Wake up," he said gently. "I'm sorry . . . someone wants to ask you questions."

Wordlessly, I looked sleepy-eyed in the direction he was

looking. I found myself looking at a long pair of legs. I traced my gaze upward over the legs, then over the torso, then to the head. It was a tall woman with black hair tied strictly back into a bun like a ballet dancer, wearing the uniform of an officer more highly ranked than Alex. She held a notepad and a recorder in steady hands. She looked apologetic.

"Your name is Kit Ward, isn't it?" the woman asked. Wearily, I nodded.

"I'm very sorry," she said awkwardly. "I know this is very hard for you, but I need to ask you some questions, all right?"

After a moment of pretend hesitation, I nodded.

I put one hand on Alex's left shoulder and pushed off it, using it for support as I stood. He grabbed my other arm, pushing it upward, as if that would help me. He looked worried. As he let go, the feeling of his touch lingered on my skin.

I stepped to the side of Alex and leaned against the plate-glass window next to him. I crossed my arms, trying to look small and scared, and glanced tiredly at the police-woman.

She looked at me pityingly and cleared her throat. She clicked the record button on her recorder and flipped open her notepad.

"When did you discover the body?"

"Ah . . . around six, I think. It was getting dark . . . ," I murmured. She scrawled quickly.

"Why were you at school so late?"

"I had a project. I was in the library . . . just down the hall . . . oh God." My eyes went wide and I pretended to be traumatized, remembering the body. I clenched my fists tightly against my thighs.

"I'm sorry. I have to ask these questions," the woman said.

"Yeah . . . no . . . I know." I wiped away imaginary tears.

"Were there any other people around?"

"Well . . . Michael . . . and the murderer . . . I suppose," I whispered dully.

"No, I mean, did you see anyone around? Were you in the library alone?"

"Yes, I was."

"The teachers were gone already?"

"Most everyone leaves by about four . . . but the school is unlocked and everything until nine."

"So you didn't see anyone around?"

I shook my head. "No."

"How did you discover the body?"

"I just . . . went to the bathroom, and he was there, on the floor." I shuddered.

"Did you hear anything unusual?"

"Unusual?"

"Footsteps, or closing doors."

"No, I didn't."

"You had an altercation with this boy last week, didn't you?"

I tensed, looking horrified.

"Yes, but I didn't do it, I swear I didn't, everyone is going to think that, but I swear I didn't, I didn't, I didn't . . . ," I wailed insistently, and leaned more heavily against the window, quivering timidly. I even managed to make myself cry some more, tears leaking out of my eyes slowly.

Alex brushed his fingertips comfortingly across my forearm.

"It's all right, Kit," he murmured. "We know you didn't do it. It's okay."

"What do you know about Michael? Did he have enemies besides you?"

I nodded quickly. Too quickly, perhaps.

"He had lots of enemies," I said.

"All right. Can you give me a list?"

"You can put the entire student body on that list, and most of the teachers," I said sarcastically, bitterly. "He was good at making people dislike him. But something like this—who could do this?"

"Hmm," the policewoman said, and wrote something down.

"It's perfect," Alex murmured. "The murder is perfect. No evidence, and there's a perfect scapegoat. There's only one murderer who does things this . . . *perfectly.*"

"There's no letter," the policewoman reminded him.

"But what if the murderer decided to kill this boy on his own? What if he had a personal grudge he wanted to settle?" Alex protested.

I couldn't decide if this was good or bad. It was good, because the police got discouraged whenever they started working with Perfect Killer cases. And it was bad because calling this a Perfect Killer case would link the Perfect Killer entity personally to Michael, narrowing the list of suspects to include me.

"Serial killers like the Perfect Killer have a consistent modus operandi, at least in terms of the letters. The Perfect Killer would leave a letter. This isn't your problem. This isn't your murder to worry about," the policewoman said with a sigh.

"Are you sure?" he asked uneasily. She didn't reply. She wasn't sure.

I sobbed into my hand to break the silence.

"Anyway—" the policewoman started.

"Kit!" I heard my mom yelp. I turned slowly to see her at the end of the hallway running toward me, pushing her way between police officers, barreling in my direction until she reached me, stumbled over Alex, and threw her arms dramatically around my neck.

"Oh my God, Kit, darling, are you all right? I was stuck in Brussels—I'm sorry I couldn't get here sooner!"

She wasn't any happier to see me than I was to see her. But we put on a good show. I wrapped my arms around her back and wailed into her shoulder. She looked around at Alex, nodding thankfully to him with little tears at the edges of her eyes—she had eye drops—and then looked at the policewoman.

"I'm Vienna Ward, Kit's mother. Can this wait?" she asked pleadingly. "Kit's tired, mentally exhausted, everything. She needs to go home and get some rest. She can't handle this right now."

"Yes, she can go home, Mrs. Ward," the policewoman said after a moment's hesitation, closing her notepad. "We'll contact her later if we have any more questions."

"Thank you." She nodded to the policewoman, then to Alex, and began to lead me down the hallway. This time the police officers scattered as she came through, and she didn't have to weave between them. She took my hand as we began to walk down the stairs.

She took it in a death grip, digging her nails into my palm, making me wince. My eyes teared up from the pain. I let myself cry—this was an appropriate time for it. Her face looked benign and distraught, but through her grip I could feel the fury and the danger inside her. Sometimes I forgot that she, too, was a killer. It was a rather foolish thing to do.

When we reached the second floor, Dr. Marcell was there, standing with a group of other teachers across the hallway.

All of them turned toward us quietly, some with morbid interest, others with pity—

Dr. Marcell looked with suspicion.

It wasn't even the mere spark of suspicion that she had looked at me with before. It was a full-fledged thought in her mind. I could see easily what she was thinking.

Did she do it?

Yes, I did.

Suspicion and doubt burned in her eyes like wildfire, raging and destructive, with not a shred of pity. She looked over me from head to toe as my mom and I turned to walk down the next flight of stairs.

I wondered if she had noticed that my eyes were barely red, that I had barely been crying.

Chapter 13

They canceled school for the rest of the week. I imagine it was a PR nightmare for Ivy High School. Well, it wasn't my problem.

Of course, my mom was furious that I had broken our code of conduct and risked incriminating myself. Not just slightly angry, but all-out furious. Throwing-things-around-the-house furious. But in a strange way, her anger was pathetic—it was the anger of a small child throwing a tantrum. She was angry for a reason that neither she nor I could quite pin down. It was Michael's murder, yes. But it also, I think, was created by something more.

It was not the dangerous anger she had felt when I had

just punched Michael. It was more childish, more fright-ened than that.

It wasn't, however, any less fear inducing.

She broke three vases and a small ceramic dog figurine from the living room fireplace's mantelpiece that reminded me of the stone dog I had seen outside Alex's police station. The mood lasted all week, and there was no dealing with her at all.

"You've ruined everything," she told me on Tuesday night as she ate dry cereal alone at the dinner table, glar-ing selfishly, desperately, up at me over the folded-up lid of the box, the shards of a teacup scattered around her feet. "You've ruined *everything.*"

The house was filled with odd bursts of cacophony and silence.

I didn't dare leave the house until Wednesday, just for the sake of appearances. I decided it was best if I appeared weak and emotionally scarred by the whole ordeal. I wanted to leave desperately. I felt like I was sitting on pins for every moment I was at home. After much thought, on Wednesday I decided that I had waited a tasteful amount of time—and besides, Michael's funeral was late that morning, and I figured that it might look good for me to go to that.

For a while I had been undecided about going, but after my mother started throwing things in earnest, I realized I needed to get out, if only for a little while; and the funeral would give me an excuse to respectably leave the house. I didn't mind funerals much, anyway. They made other people sad, but for obvious reasons, death didn't bother me much. I didn't know how to mourn.

The service was in an old, small church with a thin steeple piercing high into a cloudy sky that swirled like milk poured into tea. When I got there, people were entering the church one by one, looking down. Some were whispering to one another. But strangely, or perhaps not so strangely, considering Michael, the overwhelming mood wasn't somber. It was muddled, confused, and almost curious, as if none of the attendees could believe he was actually dead. Couldn't believe someone with such angry conviction could just vanish so easily. It was a very strange mood for a funeral. As I arrived, a few men in stiff suits walked in a line through the wide church doors, looking up at the stained-glass windows as they entered.

I gathered a few glances as I stepped out of my cab. I didn't own many black items of clothing, and I hadn't dared to borrow anything from my mom with the mood she was in, so I had ended up wearing the black taffeta dress I had worn at a Christmas party two years ago, which made a lot of noise when I moved and was too formal for the occasion. And black always made me look pale and stern. But it was the best I could manage on short notice. Looking down, imitating the rest of the funeral-going crowd, I walked through the doors, adjusting clumsily to the relative darkness of the sanctuary, and took a seat in a pew in the back of the church as quietly as I could.

The seat was hard and the back was too short.

The church was beautiful inside, in a way, I mused, that only churches could be beautiful. The ceiling was the shape of an arching triangle overhead—arching, I imagined, as if it were moving away from me, with Gothic stone carvings crisscrossing it and spreading down the walls. Stained-glass windows sent light cascading in bright rays over the floor. Images of the burning bush and Noah's ark and a few other biblical events I didn't recognize stared down at me from those beautiful windows. Somehow, they made me itch, and made me want to apologize for something, I didn't know what exactly. By the laws of the Anglican church, I was a pariah. I had so many things I could apologize for, by their rules. I didn't really feel like I should, or even could, apologize for any of them.

Absently, I listened to the muffled sounds of people talking, catching a few whispered words every now and then.

"Can't imagine . . ."

"I don't . . ."

"His poor mother . . ."

"Insanity . . ."

Strangely enough, Michael's body seemed to be of almost secondary importance.

He was laid out in a coffin on a table in the front of the church, surrounded by white roses and stuffed into a prissy black suit. I didn't think that bodies were viewed all that often at funerals anymore, but I guess I must have been wrong, or perhaps someone had made an unusual decision while planning his. That seemed the most likely explanation. This whole thing seemed so unusual that a little bit more absurdity seemed only natural.

He still looked like a prat, even in death. That creeping, obnoxious smirk of his still seemed to play at his lips, and I could still see his fluffy hair bouncing stupidly as he walked. I couldn't see his body clearly from this far away, but as I'd entered the church, I had caught a faraway glimpse of him. They'd cleaned him up. They'd wiped the blood away from his mouth and closed his lips so you couldn't see the way he'd bitten nearly all the way through his tongue when I killed him.

I'd *killed* him.

I kept looking at the windows until someone came to the pulpit and began to speak.

"Jesus said to his disciples, 'Do not let your heart be troubled. . . .'"

His voice echoed like a bell.

It was the pastor of the church, an old man with a wispy comb-over, who, to be honest, looked almost uncomfortable speaking to the crowd. I wondered how much of that was because he wasn't a good public speaker and how much of it was because he had never liked Michael and essentially had to lie when he said all the things he was required to say—that Michael had a place in heaven, that he was now at peace. I, personally, didn't think Michael even knew how to be at peace. The pastor's dislike for Michael was at least half the reason for his hesitance—you could see it in the way he kept glancing at the coffin with that same muddled expression that so many of the people in attendance were wearing.

". . . I am the way, and the truth, and the life . . ."

He was speaking about God. I was only halfway listening.

In the front row someone was crying.

It was a woman, and I wondered who it was for a while before realizing that it had to be his mother. He was an only child, and who else would cry for him, anyway? Slowly everything else faded away until all I could see were the high windows and all I could hear was the sound of her weeping softly. When she breathed in each time, she made a hiccuping noise, so it almost sounded like she was laughing.

I couldn't see her from where I sat. I wondered what she looked like, this woman who was the mother of such a monster. Did she regret it, bringing such hatred into the world? Was she blind to it? Part of me wanted to look her in the eyes and just *ask*. I was so curious. Michael was dead—

Michael was dead.

Every time the thought occurred to me, it stopped me short. I suddenly remembered my mother's screams as she picked the ceramic dog up in one elegant hand and thrust it at the far wall, just above the piano. . . .

The pastor had stopped speaking and had moved away from the pulpit, gazing entreatingly into the front pew. His eyes, set beneath sagging eyelids and thin eyelashes, were slightly nervous, anxious, uncertain. He nodded. Michael's parents stood. I watched them with morbid interest.

His father was tall and slim, and had obviously given Michael his thin frame and self-assured bearing; but he wasn't obnoxiously self-assured like his son, he was just proud, and seemed very old even though he couldn't have been any older than fifty-five. He was in a dark-gray suit and had tired brown hair like a horse's mane, wiry and wide. He was solemn. His wife was small in comparison to his height, with long hair and a smooth jawline and soft lips. Michael had his father's body, but his face was nearly identical to his mother's, though of course built on more masculine lines. It was eerie, the similarity.

Should I be thinking about Michael in the past tense now? I didn't quite know. It occurred to me that maybe I should.

His parents ascended the steps, moving toward the pulpit. They would say a few words for their son. Michael's mother was still hiccup-crying, her hiccups increasing in frequency and her hand shooting up to cover her mouth as she passed by the lifeless body of her only son. She was wearing a blue sheath dress that was too big for her, and she wasn't wearing any eye makeup. Her husband murmured a few inaudible words in her ear and pushed her gently past the open coffin.

They reached the pulpit and turned to face the crowd. And almost immediately, Michael's mother's eyes lit on me.

I was frozen. She stared over the crowd and met my

eyes exactly. She knew who I was. She might have looked for my face in one of his yearbooks when she had been told who found him dead, perhaps. However she knew my face, though, it was obvious that she did. She was still crying, and I could still hear her hiccuping, but everything else was silent. She wasn't angry. She was just confused. Her face was lit up red from the colored light coming through the window.

I didn't belong here. I couldn't stay. I shot to my feet and looked down at the Bible held in a wooden pocket on the back of the pew in front of me, focusing on the swirling patterns in the old leather of the cover, and then, after mumbling some words of apology under my breath, I darted out of the pew into the aisle. I went to the heavy door. With some effort, I pushed it open and let myself out into the midday London sun. My taffeta skirt rustled far too loudly.

Or let myself out into the London half sun, rather, because the sky was cloudy and only half the sunlight made it through the clouds onto the street. I felt tired. There was an unlit streetlamp near me. I walked to it and wearily leaned against it, pressing my forehead to the metal, closing my eyes as the church door swung shut again.

I stayed there for a few minutes, just breathing in and breathing out.

Or, I suppose, it must have been longer than that. Longer than a few minutes. Because before I moved away, the doors to the church opened and people came streaming out, quiet, one by one. The service was over. I moved my head to watch them go, wrapping my arms around the lamppost. Some of them looked at me, but most of them didn't. I felt as if I should leave entirely, but I couldn't make my body listen to me.

Michael's parents came out last, and as they came out, something jolted through me like electricity. He had his arm wrapped around her and she was looking down; but then he said something to her, something I couldn't hear, and she looked up toward his face, and in the motion her eyes found me, the teenager by the lamppost. She let go of her husband gently and walked over to me where I stood. He looked reluctant to let her go but he did, and he lingered behind. I wanted to run, but I couldn't make my legs move.

"Hello," she said quietly, with a voice like butter.

"Hello," I replied.

I kept seeing Michael in her face, and it disturbed me. I felt as if I were looking at him again, and that feeling brought me back into the moment of his death, and somehow, looking at her, I kept reliving it—I was killing Michael, again and again and again, in her deep brown eyes.

"You were the girl who found him," she murmured, offering no explanation as to how she knew that.

"Yes, I was."

"Why did you run out?"

I shuddered and sighed and looked down at my feet. What to say, what could I say?

"I thought you didn't want me there," I replied lamely.

"Why?" She sounded honestly surprised.

"You were staring. I thought you were angry."

She laughed, and then cried for a few seconds, and shook her head. "No, I wasn't angry. I was just surprised that you came."

"My friend heard about it from someone, she told me when and where," I explained, still trying to make excuses even though she wasn't mad. I still felt out of place, out of line.

"I'm glad you came. Thank you for coming. Thank you. It's good that you came." She was looking up at the swirling somnolent sky now, distracted, halfway broken.

For a moment, I was so, so sorry, not for murder, but for this woman, this survivor, but then, of course, the moment passed.

"Um, you're welcome."

There was a pause. Then—

"What did he look like?"

"Excuse me?"

"Him. Michael. When you found him. What did he look like? And don't lie to me, please, they've all been lying to me—" She glanced back at her husband furtively, like a child keeping a secret. "They keep saying he died peacefully, that there was no blood, but it's murder, and that's obviously a lie. They're trying to please me. I want to know, really. Please. Please tell me."

She reached out and grasped my left shoulder in one surprisingly strong hand, her fingers clenching around my skin and refusing to let go. I felt sorry for this woman. This poor strong woman who others assumed was so weak.

I looked at her and spoke in a quiet, quiet voice.

"His eyes were open," I said. "And he had a bruise on his temple."

She shuddered but she kept clutching, and I went on. I wasn't done.

"There was blood coming out of his mouth, a lot of it."

"Did he look like he died in pain?"

What could I tell her?

"I don't know," I replied.

"What do you *think*?"

She wanted to know. She wanted to know like her life depended on it. I felt the strange, irrational, unnatural urge to cry.

"I think it was painless," I murmured, and after a moment, she let go.

"Good," she whispered, and cried, "Good . . ."

I stared at my feet. She kept talking.

"He was a good kid, you know. People said he wasn't. But he was a good kid. If you *really* knew him, like I knew him. If you knew him, sometimes, just sometimes, he was so good, so lovely. . . ."

Her words melted into tears. Her husband came over and put an arm around her waist. He didn't look at me. It was odd. She was strange. I supposed my idea of what a mother should be was somewhat skewed—this woman believed so blindly in the goodness of her son, and I found it hard to reconcile this idea of a mother with my own mother, who had no such illusions about me.

"Come on, let's go," her husband murmured, and led her away. She didn't look back at me, just went on, leaving me behind. I imagined—correctly—that we'd never meet again.

I walked away from the lamppost and moved on.

◆ ◇ ◆

I came home late. I wandered all day through the streets of London, trying to avoid returning. I walked through Brixton for a while, and then Westminster, and then somehow I made my way to Notting Hill, and I stayed around there for a while because I hadn't been in that area for years, not even for a murder. Some streets were lined with tall white houses and reminded me of my own, but other streets were colorful little jewels, and I tried to find those. When I did find them, I took my time. I walked slowly, absorbing the color of each bright house. I tried to let them make me happy. But wherever I walked, Michael followed. I imagined him watching me, gazing from street corners, sneering from windows, laughing from the steps of houses. His image chased me through the city.

I was haunted by a memory, too, not of Michael but of a time before I knew Michael, a memory of the room where I had spent so long training with my mother—only a snippet, really. I was twelve, and I knelt over her, fist pressed to her chin at the end of a sparring match—I had won. She gasped beneath me. I remembered the anger and pompous victory that ran through my veins, burning—and I remembered the look in her eyes, defeated and wondering, as she proudly pronounced that I was done with my training. She lifted me up high in celebration—and I remembered that even though I had killed before that, the moment I knelt over her on the mats was the moment everything truly began.

It was the first moment I had become Diana.

The memory shocked me through with something akin to fear.

I watched the sunset from a street corner near Westminster Abbey, among crowds of tourists who stared at me, almost in awe of my beautiful taffeta party dress. I was an island, though; I didn't see them. I watched the sunset by myself. It seemed monochromatic to me. Everything mashed together in the sky to make one unappetizing, oversweet shade of salmon pink.

Home wasn't comfortable anymore. But eventually I had to return, because I was tired and I had to sleep, no matter how much I didn't want to. I felt like I wanted to stay awake forever.

My neighborhood was quiet, and the sky had long since turned dark. The rows of clean white houses on either side of my street stood gracefully, presiding over neatly trimmed window boxes and shining front steps in the mellow glow of the arching streetlamps.

At almost the exact moment I got home, my father happened to come home as well.

He parked his big, dark, expensive car with the clean silver wheels and old license plate outside the front door and stepped out onto the curb the same instant I was mounting the steps—and just for politeness' sake, I turned to say hello. But then I was quiet. Maybe it was spiteful, or maybe it was self-defeating, I really didn't know, but either way I wanted him to notice me before I said a word.

As he stepped out of the front seat, he was staring at the ground, thinking, maybe. Like always, I was mostly invisible to him. It was only when he walked around the car to get his briefcase out of the passenger seat that he saw me. I couldn't see any emotion in his eyes; if it was there, it was invisible.

"Hello, Kit," he said politely.

"Hello," I replied.

He opened the car door and turned away without another word. He shifted his weight from his right foot to his left and then back to his right again.

Didn't he know? Hadn't he heard? A boy had died. It was all over the news. Hadn't he even thought about it? Wasn't he even going to ask me what happened?

To my surprise, words rose up within me—words I wanted to shout at him, throw at him, make him listen to.

I am a murderer! I wanted to say. I am a killer! I am dangerous! Half of London is talking about me and my work, and sometimes I wonder if you even know my name any longer. I've punched and *killed* a classmate. I'm going to kill another. I've killed over fifty people. I'm famous. I have blood on my hands that I can never wipe away. I can think of a thousand ways to kill you just in this moment. I'm your *daughter*, I wanted to say, but when you see my face, I swear you don't even believe it.

He walked up the stairs and put his key in the lock when I made no move to do the same. I crossed my arms. I had so, so many things to say, especially now, and all of them were trying desperately to escape from my lips. I couldn't say any of them. I felt like if I tried, I wouldn't be able to stop myself once I began.

So I just said, "Thank you," as he opened the door for me, and I went upstairs before I had a chance to hear what he said in reply.

Late that night as I tried to sleep, I couldn't. I could hear voices, taut and anxious, emanating from my parents' bedroom, just below mine, and I knew my mom was explaining some of the things I couldn't say. She would be explaining Michael's death and my involvement in his discovery—she would give my father the official story, the facts, the things he needed to be aware of in order to be respectably informed. He never knew anything besides the official story. He lived in quiet ignorance.

She would explain the events of the past week because he hadn't been home at a reasonable hour since Michael's murder, and then they would say nothing more to each other.

I wondered what he thought of it all. I wondered if he even thought anything.

◆ ◇ ◆

By Saturday my mom had started giving me the silent treatment and stopped throwing things, but on Monday I was still nursing a long cut on my arm I had sustained the previous Friday when she broke a vase when I was standing next to her. Her injuries were worse than mine; the bandages on her wrists and arms were caked through with blood in places, and on Thursday I had sat with her for two hours trying to dislodge a piece of glass from deep within her palm. On Monday, I hid my cut with a long-sleeved sweater, put on a morose face, and went to school.

After I had hit Michael, the stares had been scandalous and gossipy.

Now the stares were pitying and wary.

The hallways went silent around me—they were quieter than usual to begin with. But as soon as I passed, there was dead silence—no one spoke, no one moved. I had seen a murdered body. I was special. In the worst possible way.

Well, perhaps not in the *worst* possible way. I wondered what they all would say if they knew I was the one who murdered him.

My heart went cold.

Murdered him without a letter.

Before I knew it I was at homeroom.

I stopped outside the door and hovered there. I was early. I had to go in, of course. But part of me, a large part of me, didn't want to. There were two monsters in there. One was Maggie, the other was Michael's distinct absence.

But there was no helping it. I walked inside.

The first thing I noticed was that there was nothing on Michael's desk, the one he *always* sat in during homeroom. I had imagined that people would leave things there.

Flowers, notes. I suppose I had this image of bouquets and pictures and letters overflowing from inside his desk, petals falling onto the floor, a display like I had seen once where someone had died in a car crash by the side of the road. That was what people did for dead people, wasn't it?

But there was nothing there. Just an empty desk that people gave a wide berth and stared at with wide eyes.

The second thing was Maggie. She was sitting alone, five feet from the nearest person. She was leaning back in her chair, hair loose and curly and wild, collar neat and crisp, feet up on her desk, angled toward the door so that she could see the people who came in.

Her expression was one of defiant happiness.

Our eyes met.

"Hello," she said.

The room suddenly felt twice as silent as before. A chasm opened up between Maggie and me. I felt far away. Outside, a tree moaned in the wind, silhouettes of leaves flying by the open window like a fake backdrop from an old movie.

"Hello," I replied softly.

I walked to her desk and stood in front of her, hands in my pockets.

She took a minute to think about what she was going to say.

"He's dead," she said simply, her voice barely above a whisper.

"Yes . . . he is," I replied, my voice even quieter than

before. No one looked in our direction.

She tipped her head back, hair flowing down, and breathed in. And as she exhaled, a small laugh escaped her lips. A laugh that could almost be mistaken for a gasp. Cold and merciless.

"He's gone," she murmured happily, just loud enough so that only I could hear, as I stared on in horror.

• ◇ •

I had philosophy just before lunch. I probably should have been dreading it. But I wasn't. In fact, I was rather excited for it, in a morbid sort of way. Perhaps "interested" was a better word. I knew Dr. Marcell was suspicious. No one else seemed to be. So how would she act?

I took a seat near the back of the room. At Michael's seat, yet again, there were no flowers. Just an empty space where he had been and was no more.

Making a point to look miserable, I listened to the bell ring like a church bell and watched the students settle into their seats. In the front of the classroom, Dr. Marcell stood, went to the classroom door, and closed it. All of us watched her as she walked to the middle of the front of the classroom and stopped. She looked over us, studying our expressions. After a while, she spoke.

"Something terrible has happened." Daggers. The words felt like daggers.

Terrible? How was it terrible? Sure, he was dead, and death was traumatizing, but it wasn't terrible. Michael was a bastard. He was more than a bastard—he was legitimately insane. He was dangerous. Everyone was better off now that he was gone.

"I know all of you know what I'm talking about. Here, in this classroom, with one empty desk, we can see it clearly. Now, I know all of you are required to go to therapy at least once, so I'm not going to spend any time talking about the event itself, but I want to talk a bit about something I think pertains to the situation."

No one said a word.

"Today," Dr. Marcell said, "we're going to talk about what evil is."

She looked at me. I looked down.

"I'm going to ask you a question, and I want to know what you think," she said, pacing back and forth across the front of the room. "Tell me this—is evil universal?"

For a moment, there was silence; then someone whispered, "No."

"Interesting. Why do you say no?" Dr. Marcell prompted.

The same person did not care to elaborate, so Dr. Marcell looked over the room for a volunteer. There were none, so she chose someone.

"Marie," she said, gesturing to the blond girl sitting in the first row. Marie, poor girl, didn't know what to say for a moment, but after a few seconds she came up with something.

"It's the same argument as . . . moral nihilism. Like, there's no true evil, since evil is a social construct."

"All right." Dr. Marcell paced back and forth once more, then stopped. "So, then, would you say that Hitler, for example, was not truly evil?"

"No, that's not what I meant," Marie breathed.

Damien, the boy next to me, added helpfully, "I think that all the stuff in the middle, like little stuff, like stealing a bag of chips or forging a signature on a minor piece of paperwork, isn't evil. And for some bad stuff, like, murder, it depends on what kind of society you live in. 'Cause in some places that can be evil, and in others it's normal. Some stuff is never really evil—unless there are crazy circumstances, like you steal food from a starving person or something. Some stuff depends on where and when you are, like, your society. But stuff . . . like mass genocide . . . that's evil, no matter what society you live in."

Dr. Marcell smiled. "Basically, Damien says that evil, except for extreme evil, is based on the circumstances. Can we all agree on that for the sake of argument?"

The students murmured passively in agreement.

"So," Dr. Marcell said softly and carefully, "was Michael's murder evil?"

All the air suddenly seemed to disappear from the room. Everything was quiet. Rigid. Immovable. No one could believe she had just asked that question. It was so obvious—everyone would say that it was evil, of course. Even asking it seemed almost blasphemous. Even to me. His mother had cried so passionately for him. Asking the question seemed almost to negate her suffering.

Though, as I thought about it, I probably shouldn't feel that way.

Dr. Marcell chose her next words carefully. She had to. They were dangerous words. Honestly, if anyone heard her talking, she would probably get fired for insensitivity or something. I knew she was aiming this at me. Every half second her eyes would flicker over to me and stare. I knew she suspected me. But there were more elegant ways to go about victimizing me. I didn't react.

"Michael . . . was a troubled soul," she said quietly, her words floating over us and settling restlessly. "Many people, including the police and some parents and teachers who shall remain unnamed, upon reviewing his actions and history, have expressed concern that he may have suffered from antisocial personality disorder," she said, and continued, even though we already knew what that meant. "Antisocial personality disorder is a disorder that makes a person tend to disregard the rights of others. A violation of the rights of another person, if extreme enough, could be considered evil. He had the potential to become evil. So I will repeat the question: was his *murder* evil?"

It was a question with only one answer. Of course we had to say it was evil. If we said it wasn't evil, we would sound like psychopaths. It was a trap.

"Of course it was evil," I said strongly.

She looked at me sharply.

"Explain," she said.

I was stunned.

"Well . . . how could it not be evil? Suffering from whatever he suffered from—that's not his fault. Wasn't his fault. He was only a kid, we're all only kids. Killing someone who barely had a chance to live—that's evil," I said.

They weren't my thoughts. They were the thoughts of the people around me. But still, something about the words, even as they passed by my own lips, unsettled me.

"You . . . hit him in the cafeteria two weeks ago, didn't you?" Dr. Marcell asked cautiously. I nodded.

"I did . . . yes . . . but that's completely unrelated. I didn't get along with him, but killing him—I wouldn't wish death on anybody."

Unless they deserved it, I thought.

"Is this a really necessary conversation?" someone behind me whimpered.

Dr. Marcell ignored the plea.

"So he didn't deserve death, even if he might someday do what you consider evil?"

"He didn't *do* anything!" I shouted suddenly, standing up, slamming my palms against the table—and I realized I was right.

He didn't do anything.

He hadn't killed, cheated, lied, or stolen, as far as I knew. He hadn't caused lasting harm to Maggie, even though she had been afraid. I was the one who had hit him. I was the one who had started putting things in motion. I had passed judgment.

I could give the blame to no one else. I could no longer

say that it was all right because the death was not my judgment but another's—

It was my own death. It was my own fault. I could tell myself all the excuses in the world, but in the end it was all my fault. He didn't do anything, and I had killed him. I'd known it before, had realized it before—but suddenly it felt real to me, all too real and terrible.

I looked at Dr. Marcell, and all the anger and defiance melted out of my eyes even as distrust built up in hers. She glared. The space behind my sternum felt empty. My vision blurred. I collapsed back down into my chair. I closed my eyes and reminded myself to keep breathing. I felt empty, everything felt empty.

For the first time in my life, I felt like a murderer.

"It was evil," I murmured. I didn't hear if anyone answered me.

◆ ◇ ◆

I sat back in volatile repose.

I sat in the small office with my legs crossed, leaning back in the chair, casually looking over the walls with their faded peach-colored wallpaper. Across the desk, a therapist leaned toward me. She was faceless to me. She didn't factor into my life. I didn't want to be here; I was here because I had to be. All the students had to go speak to a counselor, especially me. I had left philosophy early for this; the therapist had a lot of students to see, and apparently it was a mess trying to fit everyone into her schedule. I was grateful for the timing. After the class's jarring beginning, I didn't want to be in that classroom for a moment longer than necessary, not today.

"How are you feeling?" she asked with a touch of tiredness in her voice. She of course had already asked this question many, many times.

"Fine," I said.

I didn't really trust myself, not today.

I didn't trust myself to speak like a normal teenager. I felt too much like a murderer, trapped between four peach walls, lounging—languid and nervous, all in one. I felt too much like Diana. I felt her bloodlust, her anxiety, her cold calculation.

"It must be stressful, being surrounded by this whole mess."

"It's fine."

The faceless therapist was obviously dissatisfied, but I didn't feel like giving her what she wanted. I looked out the second-story window behind her head, out at dark treetops just barely penetrated by midafternoon sun.

"Did you know Michael personally?"

"No," I lied. The image of his crying mother came before my eyes.

"I was told you . . . hit him in the cafeteria not too long ago."

"I didn't know him."

"Kit, I can't help you if you won't let me."

"I don't want help."

"Kit . . ."

I stared back at her. Maybe she would see me as emotionally affected, scarred, unwilling to speak because I was in grief, instead of out of control.

Volatile repose. The words just kept occurring to me. It was a perfect description of me—quiet, calm, but on the edge of something vast and dark and dangerous and explosive.

"You knew him," the therapist suggested firmly.

"Maybe."

"Do you want to talk about it?"

"No."

"This will take time to recover from, I realize. But you can't recover if you don't try."

"I'm required to come here only once, right?"

She looked uncomfortable.

"I'd like it if you kept coming."

"I don't want to keep coming."

"You need help, Kit." She meant so well.

"I don't want help," I snapped back, and that was it, she wasn't getting past me, not her or anyone else; I was ice and she was beating against me uselessly. I wouldn't have it.

◆ ◇ ◆

Maggie practically waltzed through the hallways. She knew she wasn't supposed to be smiling, so she was trying to hide her grin beneath her black scarf, but she wasn't doing very well. She floated through school like some sort of fairy, smiling all the way. Anger rose up in me. I was edgy to begin with, and her cheerfulness was pissing me off.

It should have made me feel better to know that even though there wasn't a letter, I had delivered someone else's justice and not just my own. But it didn't. Her happiness just made me think about the murder more, and the more I thought about it, the more desperately guilty I felt. I followed her footsteps. She cleared a path where she walked, and I used that to my advantage.

We walked into the cafeteria and over to the table. The table where I had knocked Michael to the ground. I bit my lip and tried not to look at that space on the linoleum where he had been, that empty space.

Maggie sat down and beamed at me as I took my seat across from her. I couldn't believe it. I looked away in a vague direction, gritted my teeth, and snapped my attention back to her abruptly.

"Don't you feel *guilty*?" I hissed quietly.

"What?" she asked, her expression one of vacant, honest surprise.

"You know, looking all happy like that. He's *dead*, Maggie. It's not like he just moved away or something or went on a very long vacation. He's *dead*."

"I don't care." She smiled. "He never did anything but harass me. Why should I care that he's dead? Why should I be unhappy that he's gone?"

I gaped at her. "He's . . . He loved you, Maggie. However crazy he might have been, he loved you. Don't you have any pity?"

She didn't reply. She just scanned her eyes over the

cafeteria and laughed shortly. The same disturbing laugh as that morning.

"I don't see why they all look so sad," Maggie mused to herself. "It's not like any of them liked him any better than I did. He was an arsehole, through and through."

Those words came so easily to her now. The sharp, unkind words. I had persuaded her to say them before, but now that she was saying them with such anger, of her own free will—

I didn't like it.

My heart churned.

She looked at me and smiled, trying to make me understand. But I didn't understand. I was never happy about death. I liked the *act* of killing. It was precise. But after death—no, I never appreciated that. I could never understand her joy.

"Now that he's dead, I can finally start to *live*," she breathed blissfully.

My heart burned.

I would kill her too. Michael was dead by my hand, but I would still deliver his justice. I had accepted his request. I would not turn away now. It was the least I could do to, in some way, atone for his death.

She didn't know it yet, but she would know it eventually. And she would hate me. And that was fine. They all hated me, close to the end.

My heart felt like it was going to disappear.

Something had broken inside me. It hurt. Before, my

moral compass had been frozen at due north, completely neutral. But now the ice was beginning to crack, and things were beginning to unwind and unravel.

◆ ◆ ◆

After school I found Maggie and three other girls in the first-floor bathroom. Maggie was leaning against the far wall, watching them warily as they talked. Their words were sharp, not openly aimed at her but meant to be overheard and hurtful, and they were standing directly between her and the door. They had cornered her here just before I arrived, and showed no signs of moving.

"What a horrible thing, that poor boy dying," one of them said with a melodramatic sigh, twirling a piece of brown hair around her finger and looking pointedly at Maggie out of the corner of her eye. "Don't you think, Annie?" she said, looking expectantly at one of her friends.

I hovered just outside the door, pressing myself to the wall next to it. There was a crack between the door and the doorframe just wide enough for me to see what was happening inside. With sharp, watchful eyes, I observed them, wondering if I should intervene. For the moment I would just watch.

"Yeah, awful. I can't believe it. Everyone's all torn up about it," Annie drawled.

"Except," the third girl chimed in, "I heard this awful rumor. There's this one girl, I heard, who keeps on smiling about it."

"Fucking crazy," the first girl agreed with a shake of her

head. "What kind of insane human being acts like that? She needs to be locked up, I swear."

"Even if they didn't get along, that's no excuse. Honestly. Even the girl who punched him in the cafeteria two weeks ago is torn up about it," Annie said, sighing.

"Anyone who can laugh about a murder is a psychopath," the first girl said, and then pretended to think about that. "And a psychopath probably committed that murder," she said lightly, as if she were realizing something.

I saw Maggie clench her fists. At first glance she looked vague and disinterested, but as I looked longer at her, I saw the way she scrunched her shoulders up, the way her left ankle was shivering with tense anger.

I slunk a step toward the doorknob, readying myself in case I needed to intervene.

I had protected her thus far, at great cost. I sure as hell wasn't going to stop now. I had begun something, and I would see it through to the end.

Chapter 14

*T*hat night, I chose a letter and got dressed in black leather. It was written on thin paper, and as I cleaned it of fingerprints and other evidence, I had to be careful not to rip the paper.

Dear Killer,

I don't understand why she wants to go. I love her so much. I love her more than anything. And you'd think that'd be what she wanted—who doesn't want to be loved? I would do anything for her. I've always been there for her. Always.

But she's leaving me. I don't understand, and I think I'm going to kill myself thinking about it. I'm going crazy. I can't stand the thought of seeing her with anyone else. It makes me angry. She makes me angry. But I love her. No one can have her but me, or I really am going to kill myself.

Please. Please kill her. If I can't have her, no one can. Her name is Cherry Rose.

I recognized the name of my victim. Cherry Rose, an up-and-coming singer who sang a lot at clubs in the West End. After a quick internet search, I found that she was singing her first of a few gigs at the Ball tonight, a new club near Leicester Square. I needed to fit in, so I picked up a slinky black leather dress from my closet, the one I had bought three years ago on a whim but never worn until now. It still fit, just barely, though the skirt kept riding up and I had to pull it down every few seconds.

My mom was nowhere in sight, and as usual my dad was MIA. I left a note on the fridge for my mom—*Going to Leicester*—in case she worried, and then I left.

I needed distraction.

I took the subway to Leicester Square. I made sure to wear a sullen expression—I didn't want anyone messing with me. I wasn't in the mood. I had a long black overcoat on over the slinky dress, and I stuffed my hands in my pockets, deep in thought as the train clicked evenly through the city. I shouldn't have been thinking, probably. Thinking is always dangerous when you're me. I remember very little about that train ride except for the fact that the train was too warm and that the woman I was sitting across from wouldn't stop humming loudly along to whatever music she was listening to through her earbuds. She was fat and had a pink shirt on and she looked like a giant piece of bubble-gum. Funny the things you remember.

Leicester Square was busy. Everywhere you looked there was light and people. It was a violent cacophony of sights and sounds and smells; I felt small wandering through the crowd. Small and young. There were surprising numbers of couples in the square. They walked with linked arms, whispering in each other's ears, hanging on to each other. I wove between them. I kept out of sight. I shivered. The night was cold.

The Ball, named for the large mirrored silver ball that hung over the doorway, wasn't the busiest club on the square. Nor was it the most deserted. It was completely average, completely innocuous, with the regular assortment of couples and singles and groups of women in too-short dresses and men leaning against the wall waiting outside. The bouncer was drunk and easily distracted by pretty women and wasn't paying much attention to the people walking through the door—lame, but convenient. He would be sacked later. It would be too late for Cherry.

I slid through the black doorframe behind a pair of sickeningly cheerful couples. Everything inside smelled like alcohol. The decor was sleek and new, but the floor was dirty and the music was too loud and the lighting overhead made everyone look narrow and wan. I stopped and stood still; people pushed past me, knocking against my shoulders. I ignored them. A level below where I stood, slightly belowground, was a rolling crowd of dancers, moving like one thing. I stood and watched them briefly, and then I turned my eyes and ears to Cherry Rose.

She was on a stage, and her name fit her perfectly.

She was short and thin, with high cheekbones and pale skin like a doll's. Her hair was a bright, bright shade of scarlet, almost exactly the color of a cherry. Maybe a bit darker. She was wearing a green dress that made her green eyes seem brighter than they really were. There was something strange about her, something ephemeral. She sang into the microphone, holding it close to her lips as if she were about to kiss it.

I leaned over the railing, looking down on her, trying to figure out the words she was singing. Slowly, I removed my coat and hung it over the railing. I would try to come back for it later. Hopefully it would still be there. It wasn't like it could incriminate me or anything—things like jackets got lost all the time and didn't mean anything. And they couldn't get fingerprints off it either, anyway. I had forgotten I couldn't wear it while I was killing her, because it would be too bulky and I sometimes had to move like a dancer when I worked—oh well. No time to worry about it now.

Cherry, balanced on tiptoe, sang her heart out.

"Somewhere in the night, you're calling, I'm calling—
Somewhere deep inside, I'm waiting—

The moonlight rips through me
Like claws on my skin.
I don't know where I stop and you begin."

It was a fast-paced song, lively, easy to dance to, backed with a strong beat and a growling guitar—but it was shot through with a deep melancholy. She sang it with fervor. As I watched her lips move, I imagined how she would die. Would it be with bare hands? Most likely. She was small enough that it would be easy. Most of my smaller victims died that way. Bare hands around her neck, bare hands smashing her head into something sharp, a bare hand jamming into her temple. Or maybe she would die by having something smashed into her. A pipe. A handheld mirror. A crack against the skull or neck, that would do it—

Cherry finished the song, and I walked down the stairs.

I wove through the crowd, occasionally stopping to dance for a few seconds so as not to arouse suspicion. I kept my eyes trained on Cherry. She didn't have a clue. Just like everyone else. Not a clue.

She started into another song, and I considered my options. I looked around the crowded room. What options were there? Ideally, I wanted to make my way backstage—but how could I?

After a few minutes, I saw the way. A black door blending into the black wall and guarded by a hulking security guard with a handlebar mustache and a wide face. He wouldn't be trouble.

As Cherry sang on, I meandered my way toward the guard. I wasn't in any hurry. As I drew nearer, I slowed, blending into the crowd. I was close to the stage now, about five feet away. Close enough to see the dark roots of Cherry's hair where it was growing back brown. And I could see now that she had dark circles under her eyes. That was a tired face. And yet she sang with such passion. It occurred to me that she was an unusual person, somehow, an individual like few people really were. For a few seconds she mesmerized me, and then I remembered what I had to do.

I moved toward the man and made sure no one was watching. His mustache twitched. No one was focusing on me, everyone was focused on Cherry—how convenient. I danced my way over next to the man—I was invisible to him. Tranquilly, making sure to seem innocuous, facing mostly toward the wall, I pulled a latex glove from within my bra and pulled it on. I stayed a bit behind him, staying in the shadows.

I quietly moved my hand up to pinch my fingers around his jugular.

He gave a small gasp and, as expected, went immediately limp, unconscious. As best I could, I slowed his fall. I looked frantically around to make sure no one noticed. No one did. Everyone was too occupied with other things. I let him sit on the ground and grabbed at the doorknob—locked. Damn. I dug my fingers into his coat pocket, looking for the keys. He wouldn't be unconscious long. I had to be fast.

I found them in the second pocket—cold metal—and dug them out. With calm fingers, making sure to touch the keys only with my gloved hand, I opened the door and dropped the keys behind me. The guard wouldn't come after me. He hadn't seen me. He had been watching Cherry.

Backstage was more deserted than I'd expected. Good. Deserted was good. This was all too easy.

♦ ◊ ♦

I waited in her dressing room and looked over her possessions. I had both gloves on now, and as I drew my fingers across her things, I didn't leave fingerprints.

She had only taken possession of this room earlier that night, so of course it wasn't completely *filled* with her things—just scattered with them, here and there, enough to make it distinctively her room and not someone else's. A slightly open lipstick on the edge of the counter in front of the mirror, a black jacket slung over the back of the folding chair near a window that showed a small view of a dingy alleyway. As I waited, I took in these and other things—a bag with a phone sticking out the top, a paperback romance novel near the mirror, an empty water bottle—and I looked at my reflection.

God, I looked tired. And weak. Dark circles lined my eyes, and my skin was pale and sallow, as if I were spending too much time indoors. I was too thin. My hair was a mess too. It was tangled around my shoulders like a lion's mane. Gingerly, I ran my fingers over it. It was getting a bit long. A bit unmanageable. Maybe I should cut it. But no, maybe not. I had cut my hair when I was thirteen, and it hadn't been my best look. It didn't look chic like my mother's when it was short. It just needed a trim.

It suddenly struck me that I was waiting to kill someone and I was thinking about hair.

The letter, tucked within the neckline of my dress, pressed suddenly against my skin, feeling like a brand across my chest.

I was waiting to *kill* someone and I was thinking about *hair*.

What the hell was I?

I looked at the mirror again and saw something very different.

Instead of seeing a pitiful teenager who needed to eat and get out more, the kind that you always felt sorry for, I saw a monster, little more than a skeleton, with big, white, sharp teeth and a rough mane like a lion and hands like long, grasping claws. I saw a nightmare. I saw the creature that hid in your closet and under your stairs when you were four. For a moment, I saw myself as terrifying. I felt shocked through, as cold as ice. For a moment, I was paralyzed. For a moment I saw what everyone else would see if they knew the truth.

But then I shook my head and remembered that I was a moral nihilist.

I wasn't a monster, because there were no such things as monsters. They didn't exist. I exhaled loudly. I was fine. There was no morality. I was fine.

But my heart was still beating like a jackhammer.

Unsettled, I walked across the room to the wall the door would open on to, so I wouldn't be seen when Cherry came back in. A blind spot. My thoughts were whirling too quickly, my breaths coming too fast—

I closed my eyes and tried to relax and forget.

I shut everything out to a point where I felt like I was almost sleeping, and then Cherry came in.

She was quieter than I expected. She had been so loud onstage that I think I expected some sort of fanfare on her arrival. But she opened the door slowly, and when she came in, she was quiet and sat down in her folding chair silently.

I opened my eyes and stared into the door, the rest of my senses suddenly alert and waiting.

A harrowed-sounding backstage worker stuck her head inside the door and snapped, "Do you need any help, or can you pack up on your own?"

"I'm fine," Cherry replied softly.

I heard the backstage worker move away, and I made my breaths quiet. Even though there was such a din in the hallway that I probably wouldn't be heard even if I coughed loudly, I couldn't be too careful.

Cherry seemed content to keep the door open for the time being. Over near the counter, I heard her moving. Packing up her makeup, throwing the water bottle away. I considered my options. I could wait, keep her in the room somehow, and murder her a bit later so there would be no one to hear us from the hallway, though I would undoubtedly be caught on camera leaving later than everyone else—or I could do it now, as quietly as possible, and escape through the small window in the corner of the room into the alley behind the building if need be. I wouldn't be caught on the backstage camera if I did that, but I would probably be caught on a surveillance camera suspiciously coming out of an alley I hadn't gone into earlier in the evening.

I realized suddenly that there was no easy way out.

Sure, I had found my way in, but how was I going to leave after the fact? How was I going to escape her dead body, how—

I was trapped. I had trapped myself. I didn't know what to do. My breaths came even faster.

I pinched myself and reminded myself who I was. The Perfect Killer, for God's sake. This was nothing. I could find my way out of this. So what if I was seen coming out? I could borrow clothes from backstage and be nothing more than a shadowy figure on camera. No one had seen me come in. The cameras on the way out would see nothing more than a silhouette. Sure, it would be the first time the Perfect Killer had been caught on film, but what would that matter if the Perfect Killer was nothing more than an indistinguishable shadow, quickly lost in the crowd of Leicester Square?

Still, I would be disappointed to know that I had stooped so low so as to allow myself to be recorded.

Perhaps it was best to do this quickly. It would save

me the trouble of worrying about how to keep Cherry in the room while waiting for everyone to leave. Besides, I had never liked waiting much. Patience wasn't one of my virtues.

Cherry hovered around the mirror. With a soft breath, I raised my fingers to the door, stretched out my arm, and pushed the door into the doorframe. It closed with a barely audible click. It was so smooth, so quiet, that Cherry almost didn't notice. But she did notice, mostly because my reflection was now visible in the mirror. She gasped and dropped her purse onto the counter, then laughed softly, nervously.

"Who are you? What are you doing there?" she asked with only a touch of suspicion. So she was that sort of person. The sort of person who found it hard to perceive evil in anything. Those people irritated me.

I almost said "Kit" before I realized that wasn't my name right now.

"Diana," I murmured to her, and I think that was exactly when she realized something was terribly wrong.

I reached out and locked the door with elegant fingers.

"What are you doing?" she demanded whisperingly.

"Locking the door."

"Why?"

I just smiled.

I could see it now. The sharp edge of the counter would do it. I would take her head in my hands and drag it downward with brute force—she was smaller than me, and weaker, that wouldn't be hard—slamming it against the fake stone edge. It would kill her in one blow—

Monster.

The word flashed unbidden through my head. I was done thinking it even before I realized I had begun. I froze. I felt like I was going to throw up.

"What do you want?" she demanded timidly.

I opened my mouth to tell her the truth. I wanted to kill her and keep my place in the world. I wanted to crush her skull against the countertop.

But I couldn't say a word. Not for a few moments, before I cleared my throat and recovered myself.

"I'm going to kill you," I said, trying to make her understand. Why was I saying that? I always played with stories, never told the truth to my victims. Michael was the first one I had told the truth to before the end, and I had been sure about his death. I had held him in the palm of my hand. I didn't hold her at all. The truth was dangerous. Why was I telling her this?

She gaped back at me like a fish, fear lighting in her eyes.

"What?" she gasped.

"I'm the Perfect Killer, and you're going to die." It was too late to take back what I had already said. I might as well run with it. I was just beginning to feel like Diana. This was fine. I was fine.

"Why?" she pleaded.

Why?

No one ever asked why. That was new. Why? Because

someone wanted her dead, obviously. She knew me. She knew my modus operandi. I killed on cue.

"Your ex wants you dead because you left him," I said.

"I thought so," she murmured. "But *why*? Not him, you. Why, just why would you do this—you're so young, why . . ."

She begged with her eyes, sought to understood. There was something more than fear there. Sadness. She understood that she was going to be killed, and she just wanted to know why.

Did they all look like this before the end?

Usually when I became Diana, I ceased to see my victims as people and saw them simply as animals. As cattle. Somehow, something about her or about me as I was wasn't allowing me to see Cherry that way. I saw her as human. And it unsettled me. Spooked me. And so I had to wonder. Did they all look like her, have the same look in their eyes as she, and did I just not see it each time?

Monster Monster Monster

The thought echoed through my head, and I reeled.

What was I?

I tried to remind myself of what I believed, moral nihilism, but suddenly all I could remember was the list of names, the slide show of faces of the people I had killed. Young, old, fat, thin, blond, black-haired, brunette, green-eyed, blue-eyed, brown-eyed . . .

Monster Monster Monster Monster Monster

What *was* I?

Who was I to kill so freely, even on others' wishes, who was I to kill Michael, who was I to kill this woman, who was I to make her feel so afraid?

Blood painted my hands, left me breathless. How was there so much blood?

I fell to my knees, my eyes wide, my entire body shaking even though the air was warm.

Who was I?

Who was I?

Monster Monster Monster Monster Monster Monster Monster

Cherry knelt and stared me in the eyes. Unable to look away, I stared back. The fear was gone now, replaced by confusion, and amazingly enough–

Compassion.

I couldn't move a muscle. Slowly, Cherry placed a hand on my shoulder.

"You won't kill me."

It was the truth.

Her red hair floated around her face like blood, and she caressed my cheek gently.

"You poor, poor thing," she whispered to me. "What kind of life have you led?"

My mouth was dry. I wet it and choked out a few rasping words.

"You shouldn't feel sorry for me."

"But I do."

"I've killed people."

"That's why I feel sorry for you."

I gazed back at her, stunned. No one felt sorry for murderers. That was . . . that was wrong. And yet the pity in her eyes was genuine. That was morally nihilistic. Not exactly, but in a way it was. Or maybe it was just a judgment that some things, like pity, were more important than morals.

I realized strangely that she was one of those magical creatures who weren't quite human. One of the people you meet sometimes who have something supernatural in their blood. She didn't quite think like anyone else. She was extraordinary. Like something shining, something incredible.

And I could have killed her without even realizing it.

"You regret it, don't you?"

Yes yes yes yes yes

"Yes," I gasped. "Oh God, I regret it, I regret it. . . ."

And suddenly I was crying and I didn't know what to do and I was being held in the arms of one of my victims and I was lost and floating and I was like a little child afraid of the monster under her stairs but the monster was me and I didn't know what to do anymore–

Cherry, after a minute, let me go, stood, and picked her dark jacket up off the back of the chair. After a moment of thought, she took off her shoes as well and handed them to me along with the jacket.

"You haven't done anything tonight, but it's better safe than sorry. Change so you won't be recognized by the cameras," she said.

"You're helping me go?" I managed to ask through my tears.

Cherry nodded. "And I won't tell anyone I met you, either."

I saw in her eyes that she wasn't the kind of person who would lie.

"Why are you helping me?"

She smiled. "I don't believe you're a bad person."

"I'm a *serial killer*."

She looked at me darkly.

"I know."

"Will you turn me in if I kill again?"

Cherry shook her head. "No."

"Why?"

She shrugged. "I don't think these things out too much. I go on instinct. Leave now. Stop crying, and get out of here before I change my mind."

◆ ◇ ◆

I stood perched on the edge of Waterloo Bridge.

In the distance I could see it all lit up in the night–the London Eye, Big Ben, all the iconic pieces of London. Usually I liked all that. It was pretty and gave everything a sense of place. But not now. Now it didn't hold any charm for me.

I stood perched on the edge of Waterloo Bridge and stared at the black waters of the Thames.

What would it be like if I jumped? Plunged beneath the dark water, let it close coldly over me, sank into the blackness below? I was already leaning halfway over the railing. It would be so easy. No one would miss me. Maggie was clueless, my mother just cared about her own safety. Alex didn't really know me. My dad didn't care much about anything. The death of the Perfect Killer would be welcomed by many. If I jumped, maybe everything would be better. Maybe even for me.

The letter, still tucked inside my dress, felt like it was stinging my skin.

With a gasp, I dug it out and crumpled it into a ball within my fist. Angrily, crying out, I threw it down at the water and watched it float away. It bobbed below the surface for a moment, then floated wetly back up, hovering heavily on the surface. That horrific thing just floated on away down the Thames like it was a brochure, or something harmless like that. It just floated away like it was innocent.

Thoughtfully, I lifted one knee up and rested it on the top of the railing. The metal reverberated beneath me.

Maybe I *would* jump. It wouldn't cause any trouble, and it might fix something. Make something better.

I put my weight on that knee and lifted my other foot off the ground. I hovered there for a moment and stared down at the water, black and deep and waiting.

No, no, no, I couldn't do it.

I couldn't.

A large part of me wanted to, badly, but I couldn't make myself do it. That much was obvious. I couldn't lean over and fall, though it was so physically easy and I wanted to—I just couldn't.

I stepped back down and crumpled to the ground. I pressed my back to the railing and tucked my knees to my chest and cried into them, wailing with a sound like a train as it shrieked into the station. People passing ignored me, stepped by me as if I weren't there. No one took a minute of their time to so much as notice me. And I just sat there and cried, falling apart, burning down inside like a broken house, for God knows how long, until suddenly I felt a hand on my shoulder.

I started. And then I turned—and unexpectedly met my mother's eyes.

I didn't understand why she was there. And I didn't really care. I was happy to see her. She was my mother. I needed her, and she was there.

She wasn't angry, as I had grown accustomed to seeing her. The look in her eyes was disturbingly similar to the look in Cherry's. Pitying. But I got the strange feeling that unlike Cherry, she understood exactly every inch of why I was sad. She wrapped a long arm around my neck. Kneeling next to me in a white pantsuit, she pulled me close to her chest.

"Let's go home," she murmured in my ear, like a mother is supposed to murmur.

I wrapped my arms tightly around her and held her like she was about to disappear.

Chapter 15

We sat in the kitchen across from each other at the table. We were both drinking tea. Earl Grey, milk, two sugars, just like we liked it. Silence.

"The person you went to kill . . . will you be caught?"

I shook my head. She sighed with relief.

More silence.

"You got too close," she said eventually.

"What do you mean?"

"You got too close. You let your murders affect you."

I curled up in my chair, as if that could make me disappear. I listened to the sounds of the room. There was the ticking of the grandfather clock in the hall. There was the gentle hum of the refrigerator. There was the faint yapping of the dog two blocks away, the one that never shut up, especially during nighttime. I couldn't see much; everything was shadowed. There weren't any lights on save for the tiny chandelier over the table, which lit up my mom and me and not much else.

"Oh."

"You know exactly what I'm talking about," my mom said with a sigh. "Don't you?"

I nodded. "Yes."

"You got lost."

"Yes."

"You forgot why we kill."

I sighed and whispered, "I'm not sure I even knew why I killed in the first place."

She took a sip of her tea and set it down on the table.

"Kit." She leaned over the table toward me. "There's no one on this earth like us. We're unique. We work according to our own individual morals. You understand that, don't you?"

"Yes," I said after a moment of hesitation.

"Tell me, then. Explain to me. In plain words. Why do you kill? Or . . . well, how did you justify it to yourself before?"

She looked at me curiously. She waited.

"You know why. You were the one who explained it to me," I reminded her. I had done it for her.

"I told you what I could tell you. The rest you were supposed to figure out on your own. I want to see if you've figured it out. Because if you haven't, I think that might explain something."

I looked at her tiredly. I couldn't bring myself to truly care about what she was saying.

"I want to sleep," I told her, closing my eyes halfway. She grabbed my wrist. Her skin was cold. It kept me awake.

"Why do you kill?"

"I kill . . . I kill because it doesn't matter. There's no good, no bad. There's just . . . opinion. That's what you told me, wasn't it?"

She leaned back.

"Yes, that's what I told you."

"Was I supposed to figure something out besides that?" I snapped bitterly. "Did you just leave me with some sort of sick mystery I had to solve?"

She sighed again.

"Murder is a strange sort of self-discovery, I've learned. At least it was for me. There's a halfway secret I haven't told you, yes. But there's a reason I wanted you to figure it out for yourself. I couldn't just tell you; you wouldn't understand, at least not at first. I had to figure it out for myself. I thought you would discover it too, like I did, on your own . . . but I suppose not. Maybe because you were comfortable with the way you thought about things, more comfortable than I ever was. Maybe that was enough for you, for a while."

"I don't understand what you're saying."

"I guess I'm rambling."

"Just say whatever you want to say."

"You really didn't justify your killing any other way?"

"All I know is what you told me."

The sentence started out angry, but by the time I made my way to the end of it, my voice had faded into near silence. I didn't have enough energy to be angry. Tired, so tired.

"There's more than moral nihilism. Just that isn't enough."

In her voice I heard certainty and determination, things I hadn't seen in her for a while. Something in her had lit up, just for this moment. But even through that sudden flame I could see that she was tired.

"I guess so," I said noncommittally.

She took a deep breath in and clenched my wrist in both of her hands.

"Kit, you're a higher power."

Finally I was listening entirely.

"What the hell are you talking about?" I protested quietly.

"That something more is what you need to understand. I couldn't have told you earlier. You wouldn't have understood then. It's what I discovered, and it's what I'd hoped you'd discover, but I suppose you didn't." She looked at me with pity, incredible pity. I didn't understand.

"What the hell does that even mean?"

"Think about it, Kit."

"I don't know what you're trying to say."

She touched my cheek, and a memory of Cherry touching my cheek returned to me.

I was a monster. What was she trying to say?

I curled up further into myself and cried silently into the teacup I held clutched to my chest.

"Kit, listen to me. Try to understand."

"I don't—"

"You're a higher power, Kit. I was a higher power too, back when I killed. People need us, Kit. People need us."

"People don't *need* murderers."

"Yes, they do. They need murderers like they need police officers, or like they need bankers. They need us, even though they don't really know it. It's a crazy world out there. A violent, crazy world. Don't you understand?"

The remote for the kitchen TV was on the end of the table. Quickly, she reached over and grabbed it. In the same motion, she clicked the power button and the screen flared to life.

Someone had bombed something in Sweden. It didn't have anything to do with me. But there it was, pasted up on the television screen, larger than life. A reporter in front of a pile of rubble, talking quickly. I didn't listen to what she was saying. The volume was too low to decipher much of anything, anyway.

Death. Destruction. Didn't she understand that I didn't want to look at any of that right now?

I looked away, staring at the table. My mom grabbed my cheek sharply and jerked my face back toward the television.

"Look," she demanded.

"I don't want to."

"Look."

I looked. I looked as images flashed past. Rescue teams in the wreckage, looking for survivors. Nervous spectators. Back to the fast-talking reporter. There was something so horribly surreal about it. It looked almost like it was fake, created and filmed for the entertainment of the morbid masses, but of course it wasn't. Of course it was real.

"Do you understand yet?"

"I don't."

"But you have to."

"I don't understand," I said emphatically. I didn't. I didn't know what she was trying to say.

"Look at them, Kit. Look at the people."

I obeyed. I watched the people.

They stood near and inside the wreckage, and they watched things unfold. They all had the same expression, all of them. Tense, expectant, scared. What were they expecting? Nothing more was about to happen. It was already done. They held on to each other. They tugged on the jacket sleeves of those around them. They buried their faces in one another's shoulders. And all of them, all of them watched the rubble. They took strength from one another. They were so afraid.

I understood.

"Oh," I said.

Oh.

It was so simple.

Why hadn't I seen it before?

I was needed.

I was a higher power.

The people needed me.

Without me, they would be lost.

Oh.

Oh.

"Do you understand now?" my mom asked quietly. I nodded.

"Oh, yes," I breathed. "Oh, it's so simple. They need me. They need me so much."

There was no sound for a moment except for the excited beating of my own heart.

"Explain it to me," my mom said, testing me. I laughed breathily, and then louder, and then I settled into a slow, relieved chuckle. Tension melted away from me. I set my teacup down on the table and wiped my tears. Oh, it was so simple. Why was I so afraid, so scared? It was so damn simple.

"I'm a higher power," I said, "because the people need something to be afraid of. They need a monster under their stairs."

She smiled. I went on.

"The world is full of chaos. And it's that chaos that joins people together. Scared people are more cohesive than people who aren't scared. It's so clear—right there, in the way they hold on to each other. They *need* me. Because the people here in London start feeling so safe. And every once in a while they need a murder—just a tiny fragment of chaos—to remind them that they aren't safe, to remind them that they need each other, to remind them that in the end it's human relationships that matter. I make them better people. It's about the moral nihilism too—and the justice of the individual—but it's also so much *more* than that. This is my city. Murder is so much *more* than what I thought before."

I spoke with fervor. It was all so clear.

My mom smiled.

"Good," she said. "Exactly."

The clock ticked, the refrigerator hummed, the dog in the distance yapped. And sitting at the kitchen table in the middle of the night, I realized my place in things.

◆ ◇ ◆

Alex looked at me thoughtfully as I scraped butter over a piece of bread. We were in the same café as before. This time, though, neither of us was saying a word.

I looked around, pointlessly moving my eyes over the bird-patterned wallpaper, the worn wicker, the plates with chipped edges. I occupied my time with observation. Alex was wearing glasses again, and they really did suit him. He was in street clothes again, too, and he had a scratch on the base of one smooth wrist. I wondered for a moment where it had come from; then I met his nebulous hazel eyes and smiled.

I had forgotten precisely why we were here, why I had invited Alex out for lunch. Had there been a reason? Did there have to be a reason? I felt somehow detached from him, from everything, like I was floating far above. But at the same time, his faraway presence was pleasant. He wasn't comforting like he had been before, exactly, because I no longer needed comfort . . . but his presence was nice. I liked having him here.

Something unidentifiable in our relationship had changed, for whatever reason, I realized—perhaps it was my newfound sense of mature self-assuredness that made it that way. I no longer felt sporadically girlish and gawky around him, but rather felt more like an adult in his presence. It was as if something new was crackling through the air between us now, building, lighting us up, connecting us to each other irrevocably in a way neither of us quite understood yet.

Eventually someone had to say something. It was Alex who spoke first.

"It's Tuesday. You didn't go to school today." It was a statement, but there was a question in it.

"No, I didn't," I agreed blithely, ignoring the question.

Another pause.

"Why?" he asked.

"I was sick early this morning. Passed quickly. Nothing major. Just no point in going to school if I was going to be there for only two hours." I didn't look him in the eyes. I stared past him, out the window at the street.

"You're better now, though?"

"I invited you out for lunch, didn't I?"

"Yeah," he said uneasily.

"You seem uncomfortable," I said, not particularly trying

to make him less uncomfortable. I was simply stating a fact.

He was so small.

"You're in a weird mood," he said cautiously. I smiled.

"Sorry. Had an unpleasant morning. I guess it's carrying over."

"I guess."

"How've you been?" I asked. "I haven't seen you since . . . that whole business at school."

He laughed. "Yeah, I guess not. I've been fine. I should really ask you how you've been doing. You were shook up by it all pretty bad, weren't you?"

I nodded solemnly. "It was crazy. But I'm fine. I guess . . . I didn't like him. In the end, I know it sounds bad, but I'm not really heartbroken that he's gone."

"I understand. I've been investigating it a bit, just casually. Judging by what I've seen in the case file, that guy—Michael—didn't seem like a great person."

"He wasn't."

"Got nailed by the police for fighting three times in the past six years, did you know?" Alex confided. I laughed.

"Sounds like him."

"Was he disruptive at school?"

I narrowed my eyes at him. "You're investigating this murder more than just a bit, aren't you?"

He shrugged sheepishly and leaned back in his chair, away from me. "Actually, I'm not. Not allowed to investigate it too much—it's not assigned to me. Plus I've already got my hands full with the Perfect Killer. But I am curious.

Just a bit. Casually. I'll find my mind wandering to that murder whenever I have a free moment."

"That's a bit morbid to think about in your spare time, isn't it?"

He chuckled.

"Do you really think it was the Perfect Killer?" I asked eagerly, tension behind my eyes. I hoped he didn't. He was smart, smarter than a lot of people on the force. It was one of the things I liked about him. And if he thought Michael's murder was the work of the Perfect Killer, he might find his way to me. I didn't want that. Not now that I had realized my place in the world. I had so many things to do now.

"I don't really know. It might be."

"But doesn't the Perfect Killer always leave, you know, letters?"

"Maybe he lost the letter. Or something. Oh, I don't know. I don't know why I think it's him. It's a hunch. Probably a stupid hunch, but whatever."

"It seems unlikely that the Perfect Killer would just lose something," I mused quietly, making sure he could hear me, trying to make him doubt himself as much as I could without seeming suspicious.

"If only we knew where the letters were *coming* from." He bit his lip.

I looked over the menu silently. I didn't answer. I didn't want to play this game with him today.

"I'm getting a salad," I told him. "How about you?"

♦ ♦ ♦

I took a bath in dark water.

It was dark outside the thin white curtains, a night sky with no moon—it had been day outside when I began my bath, and so I hadn't turned on the lights. Now there was no light left except for the faint glow that came from the hallway, beneath the door, spilling weakly over the woven bath mat. It wasn't much. When I lifted my arm out of the water, I couldn't make out the shapes of my fingernails.

So the water was dark.

I exhaled, humming a few notes of a nursery rhyme that I had heard once but couldn't quite remember the name of. Something about mice. What was it . . . I sank deeper into the water, trying to recall. After a few moments I did. I tipped my head back and hummed a little louder, reminding myself of the words. Three blind mice.

Three blind mice, three blind mice,
See how they run, see how they run.
They all ran after the farmer's wife,
Who cut off their tails with a carving knife . . .

I lounged and fell silent, forgetting the rest of the words, tipping my head back into the now-lukewarm bathwater. The tips of my fingertips were wrinkled and wet. My hair clouded about my shoulders, feeling like silk on my skin. It was getting very long now. Maybe I really should cut it.

I was deep in thought. I itched for murder.

But I could still feel it, I realized. The uncertainty that

had doomed my attempt at murdering Cherry Rose. I knew my purpose now but the uncertainty still lingered, a stubborn reminder of my previous ignorance. That feeling had made its way under my skin, and it wasn't as easy to get rid of as I wished.

I should wait. I didn't want to, but I should wait. I had to. If I murdered too soon, I could lose myself again. Perhaps consider suicide again. For a while, I needed to distance myself. Go on hiatus. I had to be smart about this, reasonable. I had been thinking about this in the bath for hours, and this was the definite conclusion I had reached.

I ducked my head beneath the surface, plunging myself into water, opening my mouth to blow out bubbles and then resurfacing.

But I didn't want to! I knew the thought was childish, but I didn't want to. I wanted to go claim my place in the world *now*. I wanted to kill and be the higher power that I was. I wanted to kill, for the first time, for the right reason.

But no. I couldn't be childish.

I stood up in the bath, still for a moment, water dripping down me into the tub like I was a living waterfall. I stepped out onto the thick bath mat, wrapped myself in a monogrammed towel. I looked at my shadowy reflection in the mirror. All I could really see were my eyes, sharp and glowing and mysterious like two fireflies.

I would wait.

I drained the tub methodically, looked at my reflection

again. Again my eyes flashed at me.

Yes, I would wait.

◆ ◇ ◆

Weeks passed. I waited.

As far as I could tell, my mother didn't mind my lack of action, though of course, I had never been good at understanding her thoughts. We never talked about murder. I didn't bring it up, and neither did she. She didn't so much as mention my hiatus. Whatever her opinion, she kept it neatly to herself. I didn't mind. She could do whatever she liked. My murders weren't her problem. Not anymore.

I was drifting away from her little by little, and she knew me well enough to realize it; we talked less, spent less time together, no longer felt truly and absolutely at ease with each other. It was strange. It was not so much that I intended to drift away, but rather that I suddenly felt as if I didn't precisely *need* her any longer. Realizing that the things I had done and the things I had yet to do were so necessary had given me newfound confidence, and that confidence had led me to feel more independent than before, more truly self-sufficient. There was a strange disconnect between us now, and I regretted it.

She spent more time at home than before, for whatever reason. She took one weeklong trip to Rome with a Parisian stockbroker, but that was her only vacation during those months. She didn't go to as many parties, or see men often as she used to, or laugh like nothing mattered.

Once, I saw her dancing. I came home earlier than

usual to find her in the living room; she didn't notice me. I considered saying something, but in the end, I didn't–I only stood near the door and watched her. She was pale and faint in the midafternoon sunshine, a white dress swaying about her knees. She moved quietly across the floor, adjusting pillows, humming, and every once in a while she would say a word of whatever song she was humming, and it would come out of her mouth in a singsong gasp.

I got the oddest feeling that every word she sang took something away from her, like she was fading away in shards.

I realized, with newfound clarity, that I didn't understand her.

I tried to let Michael's murder fade out of general memory. Small murders like Lily Kensington faded away from me, and then, as time moved on, I washed away my memories of Michael's murder and began to create myself anew.

It was hard sometimes, watching the news when my mother turned it on while she made dinner, seeing blood on the television screen. The newspeople were always so preoccupied with it. Murders in London, turmoil in the Middle East, videos of people being shot in the streets, pictures of children who had vanished and were found decapitated in the woods three months later. And every time they began to talk about violence, things bubbled up within me. Many emotions, but two were the most dominant: irritation with those who killed for the wrong reasons, and impatience for the day when I would again have the power of life and death. As time went on, the second emotion grew stronger,

stronger, wilder, stronger.

In the night sometimes, when I couldn't sleep, I stood by the window and just looked out. The city was quiet. In the distance I could always see the glow of bright lights, but here, on my street, things were infuriatingly peaceful. Nothing ever changed. The streetlamps kept shining, the dog a few blocks away kept barking, and every once in a while a quiet car would pass. The moon waxed and waned, and sometimes there were clouds and sometimes there weren't, but other than that, the view was always the same.

But I saw the merit of patience even through the veil of frustration. As I woke up each morning, I felt clearer, like my vision was somehow slowly improving. And I knew that one day I would wake up and I would feel as if I were seeing everything clearly and, yes, that would be the day. I waited.

I waited. I waited.

I could barely wait.

I kept Maggie close, with invisible discomfort. I killed to bring people together. She couldn't understand that death was supposed to be scary, and that revolted me now. But I smiled and went along with her and acted like her friend, because that was what I had to do.

Alex and I were constant companions now. I was something of a consultant to him. We talked, had lunch; he talked with me about his cases, and I steered him away from my trail as best I could with smiles and wit. He was puzzled about the lack of Perfect Killer murders, which usually happened every several weeks, speculated even that the murders were done for good. I pitied and envied his optimism. October came. Gray sky hung over London, low and oppressive, trapping me. The year as a whole had been an unusually cloudy one, though strangely there hadn't been much rain.

I had terrifying moments when I worried about Cherry. She knew my face. She could turn me in to the police. Sometimes I doubted her, thought she might actually do it. But in the end she never did. Cherry told the truth, and Cherry kept secrets well.

Most of the time I actually managed to forget her. I passed through my day-to-day life slowly, calmly, and I remembered her only when I saw a poster for one of her concerts stuck up on a small, easily rented billboard or tacked up on a lamppost, the corners peeling and her face looking oddly pallid printed on paper.

I did well in school, but not too well—I was friendly and fun, but not too friendly. I wasn't Dr. Marcell's favorite student anymore, not at all. I think she liked me less and less with each passing day. I think that I confused her the more she thought about me. I think I was a mystery, and I think she didn't like mysteries. Maggie and I were inseparable, like two halves of a whole, and I think that strange friendship bothered her too.

Days came and days passed. The world moved on.

And eventually November came, and I stepped from the shadows.

Chapter 16

High heels, businesslike hair, sunglasses, black leather gloves, and a hat to hide my face. I had been waiting for a day like this one for this particular murder. Sunny but cold—the kind of weather that could make a disguise seem normal, and a school holiday too, so I could be here without breaking any rules. The police already knew I was a student, thanks to my insight, so I supposed it didn't matter if I killed today. It wouldn't give anything away.

It was morning, and everyone was half asleep. I don't think any of them would have noticed if I had walked among them wearing Christmas pajamas instead of a disguise. Dressed in black and gray and tan, I was truly indistinguishable from the crowd as we filed like ants, one after the other, like parts of a greater machine, into White-vale Tower, a newly refurbished office building,

My mother didn't know I was back in the game. I wouldn't tell her; she would hear about it on the news later. I wasn't trying to neglect her or anything. There was just something about this whole thing that felt like it had to be a secret, at least until the deed was done.

It was to be my first murder since my . . . well, I suppose it was a revelation. I had actually been halfway planning this murder before that revelation, but not with the real dedication this kind of public murder needed. I didn't plan often, but for this one I actually had to do a little research about building schematics and such—not too much, because as always I left much to chance, but more than usual. This was a dangerous job. And yet, it was perfect for the moment. Thrilling. Terrifying. A grand reentrance.

There was a strange quietness to it all, as I trailed along behind a man in a dark brown suit, watching his hair flip up slightly in the back as the wind caught it. I wasn't anxious anymore. As I went through the sliding doors, I matched my footsteps to the rhythm of everyone else's. I didn't take off my sunglasses. I wanted my eyes to be hidden. People couldn't recognize people easily without seeing their eyes, and so the glasses were a precaution.

There was a series of gates at the far end of the smooth gray lobby—the small kind you had to swipe your card on to get past to the elevators. Naturally, I didn't have a card. I thought fast. I kept just behind the man with the floppy hair.

As he approached the gate I watched his steps, counted them, memorized their cadence—he approached the gate—step-step-step—he swiped the card, the gate opened—

I fell forward, stumbling past his shoulder, putting on a face of startled apology.

"Sorry!" I yelped as I stumbled, letting my ankles buckle. I fell to my knees just in the middle of the gate. The floppy-haired man stopped. The gate had sensors—it didn't close on me.

He was thirtysomething, inconsequential, and he reached a hand out to me. Shakily, I took it, feeling his fingers through my gloves. He had wide hazel eyes, innocent eyes.

"Are you okay?" he asked. I made sure to stand in the gate, so it stayed open.

"I'm fine," I laughed. "Sorry."

I let go of his hand and slipped away from him.

And I was inside the gates, just like that, just simply. Of course no one suspected a thing. I was a poor girl who had fallen, that was all. None of them would put two and two together and realize that I had gotten through without a card.

The man nodded at me politely and faded away into the crowd. I went toward the elevators. I didn't need a key card for those, it looked like, so I didn't have to worry about getting to my floor. Good. I stood next to a tall, tall woman with dark hair; I pulled out my phone, flipping through my contacts until I found the one I was looking for.

It glowed from the screen up at me. It was more a

reminder than a real contact, a little note with all the information I needed. Henry Morrison, suite 2948–twenty-ninth floor. Left down the hallway once I got out of the elevator; I had tracked down the schematics of the skyscraper, with some difficulty, from old building records. My victim was a high-ranking businessman who had cheated a young man out of his money, at least in the young man's eyes. The letter was inside my zipped jacket pocket.

Dear Killer,

Six months ago Henry Morrison helped me invest in some stock. I hired him to do that. I don't know much about that sort of thing, so I let him do what he wanted with my money, and I trusted him, I really did. Apparently that was stupid.

Since then basically every single thing he invested my money in has gone down a shit-ton—he says he's sorry, and that times are tough for everyone, but I don't think he means it. I think he was out to get me from the beginning. I don't know why. But you can't trust anyone in this world, you know?

I'm nearly dirt-poor now, thanks to him (arsehole). I don't know where he lives, but he works in Whitevale Tower, in one of those fucking annoying corner offices. For the love of God, end his sorry little life.

Henry Morrison, no doubt, had a secretary. I hadn't dealt with that sort of thing before. It would be interesting getting past that little roadblock. But oh well, I was Diana—or would be—and I could handle it.

An elevator near me slid open. People filed in. I just stood for a moment, wondering if I would fit inside. I decided that I would. I nudged alongside them, just through the door, slipping into a small spot near the wall, murmuring "Twenty-ninth floor, please," to a man standing near the buttons. I did my best to hide my face.

People crowded around me. Suits, trim dresses. The doors slid shut with a quiet whir and we began upward. The people murmured, rustled, some of them messing with their phones. I was silent. I breathed. I tried to calm myself, slow my breathing. I was excited.

So very excited.

It had been so long.

The elevator slid upward, and the doors opened and shut at each new floor. People emptied out. I thought about strategy. I had done some planning beforehand, but like always, I loved to act in the moment. I played with my phone inside my pocket, and as we rose, an idea occurred to me.

I was standing just behind a man—I needed something from him. Behind my sunglasses I ran my eyes up and down his body, looking for it, in his pockets, perhaps just inside his brown messenger bag. His phone. I needed it.

Ah, and there it was, tucked just inside his bag, next to a slim laptop case. The screen glistened just slightly. I slid more into the corner of the elevator, sinking in between the bodies until I disappeared between them. I was close to his back and mostly hidden from sight, so no one noticed as I tugged my black leather gloves to make sure they were all the way on and raised my right hand up by my side.

I held my breath as I slid my hand into his bag and plucked his phone out like I was plucking a weed.

A gray-suited woman next to me cleared her throat, and for a terrible moment my heart nearly stopped, thinking she had noticed me. But she hadn't. She was looking elsewhere. As I took the man's phone from his bag and put it my pocket next to mine, I exhaled softly, casually straightening my sunglasses. And I smiled, slightly sheepish that I had been nervous at all. I wondered what kind of smile it looked like from the outside.

The man with the bag shifted his weight a little, but I was like a ghost, and he hadn't felt me. I was settling into it again now, the naturalness of murder. I was regaining my footing. I ran my fingers over the two smartphones, wondering if I should have put the man's phone in my other pocket so my jacket didn't bulge so much on the right. Oh well. Switching it now would look suspicious. I didn't think anyone would notice.

Eventually the elevator arrived on my floor, and with a demure, inscrutable expression, I nudged past a few men into the hallway, pushing my sunglasses back on my head, and the elevator closed behind me, and there was no turning back.

The twenty-ninth floor was the kind of place that tried

to look stylish and high-class but just missed it by a little bit. The walls were paneled with sleek wood the color of amber; the light fixtures were modern, large bulbous things that looked almost like jellyfish. But the cubicles filling the office space were old and graying, and the people moving through them looked haggard and overworked, their movements tight and fast, which didn't lend much of a pleasant air to the whole scene. I had timed my entrance well. It was morning, which meant that people were both arriving and tired. Everyone was settling in for the day, and no one was quite awake yet. Which meant that no one was quite in the right state of mind to notice unusual things.

Still, it was probably best not to be seen at all. There were no cameras, so I was safe from that, at least.

It was too open here. People were milling about around their orderly little cubicles. Just in front of the elevator everything was open, and I felt unguarded, like a deer in the open. To my left about twenty feet down, the narrower hallway began. I turned and walked toward it, quickly but not too quickly, as if I knew what I was doing exactly. Confidence was the key to invisibility.

Logically, I knew this was too dangerous. I was too likely to be seen. There weren't any cameras, but people had eyes, and memories. It wasn't safe. I should have found Henry Morrison at home, or on the street—I was clever enough to do that. Being here, in this office, killing him with so many spectators, was absolutely stupid.

But I felt electric, invisible, invincible.

I was so powerful. I couldn't be caught, not here. I was so sure. I would remain free. And I wanted to prove that to myself. I wanted to be dangerous, and I wanted to be obvious, and I wanted to be a shadow that crept into the heart of things and took a life with me and left terror behind. And I would be. That was what I was meant to be.

Everything was so clear.

I entered the hallway. A few offices opened off it, the large offices of the company bigwigs, and at the end of the hallway I could see the office I knew belonged to my Henry Morrison—the number 2948 glistened in large silver letters to the left of the door, giving it away. It was the corner office, and his secretary's desk was just outside. She was talking on the phone, staring down at her shiny new-looking computer, scheduling something, presumably. She didn't see me.

I took in a few details, very quickly, the important ones. New, sensible shoes, meticulous makeup but an old tweed jacket fraying at the hem of her left sleeve. She was a bit tense, and the door to her boss's office was shut, with the windows looking from the office into the hallway covered with heavy forest-green curtains.

There was a small gap in the wall to my left, situated just where I knew it would be from looking at the building schematics. I quietly slipped inside it, drawing back into the shadows. At the end of the alcove there was a door to the emergency staircase. I stayed a few inches from the door handle, lest I accidentally open it and set off the emergency alarm.

I thoughtfully considered the secretary. New shoes, perfect makeup, old jacket. She was trying to make herself look her best with a minimum of money. And the makeup was too textbook perfect, too neatly painted on for a normal morning—she was new to the job, and trying to make a good impression. But that tense position, paired with the closed door and curtains, told me that it wasn't going well. Henry Morrison was most likely standoffish, and maybe even a bit rude, by appearances. This secretary was desperately trying to get things right, probably grasping at straws by this point. I could use that.

Someone passed though the hallway, heading back toward the elevator. I froze, watching, my eyes wide and careful. He stared at the ground and didn't even look in my direction. Once I was absolutely sure he was gone, I reached into my jacket and took out both phones. With mine I did a quick internet search and found Henry Morrison's phone number, or more accurately, his secretary's phone number, which was of course exactly what I wanted.

I didn't send the call just yet. I dialed the number, put my own phone back in my pocket, listened, and waited.

There was a brief moment of silence in which a thousand things occurred to me, the same way things always occurred to me quickly when I was about to murder, or was planning a murder. The first was Cherry Rose, and then my mother, and then Maggie, with her brilliant smile and shallow imagination. It was Maggie's face that remained the longest. Perhaps it was because the secretary had something about her that reminded me of Maggie, because that was true—more likely it was that murder in any form was now irrevocably linked to Maggie in my mind. Every drop of blood, every bruise, every vicious thought. Those were all Maggie, I realized. She permeated even here, in Whitevale Tower, even in the midst of my work.

I was bound to her. I couldn't walk away from her. Her journey was locked to mine, and I couldn't break free.

It irritated me.

"I'm so sorry, he's here but he's on a call now, and he's booked up for the rest of the day. He has a ten o'clock opening tomorrow," the secretary chirped efficiently. She had the same sound to her voice as Maggie, a little bit, happy but in an uncomfortable way. And she was loud; she was really quite far down the hallway, but I could hear her as clearly as a bell.

"No, that doesn't work for you? He has another opening at four tomorrow, but it's only twenty minutes or so—that works? I'm so sorry I haven't got anything before then, he's so busy. Okay, lovely. Thank you very much."

I heard a click as she put the receiver back into the body of the outdated office phone, which looked so strange sitting next to her shiny laptop. I waited a few seconds, making sure she didn't have another call coming in. All I heard from her was the soft clicking sound of typing. I waited for a few more seconds, and then I sent the call.

I heard the phone ring at the end of the hallway. It was barely half a second before she picked it up.

"Henry Morrison's office, how may I help you?"

The voice echoed twice through my ear, once from her actual voice and once from the phone, slightly delayed. It took me a moment to orient myself.

"Hello, may I speak to Henry?" I said familiarly, making sure my voice wasn't loud enough to be heard at the far end of the hallway. I made it a bit higher, a bit breathier than usual, so it couldn't be identified later.

"I'm sorry, may I ask who this is?"

"Oh, sorry, this is Jaime."

"Who?"

"His sister," I said, as if that should be obvious.

"Oh, I, eh, didn't know he had a sister."

"Well, he does," I replied shortly. "Look, can you do me a favor? I'm in town next week from Tuesday until Friday, and I'd love to have lunch with Henry—just pencil me in somewhere, okay? My schedule is pretty free, so whatever works for him. We haven't talked in a while."

"I—ah, I didn't know he had a sister," she said again, pathetically.

I laughed as if I were talking to a small child.

"He *does*. Obviously. We're not particularly close, but we are siblings."

There was an uncertain silence from the end of the hall. She was beginning to believe me.

"Look"—I sighed—"I'm seriously his sister. You can check with . . . oh, what were their names . . . John, or Katie. I met them at a party a few years ago. They know me."

"John Reese?" she said slowly. I had been assuming that there was someone in this office with a name as common as John, but I still breathed a sigh of relief.

"I suppose so. I never got his last name."

"Tall . . . brown hair?"

"That's the guy."

"Ah . . . ehm . . . hold on a moment."

She put the phone on hold and rose from the desk, and I smiled wickedly.

And just as I expected, she walked away from her desk, down the hallway toward the cubicles, past me without so much as glancing in my direction, looking for John Reese.

I put the stolen phone back in my pocket. I would dispose of it once I found a way. The screen glowed for a moment and went dark. Once I was sure she was gone—she would be searching for John for a few minutes, judging by the size of the office and the number of people in it—I walked out into the hallway. I snuck quietly up it, to Henry's door. I took a moment to glance into the two offices bordering his. There was no one there. The other higher-ups, with their private, windowed offices, were apparently taking the opportunity to come in late. Convenient, convenient. Of course there would always be a way to dispose of him quietly, but being alone and being able to dispose of him loudly left so many other options open.

It occurred to me that this was another detail that I hadn't considered beforehand—what if Henry Morrison hadn't come in this early? What if I had come and he simply hadn't been here? The thought made me feel cold.

But it was all right, I thought—I didn't need to worry about could-have-beens. He was here, unlike his neighbors. My luck hadn't forsaken me yet.

After a long, thoughtful moment, I opened the door and slipped inside.

I had a strange flashback to the moment I'd walked into Cherry's dressing room; it wasn't an altogether pleasant flashback. I shook my head, banishing it; it didn't matter, not now—this was different.

And there he was, Henry Morrison, standing by the window.

He looked out over London with the air of a tired king, as if he owned it all. He had one hand in his pocket. The other held a cell phone to his ear. He was silent, listening to whatever the other person was saying. He didn't notice me. So I stood still. I drew my gloved fingers across the door to find there wasn't a lock, at least not one that locked from the inside. I would deal with that in a moment.

He didn't know I was there. I stood like a ghost, arms crossed in front of my thighs, a faint smile touching my lips. I looked around the room, making sure there weren't cameras—I didn't think there were, since there hadn't been any anywhere else in the building except for a few in the lobby, but it was always good to check. There weren't any–I was right.

"We can't have that," Henry Morrison said in a slow voice. "No."

He listened for a moment longer.

"Well, tell him he can't have that."

More listening.

"Just . . . do something."

He hung up the phone, putting it wearily in his jacket pocket, and rubbed his eyes. He stared out at the wide city for a moment longer, resting there, taking a moment for himself, away from the world. I could understand that. For a moment I had the strangest sensation that we were very much alike.

His desk was antique, but there was a largish, silvery modern statue to his left, next to the window, a sort of graceful dancer-type thing. His furniture other than the desk was sleek and stylish; but he had a collection of worn leather-bound books on his bookshelf. The entire scene felt timeless.

Henry Morrison leaned against his desk, putting his hands in his pockets. As he leaned, the desk shook slightly–the pens in his glass cup rolled around the rim, his computer screen bobbled.

London glittered in the cold morning sunlight. It shone radiantly, glass windows and water and metal sparking in the sun, like a jewel, like a thousand jewels. There were clouds, but they were high up and far away on the horizon. The sky was a dusty blue. A perfect day. Henry sighed.

And I sighed too, and I let myself fall, and I took a deep breath in, and I snapped, and I was Diana again.

Everything was *fresh*.

"Beautiful, isn't it?" I said.

Henry turned, startled. He saw me and looked confused, but he didn't say a word.

He had an ancient feeling to him, seen from the front, even though he couldn't have been older than forty-five. He had deep-green eyes and was wearing a trim gray suit that made him look like he had been plucked out of a catalog. He sort of seemed . . . fake. Like he wasn't a real person.

"It is," he said. He was quiet, caught off guard, but I could see the sharpness that had intimidated his secretary lurking behind his eyes. "I'm sorry, who are you?"

I looked at the ground, smiled, and moved toward him like a cat.

"Just a girl," I said coyly. "And you're Henry Morrison."

"Yes, I am. Why are you in my office? Why did Louisa let you in?"

"Louisa, is that the secretary?"

"Of course," he snapped. Oh, there it was, the anger that had scared poor Louisa. I chuckled.

"Louisa's a silly girl. You should fire her."

I paused, leaning over the desk toward him pensively. How should I do it? The corner of the desk, suffocation by the pillow on the armchair in the corner of the office, slamming his head against the wall? No, none of those seemed right.

And suddenly, with a flash of inspiration, I found it. It was perfect. Drama and darkness and sickening brutality, and so simple.

There was a small chair next to me. I took it and calmly wedged it beneath the doorknob, so at least there was some sort of lock on the door.

"What are you doing? Who are you?" Henry demanded, but he didn't do anything to stop me.

I turned back toward him, pulled at my gloves to make sure they weren't coming off. I wasn't quite ready. I walked to the desk and drew my hands across the edge of it thoughtfully. He was silent now. I don't know why. He had suddenly forgotten words. He just stared at me, waiting perhaps. He knew something was coming, but he didn't know what.

I took a few steps around the edge of the desk, grabbed the top of his shiny modern sculpture, and tipped it, with as much force as I could muster, toward the window.

It hit just right. The statue was heavier than I had expected, and more effective. As it slammed against the glass, I stumbled away from it, momentarily unsteady in my high heels. Instantaneously, cracks appeared—sharp, webbing wildly in every direction, deep, making the glass fragile. The window made a weak creaking noise but held, just barely, just for the moment. The statue leaned against it heavily, glimmering, threatening.

Henry Morrison looked at the statue, mouth open, face reddening. Something lit up in his eyes. I don't know whether he realized exactly what I was going to do, but either way, something caught fire in his eyes the same way something had lit up in Dr. Marcell's eyes once, and he suddenly came out of almost indifference and looked angrily at me as if I were a bug, or an itch, or some other small irritation.

But I wasn't.

I was so much more.

Before he had a chance to react with words, I walked rapidly to where he stood.

Grinning, I grabbed his tie and pulled him down toward me. I had it all in hand now, I saw the end. I didn't have to be careful any longer. He was mine. This would be a clean murder, just like the rest. There wouldn't even be any blood. Not here, at least.

Still, I should be quick, just to make sure I wasn't interrupted.

He gasped, and he was angry, and he was surprised. He was about to say something else, presumably quite loudly. I put a finger to his lips. I smiled, and whispered, as convincingly as I could, "Shhh . . . ."

And Henry Morrison fell silent.

We stared into each other's eyes, the man and the murderer.

"You are mine," I hissed. "I am Diana, and you are mine."

I stepped away from him, letting go of his tie. I leaned up against the desk, judged my distance, and without another word, with the desk as leverage, kicked him toward the plate-glass window. The window, weakened to its limit from the cracks made by the statue, resisted for a small moment, and then splintered and burst wide open.

Twenty-nine stories is a long way to fall.

He cascaded down along with a million shards of glass, hurtling, careening, glimmering in the cold morning sunlight that lit London so beautifully. If he screamed, the sound vanished as he fell away. He was a falling stone. There was no hope of survival. The wind blew through the space where the window had once been. Before he even hit the ground, I took the letter in my hand and extended it through the empty space. And then I let it go.

The letter floated away, down toward the street, toward Henry, like a white butterfly.

"Mr. Morrison!?" Louisa cried from outside the door, returning already from looking for John Reese. She had heard the sound of shattering glass through the wall, no doubt. "Mr. Morrison, what's going on? Henry!"

Shit.

I hadn't really thought this through all the way.

Now how in God's name was I going to get back to the elevator without being spotted by her? No, no, I had to calm down, I was Diana, I could outwit some stupid little secretary, I was fine. The walls were thick, neither of the people in the neighboring offices was here yet, and we were far away from the majority of the office workers, so at least I had a little time until other people arrived.

"Henry! Henry Morrison!"

She was trying to get through the door now, and realizing that she couldn't. The chair rattled. It wouldn't hold forever. I had to hide, and I had to hide *now*. There was an armoire near the broken window. It was small, but it would have to work. I made a beeline for it and just barely managed to crunch myself in between his coat and a low shelf before Louisa came through the door, the chair skittering aside.

I couldn't close the door entirely, because it wasn't made to be closed from the inside. There was a small crack that I could see out of. I saw a thin sliver of Louisa; she stood in the doorway, looking stunned, horrified, and altogether unsure what to do, her mouth gaping open like a fish.

"Mr. Morrison?" she murmured, as if that would help, wandering absently toward the window, dropping out of my very narrow field of vision. Her feet crunched on shards of glass. She sounded muted, as if part of her were floating away. There was a moment of silence, and then, suddenly, she gasped and fell to her knees near the statue, which had miraculously managed not to fall out the window. I was sure she must have cut herself, but she didn't seem to care.

"Henry!" she yelped. "Oh my God, oh my God." Her breaths became coarse and shallow and desperate.

It was too small inside the armoire. I could already feel my legs and back cramping painfully; I winced. As quietly as I could, I tried to stretch out, pushing my head up against the shelf above me. It wasn't enough—I had to get out. I wasn't claustrophobic. It was purely a physical concern. If I stayed in here, I wouldn't be able to move like I needed to when I needed to.

I moved my head up a bit farther and realized the shelf above my head was removable, and moreover, empty.

Convenient.

I could hear Louisa muttering faintly to herself. Again, Maggie occurred to me, and again, I was overwhelmed with annoyance. I pushed the useless, hotheaded emotion away; I could be annoyed later, but now I had to work.

I felt cautiously along the shelf, trying not to make noise. For a moment I paused, disconcerted, unsure whether I should really cause collateral damage, since it went against my normal way. But I had to get out, after all. I carefully eased the shelf down into my lap, and there it sat for a short moment while I stopped breathing so I could pinpoint Louisa's exact location through sound.

When I listened, I could hear the sounds of screaming from the road below. Piercing, terrified, perfect. Beautiful. And Louisa, judging by the sound of her sharp breaths, was about five feet from the window and kneeling.

I gripped my hands around the long shelf, inhaled, and leaped out from the armoire.

She didn't even have time to turn, or scream, before I was swinging the shelf like a baseball bat, and it collided solidly with the back of her head. She exhaled quietly, squeaking like a mouse. She fell to the floor with a soft thud, face turned sideways, glass cutting into her cheek in long gashes.

She wasn't dead, and wouldn't die from the blow, though she might be unconscious for a while, and she might even have scars from the glass. It wasn't that easy to kill someone. The hardest part about killing someone is actually killing them, as strange as that sounds. Human bodies are resilient, and they do not want to die. She'd be a bit fuzzy when she woke up, and she might lose a few memories, which could be very good for me, depending on whether she had connected Henry's mysterious sister with the person who had kicked Henry out the window. But she would wake.

She lay flat over the floor. I dropped the shelf next to her and felt momentarily apologetic.

"Sorry," I said.

For a moment I looked out at London again, London, gleaming in the sunlight, London, sparkling.

And I felt like laughing.

Because I was the queen of it all, a queen looking out over her kingdom, because they were all bent to my will and marched to the beat of my murderous drum. And of course they didn't know it, but I knew it, and that was what mattered–

I felt like laughing. But I had to go.

I pressed myself against the wall next to the door, just inside the office, and soon enough, office workers began to flood down the hallway toward the scene of the crime. As they came inside the room as a frantic, shivering crowd, none of them noticed my presence; and as they all gathered together in panic, I slipped out the door, unnoticed in their midst, one unimportant figure among many.

I left Henry's office with clicking, confident steps.

And from here on I was safe.

I walked down the hall, head downturned, and took the elevator to the lobby. Outside the building's glass front doors, the police were already beginning to arrive, but they hadn't organized themselves yet, and people were still streaming in and out of the building like ants, most of them oblivious to what had happened.

I was exultant.

I tucked my head down into my jacket collar and stared at the ground so no one could see my face. I moved with the flow of the crowd. No one noticed me. The police officers were emerging from their police cars now, looking frantically around, their eyes alighting in horror on the corpse of Henry Morrison a half block from where they had stopped at the curb. One of them had a megaphone and was beginning to shout orders to startled civilians, but no one was really listening. The people along the sidewalk who had realized what had happened all hurried away. They were scared and reluctant to become involved, and I went with them, invisible.

I looked through the gathering crowd for Alex. I didn't see him, but I was sure he was there. Somewhere. He always was.

I disposed of my gloves and the stolen phone in a Dumpster in a quiet alley not too far from my house, after first destroying the phone by throwing it forcefully against a brick wall where no one was watching. The screen splintered into a thousand pieces. Just for safety. The gloves I managed to rip to shreds, as if a dog had been chewing on them. I targeted the fingertips especially, destroying whatever fingerprints might have been inside.

It was there, in the shadows of small houses, leaning against a tall green Dumpster, that I finally let myself laugh.

And oh, how I laughed—

Nothing could touch me.

Chapter 17

I wandered the streets the rest of the morning and afternoon and far into the night. I didn't have anywhere in particular to go, and I didn't mind. I just wandered, and wandered. I didn't feel like being home, and I didn't feel like staying still, so I walked through the streets of London and let the city swallow me up as everything turned from daylight to darkness.

I walked through Chelsea in a black down jacket while the sun still shone—the season was growing cold—and once the sun set, I crossed the spooky nighttime Thames and found myself in Battersea Park for a while. The trees seemed to move around me, like people, reaching in. I walked across the grass, wet with dew, my ankles damp. I

saw only one other person clearly, though I saw many silhouettes and shadows—a man, and he passed quickly, with
his eyes firmly downcast and his lower lip pouted like a
petulant child.

Eventually I left the park and walked along the Thames.
London passed me by. My London. The city lights here
reflected vibrantly off the water. I passed more people, and
avoided all their eyes, and they avoided mine.

I walked a long time. I walked past bridges, across
streets, past Waterloo Bridge, through the very heart of
London, crowded with tourists, bright and beautiful. I
walked until my feet hurt, and then I kept walking, because
I was tired but I didn't want to go home.

And eventually my feet took me where I half expected
they would, to Whitevale Tower.

The police were still there, but the firemen and ambu-
lances were gone. Henry's body was gone too, though a few
police officers were gathered where it had fallen. The police
flooded though the building—I could see them through windows, all over. And twenty-nine stories up was the shattered
window, looking strange and disjointed, and not at all like
the scene of a murder, somehow. It looked abnormal; but
from far away, like many things, it seemed harmless.

For a moment, instinctively, I wondered if Alex was one
of the many men inside the evacuated building, but then I
spotted him. He was standing by the front door, aloof from
a group of other police officers who were conversing quietly.
He bit his thumbnail and looked very old. In his hand, in

a plastic bag, he held the letter that had condemned Henry Morrison—I recognized the way it was folded. His hair was uncombed and scraggly and zigzagged wearily down into his eyes. He needed a haircut. His gray suit, in style very like Henry Morrison's suit, had been worn too many times since it was last cleaned, and there was a stain at the hem of one leg.

Something panged through me—regret, I realized after a moment—not remorse, but regret, because it was my fault that he was this way, tired and beaten. Uniquely and individually my fault. This regret was followed closely by a desperate and selfish prayer, sent silently up to some nameless god—*please please please don't let him ever know what I am, I don't want him to know, if he knows he'll hate me, and I don't want him to hate me, please, that is the last thing in the world that I want, please please please.*

His eyes were deep and dark and dreaming. He didn't see what was in front of him.

He didn't see much of anything.

Oh! And what shadows lurked behind him he couldn't know. He was a gleaming spot of light in a vast darkness. Alex, always Alex, always so pure and righteous. But he couldn't see the shadows, no matter how he tried, and that was his most important flaw.

I was standing just behind a lamppost, and the light didn't quite reach me.

For an insane moment I imagined going to him. Simply walking across the street to meet him. Talking to him.

Engaging him. It would be lovely to hear his voice, to stand by his side. I might even be able to make the night a little less dark for him. Poor Alex, sometimes I just felt so sorry. I only wanted to help him, to speak to him, to be near him. . . .

But of course I couldn't. What time was it now? Midnight? Two in the morning? If I went to talk to him, he would have so many questions, about why I was out and why I was here, of all places, and questions were dangerous. No, I couldn't go to him. The savage night was an animal all its own, and even I dared not disturb it.

My phone, set on vibrate, buzzed quietly in my pocket. I turned away from Alex, so he couldn't see my face if he happened to glance in my direction. I picked up the call without looking at who was calling.

"Hello."

"Where are you?" my mom snapped at the other end of the line.

"I'm out."

"Why the hell are you out? Where? It's four in the morning, Kit."

Four, was that the time? I had been walking awhile.

"I wanted to be out."

"Well, come home."

"Why?"

"What do you mean, why? I'm your mother. It's four in the morning. Don't ask stupid questions. I know what you're feeling, I really do, but you can't just stand there and gloat."

I leaned against the lamppost, my back edging into the light.

"I don't want to come home."

There was a sigh, and then a silence.

"Kit, please," she said, but as always, there was a sharp edge to it.

She was grasping for the control she no longer held.

I turned back, looked at Alex again. He hadn't moved an inch. He was a statue. The cops near him glanced at him carefully, one by one, but he didn't notice.

"Fine, I'll come home," I said. I was doing her a favor. She needed me to obey. She needed just that much, just that small kindness, and I granted it to her because it meant nothing to me.

I hung up the phone.

The walk to Whitevale Tower had been almost magical, in a way, but the walk back home was boring and lifeless. The streetlights reflecting on the water were just streetlights, and Battersea Park was no longer a forest of dancing shadows. I went home to my upstairs bedroom. Downstairs my mother was listening to Cherry Rose. The curtains were red, and the sky outside was dark and everything was pale, muted, almost like a painting.

◆ ◇ ◆

"Oh my God, we're going to get soaked!" Maggie laughed, standing with me beneath an awning outside a deli with forget-me-nots painted in the bottom corner of the window, both of us wrapped in my black raincoat. It wasn't enough to keep us dry if we came out from beneath the awning. Neither of us had expected it to rain quite this much, and we had both forgotten umbrellas.

Rain pattered steadily over the asphalt, across the windshields of cars, dripping through the corners of the awning we were beneath. It was a cold, cold rain.

I laughed in agreement. Yes, we were going to be wet. We both had things to do, and we couldn't wait for the rain to stop to return home. We had to go out. It was going to be cold.

"I should have brought that umbrella. I was thinking about it, but then I decided against it, stupid me," Maggie groused, running her fingers through her hair.

"Stupid," I agreed, looking distractedly up at the clouds sitting overhead, stubborn and unmoving. They were a flat sheet of dark gray. They weren't going anywhere.

"Do you think we have time to go find an umbrella to buy or something?"

I shook my head. "No, I've got to get home. I guess you could go find an umbrella alone, if you wanted."

"I'll stay with you," Maggie said. "Oh God, I don't want to get wet!"

"We don't much have much choice, do we?"

She laughed freely. "I guess not."

I leaned forward and peeked out up at the sky again, a few drops of water landing along the bridge of my nose.

"Winter's coming, I guess." I shrugged.

"Think there will be snow?"

"I hope so. I like snow. There's got to be at least some."

"I'm actually really excited for it. I really hope it snows." Maggie giggled. "I want to go everywhere when it snows, to all the tourist spots and everything. I want to be a tourist in my own city, you know? Because everything looks different in the snow." She was only half aware of what she was saying; her eyes stared off into nowhere, into the rain. Her words sounded pretty to me. Almost poetry.

"We're putting this off," I said.

She groaned. "Oh God. Can't we keep putting it off?"

I laughed and hooked my arm through hers, pulling my raincoat up so it covered us as much as it possibly could. She shifted her weight comfortably.

"No," I said cheerfully.

"Oh no."

"Oh yes."

"I don't want to—"

Laughing, I pulled her out into the rain, and we were instantly soaked through, our hair and our arms and our legs, and the raincoat did nothing, but we kept holding it up. We laughed like little girls as we ran down the sidewalk through the downpour, alongside shop windows and taxis and buses and people huddled underneath umbrellas. We skipped across puddles. We were the best of friends.

But still, as much as she was my friend, Maggie was my enemy. I held that fact close to my heart, never forgetting it, never forgetting what she meant to me, what I was and who she was meant to be. She was a victim. She would die by my hand—I had decided to kill her, and so I would. I couldn't let myself forget that. And so that darkness blossomed, growing ever larger, ever more prominent, waiting for the day when it would become too large for me to ignore.

Maggie mimed a scream as she stepped ankle-deep into a dark puddle, and I laughed.

Chapter *18*

A few days after the murder on the twenty-ninth floor, at five thirty in the evening, Alex came to visit.

It was an unannounced visit. My mother was standing silently at the stove, hovering over a pot of pasta, the steam wafting near her face. I imagined that the heat wasn't comfortable. I was at the kitchen table, observing her.

There was a quiet knock on the door, not even the doorbell. I heard it, but my mom didn't. For a moment, I thought I had imagined it. But then the knock came again, a bit louder, still timid and echoing, and I stood.

"What is it?" my mom said, speaking to me as if I were a silly child. I grasped the edge of the table tightly, restraining myself. I hated her when she treated me like this.

"Knock on the door," I replied shortly. She nodded. As if she knew that already, before I told her, and she was just asking to make sure I could give her the right answer. She wanted to feel superior. I hadn't seen through her before. I saw through her now. She was transparent.

I went to the door and opened it, and was surprised to find Alex outside, dressed casually and standing stiffly. I was momentarily taken aback, both by the fact that he was here unexpectedly and the fact that his presence, even when I was expecting it, threw me a little off-kilter, changed the feeling in the air.

And God, he really was attractive. I mean, I knew that already, but as I looked at him there on the steps, the fact hit me like a ton of bricks.

I honestly hadn't expected him. We had met many times in coffee shops and bistros and police stations, but he hadn't been to the house since we'd first met.

"Hello," he said, smiling cordially.

"Hello. What brings you here?" I replied, making my voice as friendly as I could manage. Despite my excitement about his sudden arrival, I was still seething a bit about my mom's condescending demeanor. But of course it wasn't Alex's fault—I should calm down, and I shouldn't take it out on him. He didn't deserve that sort of thing; he was too good for that. He looked uncertain, standing on the front step. He stared at his feet.

"What's wrong?" I asked. Obviously something was. He looked startled.

"Nothing's wrong."

"I can read you like a book, stupid. What's wrong?"

He shook his head. "Nothing's wrong."

I bit my lip. Oh well, he would tell me eventually. He always did.

"Come in," I said, stepping aside. He moved through the door on wavering feet.

"It's Alex," I called to my mom, and there was no reply. I turned again to Alex.

"Would you like some tea?" I offered.

"Ah—no, thank you."

"Oh, come on. I'll get you some tea," I said with a laugh.

We walked into the kitchen. Standing halfway in front of the refrigerator, my mother was very calmly turning off the stove, not glancing my direction. Wordlessly, she picked up the pot. Her ankles, pressed tightly together, quivered silently, and her eyes were unreadable. Trying to escape notice, she smiled an easy smile and poured the pasta into a strainer set in the bottom of the sink.

"Sit down at the table. I'll be right with you," I said to Alex, heading for the kettle, looking at my mother curiously. I took the kettle, which was sitting on the stove near the pot, and began to fill it with water. Alex stared at the table and into space.

"What are you doing?" I muttered to my mother, who still wasn't meeting my eyes.

She smiled inscrutably and brushed her hands against

her skirt as if they were dirty. She whirled as I set the kettle on the stove and turned on the heat.

"I'm going out," she announced grandly, taking off her red apron and putting it atop a bar stool. She laughed. "I won't be long. Just running down to the grocery store on the corner. I wanted to put Parmesan on the pasta, but I forgot to get any, I just realized."

I smiled so no one could see, because, in a strange way, I was proud of her. She saw it. She saw that she would only be a third wheel. Not in a romantic sense, of course, but a third wheel in the sense that Alex and I had a . . . rapport, perhaps, that she could never share. She was not a part of us. She realized that, and would leave.

"Oh, really?" Alex said distractedly. She nodded and made sure the apron wouldn't fall off the bar stool.

"I have some errands to run."

"I'll take care of you, don't you worry," I said to Alex jokingly. He smiled very slightly; the crookedness of the smile was endearing.

She left us quickly. As we heard the front door slam, I leaned against the stove, waiting for the kettle to boil.

"Is it the Perfect Killer case?" I ventured. Alex didn't reply, just ran his fingers wearily through his hair. Even though he looked vaguely depressed, his movements were still captivating to watch, I realized—sharp and insistent and at the same time inherently graceful.

"Well, is it ever anything else?" I said wryly, looking away from him.

I don't think he heard me, and if he did, he didn't reply.

He breathed deeply, thinking deeply, hunched over at the kitchen table like he was holding the weight of the world on his shoulders.

"Don't you ever consider just giving up?" I asked.

He breathed out jaggedly. It took me a moment to realize that he was laughing.

"Never," he said.

"It's never crossed your mind?"

"Never."

"It would be easier."

"I don't care."

"You wouldn't have to worry so much."

"I don't care."

Silence.

"God, you're not in a talkative mood today at all, are you?" I said, joking, of course, but with an edge to it. I realized suddenly, unpleasantly, that I sounded almost like my mother at her worst.

I didn't want to be like that, not with him, him of all people. I wanted him to think well of me.

He was silent. The kettle whistled.

I made us each a cup of tea, struggling to find a cup or mug that had been washed recently and didn't have the remnants of my father's coffee painted on the ceramic. I remembered that Alex didn't take any milk with his, but he took sugar. The cups steamed cozily as I set them down on the kitchen table.

"Thank you," he said, taking a long sip. I sat down opposite him and drank too, looking curiously at him from beneath my eyelashes.

"You really don't ever think about it?"

"Giving up?"

"Yeah."

Slowly he shook his head.

"It's really never occurred to me. I'm not like that."

"I admire you for that."

"Thank you, I suppose."

"You're welcome, I suppose." I smiled faintly. "You look tired, though. You should get more sleep."

"Maybe." He stared off into space.

"Are you even listening to me?"

"Yes, I'm listening."

I took another long sip of my tea, tasting the faint bitterness beneath the sweetness of sugar, and leaned back in my chair. I observed him. He remained quiet.

"How've you been?" he said suddenly, meeting my eyes. And again, there it was—that sudden electricity in the air.

"I've been fine."

"You've been . . . school?"

"Oh, yes. School and homework, school and homework."

"That's good."

"It is."

"That's good . . . ," he said again, his voice barely

above a whisper. He stopped talking, done with attempting conversation; he didn't seem to be capable of it today. I wasn't quite done with *him* yet, though. I didn't like silence, especially with only two people in a room; it made me uncomfortable.

"Why did you come here?" I asked, as casually as I could manage. He didn't like the question; he suddenly looked as if he were sitting on a thumbtack.

"It's nothing."

"It's something. Alex, what the hell is going on?"

No reply.

His expression was dark, and his eyes were half closed and tired. Dark circles lined them, I noticed. His mouth hung distractedly half open. He wasn't entirely here.

"Seriously, are you stressing about the Perfect Killer case? Because I know the murderer's back, pushed a guy out of the window—it was in the newspapers."

No reply.

"Alex, just tell me. Do you need moral support? Are you about to break down or something? Do you need help?"

No reply.

"I'll get you more tea," I said, picking up his teacup, which was empty now, moving toward the kettle again. I put more water in it—there wasn't enough left for another cup of tea—and set it on the stove, watching the flames flickering beneath it. I didn't want any more myself.

"You can talk to me about anything, you know."

He stood suddenly. I turned to look at him. He stared

back at me, mouth open as if he wanted to say something but couldn't. The words were stuck.

The look in his eyes made me sad, and I didn't know why.

"I should go."

He was wearing a long coat, and as he turned to leave, it swished rather dramatically around his legs. I was so confused. What was wrong, what was wrong? I was always so good at reading people, and Alex in particular had always been rather see-through. But today, he was impossible to understand. It wasn't just the Perfect Killer's reemergence; it was something more.

"Alex," I called after him, darting into the hallway behind him as he made a beeline for the door. He stopped, hands folded in front of him, quiet, as if he was waiting desperately for me to say something.

I looked at him, and then around the hallway, even up at the ceiling, looking for something to say to make things less uncomfortable before he left.

And then I happened to glance back behind me, into the kitchen, at the kitchen table, and with an almost physical shock, realizing what was bothering him, I understood. My arrogance, my pride vanished. I felt something else. Fear.

"Oh," I breathed and slowly, very slowly, looked once again at Alex.

"Oh," I repeated, louder. He visibly shrank two inches, wanting to disappear. Understandably. Oh, Alex.

"You took my teacup," I said, just to hear it out loud and make sure he understood that I knew.

"It wasn't my idea," he said, trying to defend himself, but there was no defense for this sort of thing.

I couldn't say a word. And this time it was Alex who tried to fill in the silence with speech. He turned to face me helplessly, turning the teacup over in his hands, making sure not to touch the rim. Of course, of course.

I had no right at all to feel betrayed, but I felt betrayed anyway.

"It was the higher-ups. I'm investigating this case, but technically I still take orders, I'm still low-ranked. They're getting desperate, you know, they need a lead, and you're not a lead, not really, but you're the closest thing to a lead they've got, what with you being there at that kid's murder scene—and they found a bit of DNA at the crime scene at Whitevale Tower, and all they wanted was a bit of yours, to make sure it wasn't a match—I'm so sorry, Kit, really I am, I can't even say . . ."

He was sorry too. Honestly and truly. His upstanding heart couldn't handle this sort of thing, this trickery, and it was killing him to see the shock in my eyes. I was sure I looked pitiful. I felt pitiful. But I had no right.

"Oh, Alex."

He didn't know—he couldn't know—how important that cup was. It was small and white, and as he turned it over and over in his hands, I couldn't move my eyes from it. That cup, the DNA from my lips on its rim, was my death, my downfall. And he didn't even know.

"You could have asked," I told him. "You didn't have to steal."

"God, Kit, I'm sorry, I just didn't want you to know, and worry about it—it's not like you're a suspect; they're just grasping at straws here."

"Is this even legal? Don't you need a warrant for this sort of thing?"

"You do."

"You're breaking the law, Alex."

"I know. But I have to follow orders," he said softly, and he was practically breaking in half. For someone like him, this sort of thing was unthinkable. Going against the law violated every rule he had ever set for himself. The only thing that could override his yearning to follow the law was his need to follow orders, and that hierarchy was a very close thing.

Not to mention the fact that he was betraying a friend.

This internal conflict was why he had come here of all places, I realized. We had lunch so often, and coming here was so unusual—he was setting me up to be suspicious and setting himself up to be caught. He was smart—he could do better than this. He could have very easily stolen a fork from the side of a lunch plate without me noticing. But he wanted to be caught. He wanted to be called out for his trickery, wanted to be punished for his dishonesty.

"I could have you arrested. Fired. You'd never be a policeman again." It wasn't a threat, just a fact. The look in his eyes was excruciating to see. I knew I should be cunning, I knew I should figure out a way to slither out of this. But somehow, somehow, I simply couldn't. My mind was blank. My heartbeat was slow.

I was just as heartbroken as he was. He had been trying to trick me, ruin me, go behind my back. It startled me to realize how much I cared. If it were anyone else, I could trick him out of the cup, or even force it away from him, but things were different with Alex. I felt an abiding sadness as I looked down the hallway at him, watched him turn the cup over and over and over.

"Are you going to take it?" I asked. "Are you going to leave and take it with you?"

"It doesn't really matter to you, the cup, does it? It's not going to incriminate you. It doesn't matter." He avoided the question pleadingly. His eyes begged. I wouldn't let him have the cup.

"That's not the point."

"God, Kit, I'm so sorry I tried to just steal it, but can I . . . oh God, I'm being horrible, aren't I? But can I take it, Kit, please? It doesn't mean anything to you. I'll return it once they're done. I'll make sure I get it back. It's not going to be a match."

And then, with a sudden snapping feeling in my chest, I truly understood the danger I was in. I would go to jail. There was no death penalty, but I would spend a lifetime in a cell, perhaps in solitary, wasting away, if I let the man in front of me walk away through my front door. I was angry with myself. What DNA had I left? A hair, a bit of blood from some cut I had gotten from the broken glass?

But I still felt frozen. I couldn't talk my way out of it. I didn't have the words.

"I am so sorry," he breathed, hunching his shoulders so he appeared smaller than he was. I moved to the wall and leaned against it. I stared at my feet. Numbness seeped through me like a disease, like a quiet flame, overtaking me insidiously. Pure numbness.

"So this is what you are," I said senselessly.

The words struck him, one by one, and I could see they were hurting him. But it was his own fault. I looked into his eyes.

"I'm so sorry," Alex whispered

"I'm the one who's sorry," I replied.

Or would be sorry.

He clenched his hands tightly around the cup. For a moment I thought he was going to break it. A silence opened up between us, as I drew into myself, counting my breaths, and he struggled with a thousand different virtues within himself.

My heart began to pound out a quick one-two-one-two, like drums. I stared at Alex. My eyes were wide, and all I had was a faint hope nestled between my ribs that perhaps he valued me more than his need to follow his superiors' orders. Oh, Alex. He couldn't know.

"It doesn't matter to you," he begged.

I shook my head, very slightly. I couldn't tell him that it

did matter. I couldn't tell him that it mattered so much, that he almost literally held my life in his hands. I wanted him to understand, but I knew that if he understood, everything would be lost in the same way that things would be lost if he walked out the front door with that cup in his hands.

I stared Alex down with immense regret.

He shuddered, his fingers twitched, and then he was still. He breathed out, clasping the cup in white knuckles, and this time I was nearly sure he would break it.

"It's not worth anything," he said unconvincingly.

Put it down, put it down, put it down, put it down.

I pleaded inwardly, screamed out at him, trying to somehow make him understand what I needed.

And then, very slowly and suddenly, with a last broken glance into my eyes, he took the teacup and set it down on the hall table. He walked away out the front door, slamming it shut behind him.

It was quieter with him gone, but strangely it seemed louder. With soft footsteps, I walked down the hall, took the cup, and went into the kitchen. I walked to the sink, meaning to wash the cup, meaning to wash it all away—

But as I stood over the sink, the cup slid out of my fingertips and fell, shattering on the white porcelain near the drain, splitting into shards, and I couldn't even bring myself to care.

◆ ◇ ◆

Two weeks later Alex invited me to lunch again. It was a mostly silent and awkward meal, but I appreciated the invitation. Not, of course, that I didn't know why I had really been invited.

It was a surprisingly sunny day, with blue skies all around. As he ate a ham sandwich, I made a point to finish my tea and pasta early. I laughed at his jokes as best I could; slowly, the ice that had formed between us was beginning to crack again. But every now and then I saw the darkness, the fear, the misery creep into Alex's eyes. Because, of course, he had to follow orders, no matter the law—since sometimes the law did get lost, in cases like this, when the police got anxious about things. He still had to get that DNA sample from me, because he had been told to. He had failed once but was not allowed to fail again. I sometimes forgot that he wasn't really in charge. It was not a good thing to forget.

But I was ready for him this time.

Slowly, smoothly, with confidence, so he didn't realize what I was doing, I took each piece of tableware that I had touched and brought it down one by one into my lap on top of my napkin. I had prepared two bottles beforehand. I slipped them quietly out of my purse. One, hydrogen peroxide, and two, a human DNA sample I had stolen from a science lab at school, diluted in water—there was a student in my grade who was doing an independent research project with it, and he had a few extra samples he wouldn't miss too badly.

Alex chatted at me, and I gave innocent replies.

But beneath the white tablecloth, with small,

unnoticeable movements, I put hydrogen peroxide on each piece of tableware to destroy my own DNA, dried each with my napkin as best I could, and put a small amount of the bottled DNA on each where my own DNA would have been. I put each back on the table with care. And Alex, nervous as he was, was too distracted to notice a thing.

As we left, he carefully slipped my fork into his sleeve. I think he thought he was being secretive, but I noticed. A part of me wondered if he *wanted* me to notice and catch him like I had caught him at the house. But no, I wouldn't confront him again.

As he walked stiffly away down the sidewalk, in the opposite direction from me, I decided to forgive him. I would forget this. We would still have lunch, talk like friends, confide in each other. I wanted that. I wanted to forget this. I wanted us to go on beyond this. He would forget too, because that was who he was. Alex was Alex, after all. He loved to think well of others, loved to be their friend. His morals were impressive. He was nothing like me.

I envied him his naïveté.

And somehow, I told myself, despite everything, he might still prove to be useful.

◆ ◇ ◆

Maggie and I sat on a bench overlooking the Thames, silent as we ate identical vanilla ice creams even though it was probably too cold for it. I hadn't seen Maggie for a few weeks; I had been preoccupied with Henry Morrison's murder and Alex's suspicions. I was calmer now, less tense, because things with Alex had been cleared away. It was cloudy today again, a brownish sort of cloudy, pollution tainting the sky like it often did when there hadn't been quite enough rain.

Maggie's cheeks were redder than usual, and her hair seemed darker than when we had first met. Her clothes were tighter, her eyes were older and more alive. I found myself looking at her feet as we sat in silence—she had small feet. Unusually small, almost, tiny feet in small brown boots crossed at the ankles.

"Kit?" she asked, brushing some hair off her cheek. I looked up and saw her bared wrist and, for a moment, imagined the blood throbbing through it, the blood I would someday spill.

"Yes?"

"Do you think Michael really loved me?"

It was an unexpected question, and it caught me off guard and without words. Michael? I hadn't thought about him in a couple months. She caught my expression of surprise and shrugged.

"I mean he was sick, if he did. But in his strange way . . . I was wondering. I never really knew, I suppose. He told me he did, and he was really attached to me for some reason, but I never really knew if that was love or just obsession. I think there's a difference between those two things, don't you? I was just wondering what you thought."

I stared into my ice cream, looking at the melted bit at

the bottom of the paper bowl.

What could I say? I didn't know. His letter had said that Maggie had broken his heart. But what did that mean? Michael had been unstable, irrational. Did any of his words ever mean anything? I could never tell anything from his actions. I don't think he had ever said what he thought, or, perhaps more accurately, I got the feeling that his thoughts had changed so quickly that it had been impossible for him to say what he really meant when he had meant something different every three seconds.

"Does it matter now?" I asked eventually.

She looked at the Thames as it bobbed and splashed against its banks.

"I suppose not."

She didn't sound satisfied.

I sighed and leaned against the back of the bench. I breathed in and closed my eyes. I could hear cars and the faint lapping of the Thames and smell the musty unnatural smell of the dirty water; I could taste the acrid taste of pollution and feel the coldness of ice cream under my fingertips. Had Michael loved her? How was I supposed to know?

"Why are you asking now?" I asked her.

"I suppose now I'm just ready to face it."

This surprised me.

"You were facing it pretty well when it happened," I pointed out, opening my eyes. "I remember you were laughing."

She shrugged. "I was. But I don't think I really *got* it back then, you know. I sort of understood but I didn't, really. I thought I understood what his death meant. It meant freedom for me, I thought. He scared me. But he was a person too, I suppose. He was more than a body when he died, he was a dead person too. I think I've realized that. Oh, I don't know. I'm not making sense. I don't know what I'm saying."

I stared at her feet again, vaguely remembering the face of Michael's mother.

It occurred to me that Maggie was wiser now. In the same way I had changed, she had changed, and because she still had the same stupid smile and made the same stupid sort of conversation and laughed the same stupid way, I had thought she was the same stupid girl I had befriended those months, years, centuries, eons ago. But she wasn't. In this moment, I could see she wasn't. She wasn't wise yet, she was still only brushing the surface, but I could see that now she had the potential to be wise someday. She was finally beginning to ask the right questions. I met her eyes. She stared back at me.

"What do you think?" she asked again, almost sadly.

I broke eye contact and looked at the Thames and felt the coolness, coldness, iciness, freshness of the ice cream under my fingertips.

"I think he loved you," I said quietly.

All I could hear was the sound of water and Maggie's breathing, slowing, thoughtful.

Chapter 19

I killed abundantly and well. My murders echoed through the city. Six more people died before the end of that month. Two women and four men, only one of them over the age of forty. The first one died smashed against a mirror, one more was knocked out a window, three I killed with my bare hands, and the last one I pushed against the sharp edge of a table, too strongly and too quickly for him to escape. I was picking up the killing pace now—I was sure of my motivation and my abilities, and I felt no need to kill far fewer people than I was able to. Maggie would die too, eventually, of course, but before that could happen, I had to let Michael be forgotten completely. If people really made the connection between Maggie's murder and his, it could be dangerous. So I waited. I killed, and I waited.

Sometimes, in the darker nights, Michael haunted me. I awoke on the verge of a scream, tangled in my blankets. Only in the darker nights, but there were enough of those to put me on edge.

The seasons changed. Late fall slowly turned to true winter. The skies changed from a mild gray to an angry one and the streets turned white, coated with ice and snow. It was odd, that snow—usually we just got the fading sort that lit on the sidewalk for a few hours a few months a year and then vanished. But that year's snow was a different sort altogether. More permanent, more stubborn, more erratic— melting into water, freezing into ice, covered by new snow in an endless unpredictable cycle.

The sidewalks were slippery and the air was cold, and I took my heaviest jacket out of storage earlier than usual, because winter seemed to be in a hurry.

I saw Cherry Rose in Harrods once.

It was a shock. I was only killing time when I saw her—I realized that it was probably best if I didn't buy anything from Harrods even though I had the money, because everything there was so luxurious and people would ask questions—but I liked to go there anyway. I liked to pretend I would buy things. I tried on jackets and dresses and asked to see pieces of jewelry in cases, but I never brought anything home.

When I saw her, I was standing at a table of colored hats, trying on one after the other, looking critically at my reflection in the mirror standing a few feet to my left. The red hat overpowered my features, the blue hat made my skin look sallow.

I was just putting on a yellow fedora with a wide brim when she came into view twenty feet away. And of course, I was staring at her before I even really knew I was looking in her direction. My eyes, staring out from beneath the yellow fedora, were like brown cameras, watching, recording her every move. I was transfixed and stunned. I studied her. She didn't know.

She looked washed-out beneath the glow of the recessed lighting. Her red hair was bright, seemingly impossibly so, brighter even than I remembered. She was looking thoughtfully at a rack of gray coats.

Action went on around Cherry Rose, but she was still, and she was all that mattered.

It was almost strange, though, seeing her. It felt unnatural. Her existence for me was anchored firmly in the night I'd considered suicide off the Waterloo Bridge. Seeing her anywhere else felt almost sacrilegious. She had been a mythical creature to me then, and sure, even here, in Harrods, I could feel her faint inhumanity in the way she stood like a foreign creature next to the gray coats; but she wasn't quite as inhuman now.

I wanted her to look over at me. I wanted to meet her eyes, and I wanted her to meet mine. I wanted to see whatever it was in her eyes that was so spectacular and be reminded. Because, as I looked out at her from beneath the brim of the yellow fedora, she seemed nearly human.

But she didn't look up.

She put a gray coat back on the rack and walked away toward the escalators and past them, retreating, and my eyes followed her until she disappeared behind a long shelf of silk shirts. I felt like shouting after her as she vanished, but of course I didn't. I let her go.

It left a sour taste in my mouth.

Soon the city was thrown into a Christmas fervor. Lights went up and Christmas trees appeared everywhere along with other things, small Nativity scenes in houses and wrapping paper advertisements in newspapers and cartoons of Santas pasted in drugstore windows. Couples strolled hand in hand down Kensington High Street, snow dusting their hair like sugar. It really was a cold winter. I checked my mail in late November and killed four people from that batch of letters between then and Christmas. The ones I left outside froze quickly, leaving them like human-shaped statues. I was more confident now, but still—there was something about their eyes in the snow that unsettled me a bit. Wide, wild, staring. Unseeing. Cold.

The first one I killed in the snow was named Stacey Hill.

Dear Killer,

Stacey Hill is my older sister. She lives at 68 Dahlia Drive, in Mayfair. We were never close. Honestly, she was always a massive bitch. I could never stand her. But until about three weeks ago, I could deal with that. Until three weeks ago, I was engaged to someone.

But Stacey, being the massive bitch she is, stole him. She literally just took him. Waltzed off to Rome with him wrapped around her pinkie finger. I mean, he's halfway to blame, he's a bastard too, but how could she do that? She's my sister. Sisters are supposed to have each other's backs.

Well, I guess if she's going to play mean, then I'll play mean too.

Kill her. Kill her. I can't stand the fact that she's even alive. The bitch.

She had clouds of light-blond hair, like wheat. I remember her especially because she begged for mercy. They never begged for mercy. She reminded me strangely of Cherry, who was the first one to ask why. It was strange to hear her words—"Don't kill me, don't kill me, don't kill me"—because, honestly, I had never heard them before. No one except Cherry had ever spoken to me as Diana, and Cherry didn't count. But of course the begging didn't help. I slammed her in the head with a brick and put her in a Dumpster with her letter tucked within her jacket collar. I'm not sure if the police ever found her.

♦ ◊ ♦

I walked down Kensington High Street a week before Christmas, staring into shop windows, considering Christmas presents.

I shivered inside my blue down coat. It was winter break now, so I was shopping at noon in hopes that it might be warmer than later in the day. It wasn't really. I was wearing several layers and I was still cold; I had cut my hair short so it looked almost like my mother's hair, though it didn't curl the same way. The new haircut revealed the nape of my neck. Wind blew across it, sending chills down my spine. It had been a good idea to cut it. Short hair had looked silly on me when I was younger, but now that I was older, it made me look almost chic.

I had to get my mom something, but I didn't know exactly what. A scarf, maybe? But I got her one last Christmas. Oh, I didn't know. Whenever she wanted something, she bought it for herself. She was impossible to shop for. And my dad. I would just get him a tie, like always. It wasn't like he would use anything I bought him anyway. He seemed to make it a point not to. Something for Alex too. I should probably get Maggie something as well, I guessed, since she was basically my best friend. Oh, that was sad. My best friend was a victim.

I stopped in front of a shiny window, staring inside at leather purses slung over the shoulders of slim mannequins.

Maybe a purse for my mom. She'd like that, if I picked the right one. And I had a lot of money now that the mailbox had been so full lately. Maybe something red. She liked red. I'd probably have to get something less expensive for Maggie so she wouldn't get suspicious. And definitely something much cheaper for Alex.

I gazed at the window display thoughtfully. The mannequins were twiglike, painted white and twisted into strange, unreasonable, grasshopper-like positions.

My phone rang suddenly. I jumped at the sound. I took it out of my pocket and picked up without looking at the caller ID, still staring into the window.

"Hello?" I asked.

"Kit?"

"Oh, hello, Maggie." A squabbling couple passed by me, their voices shrill and shrieking.

"Where *are* you right now?" she asked, hearing the fight.

"Kensington High Street. Shopping."

"Oh. I was wondering if you wanted to go shopping with me later this afternoon, but I suppose not," she said with a casual laugh.

"Ah, sorry," I apologized. "If you'd called me just a bit earlier, we could have gone."

"Yeah, I missed my chance."

"Do you want to do something tomorrow instead?" I suggested.

"I can't—I've got to go visit my grandma, remember?" she reminded me.

"Oh yeah, I forgot. How about later this week? We've got the week off, anyway."

"Maybe. I'll have to see what happens with my family, what they want to do—they're all coming to visit after we visit my grandma, you know. They're likely to want to do something." She sounded excited. Her home life was usually boring, I remembered. Good. Excitement would be good for her.

"Well, hopefully we can go do something. I'll have already done my shopping, but I'll window-shop with you."

"Hmm." Maggie was thinking about something.

"Yeah?"

"Are you having any family come in for Christmas?"

I shook my head and then remembered that she couldn't hear that over the phone.

"No, no one's coming," I said.

"Oh no, why?"

I laughed. "Don't sound so worried. My mom and I will have Christmas together, just us two. Like we always do. It's nice."

"Why isn't anyone coming? What about your dad?"

"Well . . . my dad isn't really the Christmas type," I said slowly, not feeling the need to explain. "My mom doesn't have any surviving relatives on her side of the family, and we aren't really close with my dad's side of the family. Alex might come over. He's staying in London for Christmas, though I think he's spending most of Christmas with some other friends of his. His family's sort of far away, up in the north, and he doesn't have time to visit them." I could hear Maggie breathe in, about to launch into some sort of speech. "Really, don't sound so worried, though. It's fine," I said quickly, stopping her. She was uncertainly silent for a moment.

"Are you sure?"

I laughed.

"Of course I'm sure. I'll have a wonderful Christmas. I always do." And it was true. Most people's Christmases were loud party-type events with screaming and piles of presents and lights strung on window ledges, but my mother and I just had quiet ones. And they were wonderful.

I remembered being twelve years old, sitting under the lit Christmas tree on Christmas Eve with my head on my mother's shoulder, singing "What Child Is This?" under our breaths so we didn't wake my father, who had gone to sleep upstairs. I remembered mugs of eggnog and warmth. I remembered a fire that flickered from across the room, sending brilliant light cascading across the floor. I remembered never wanting to sleep, never wanting anything to change, and I remembered falling asleep at two in the morning with my head in my mother's lap.

"All right," Maggie said, deciding to believe me. "Well, we'll try to coordinate shopping for later this week."

"Sure thing."

"Sorry, I have to go, my mom's calling me from the other room."

"No worries, go." I smiled cheerfully. "I'll talk to you later."

"Right, laters," Maggie said, and hung up.

I heard the dial tone and pulled the phone away from my ear. Slowly, I lowered it down in toward my legs, staring at the screen that told me "call ended" and thinking. The screen lit up my blue jacket with glowing light.

Michael's memory had vanished from everyone's mind, even from Maggie's, mostly. She hadn't mentioned him in weeks, not since that moment by the Thames. Maybe it was time. Maybe, maybe, maybe.

I was floating away. I was like a boat adrift on a lake with no way home, and I didn't regret it.

◆ ◆ ◆

"I'm home."

The house was empty, and no one responded. My voice echoed through the hallway loudly. At the end of the hall, the grandfather clock struck four.

Sometimes the house seemed so big.

I felt like a child. The steep stairs and the expensive photographs loomed over me like something unfamiliar. My feet, like always, sank too deep into the hallway rug. My feet made no noise. I could see only shadows now. Shadows of pale curtains and sleek polished wood tables. Shadows of glass vases and fresh roses and spare, modern bookshelves. Shadows of a place, nothing more.

With effort, I carried my bags upstairs, doing my best not to crunch them together too much. In the end, I had gotten a purse for my mom, a tie for my dad, a wallet for Alex—I had noticed the last time we had lunch that his was falling to shreds—and a beautiful dress for Maggie. It hung down in watery drapes from a wide neckline, trimmed in at the waist, and flowed out into a graceful skirt, longer in the back than in the front; it was made of ice-blue silk and chiffon and looked like it would rip when you held it, even though it was actually quite sturdy. I had tried it on for size in the dressing room, because we wore the same size even though she had more curves than me–I was taller than she was, so it balanced out–and when I twirled, the dress caught the light and glimmered like moonlight on the Thames. Maybe it was a bit too expensive, but when I saw it, I absolutely had to get it. It was just exactly her. I'd had Harrods wrap it in an icy-blue wrapping paper that almost exactly matched the color of the dress itself.

I put my bags on my bed, shed my jacket, and went to the bathroom. As I washed my hands, I stared in the mirror. My light-brown eyes, which changed color just a bit from day to day, were flecked with the faintest touches of gray around the edges, like Alex's eyes. They looked nice today. Pretty. I combed my hair back behind my ears neatly, enjoying the look of my new cut.

The house phone rang, jolting me. It rang again. Remembering that I was the only one home, I walked into the hallway–where it was–not in any particular hurry, and answered it. It was probably someone trying to sell something. No one ever called the house phone anymore except for people trying to sell something.

"Hello," I said flatly.

A voice I had not been expecting replied.

"Vienna?" My mom's name.

It was my dad. I hesitated, stunned, before answering.

"No . . . it's Kit."

"Oh." There was a silence. "Is your mom home?"

"No."

I hadn't talked to him properly in months, I realized. I didn't even know where he was now. America, China, Spain, Portugal, Germany? He was gone so often so long that I sometimes forgot to wonder. It was strange to hear his voice.

"Oh, well, deliver a message to her, will you?"

"Sure."

"I won't make it home for Christmas this year, sorry. I've got business."

"Oh," I said.

"I'm sorry. I really tried to change it, but I have to be in New York the whole week before Christmas," he said, with a lame attempt at apology. "I know it's terrible. I should be home, I shouldn't be away, but I have to be. I really feel bad about it."

"It's fine," I replied.

"I'll get back home soon. Not before Christmas, unfortunately, but soon after. Okay?"

"Okay."

"You two will be fine alone for Christmas?"

I smiled. I didn't know why—he couldn't see me or anything.

"Oh, sure. Don't even worry."

"I'm sorry for missing it."

Missing it *again*.

This absence was unusually bold, though. Usually he

showed up for at least part of the time. A complete absence hadn't happened before. He really did sound sorry, though, which was strange. He rarely betrayed emotion.

Not for the first time, I hopefully wondered if he actually did care. But it was a sad hopefulness, the kind of hopefulness that has little point. Even if he did care, he wasn't around enough for it to matter.

"We'll be fine," I assured him. "Don't worry."

"I'll see you in January."

He meant "I'll see you in January, maybe."

But he didn't say it.

"Okay," I said, as if I believed him.

"Bye."

"Good-bye."

As I said good-bye, I got the strangest feeling that I was saying something more than that. Something final. Something larger than the word good-bye. The feeling hung over me, and I couldn't put it into words.

He hung up, but I still felt as if his voice lingered in the air.

As I put the phone back into the receiver, I suddenly felt very small.

◆ ◇ ◆

Blood seeped over the asphalt, too close to the tips of my toes. I stepped backward, and as I exhaled, my white breath rolled upward toward the sun. The sky was clear today. No birds disturbed the air, and the clouds like melted glass were still.

I looked impassively down at the man at my feet, whose neck was striped black and blue from where my hands had clutched him so tightly as I bashed his head again and again against the ground until it cracked like an egg into a frying pan. I had long fingers and made big handprints, like a man's. He was tall, with wide shoulders, which had posed a challenge at first. He had knocked me about a bit against a nearby Dumpster and across the alleyway before I gained control—but once I had swept him off his feet and onto the ground, he had been mine. His eyes were glazed over and open. His hands, too, were open and turned up toward the sky as if waiting to hold something.

I took the letter out of my pocket and folded it into his left hand, curling his stiffening fingers around the paper so it wouldn't fly away.

Dear Killer,

My family has hit hard times. It's getting worse. We can barely keep our flat. My husband has a nice job, and I work too, but my father recently died and left us with a lot of debt, so we're still having trouble. And it's hard on us all. I love my husband. I really do.

But I want you to kill him.

I'm not doing this because I hate him. I'm doing this because I love my children. He has life insurance that could create a better life for us—don't you see? And I don't think he'd really be mad if he knew I was writing this letter. God, that sounds strange, but he loves us so much. He would do anything for us. Including die, I think. I love him too. With all my heart. But I need the best for my children.

His name is William Cole, and he works at the Harton Finance office in Chelsea. I don't want to tell you where I live.

I removed my gloves, tucked them into my pocket, and rubbed my hands together and shoved them under my armpits for warmth. Twenty feet down the alley, cars and people moved along obliviously. Snow fell down through the dark alley. A car honked. Above, the latticed shadows of fire escapes crisscrossed like jail bars.

I looked down at him a moment longer, and then I walked up the alleyway, back toward the rest of civilization. The crowds were large enough that I could slip back out onto the street without raising suspicion from onlookers, and the entrance of the alley was hidden from surveillance camera view behind a tall newspaper stand. I'd chosen this place carefully. I'd just watched him for a few days, mapping his route home from work, the timing, the places, figuring out when and where I needed to be to intercept him. He'd been so willing to come with me when I'd told him I worked nearby and needed some help with heavy lifting; he had been the kind of person, I supposed, who had loved to help.

This was a familiar neighborhood. The Chelsea Police Station was only a few blocks away, and the bistro I had met Alex in so long ago and a few times since, with its bird-patterned wallpaper and fraying wicker chairs, was directly across the street. I paused on the sidewalk in the midst of the crowd, staring at it, remembering the first time we had eaten together. Remembering how weak he had been as he told me he was afraid, remembering his handsome face torn with fear. I had been weak then too. The bistro had white shutters and pots of plastic orange flowers on the steps out front. They looked strange and unnatural in the snow.

I was just standing there when the door of the bistro swung open and Alex came out into the cold.

Oh God! He could see me, I was sure. But no, he wasn't looking in my direction, not yet. If he saw me, he would call out to me. He was alone and was looking up, memorizing the sky. He was wearing work clothes—he must have come here for his lunch break, stupid, stupid, shouldn't I have taken that possibility into consideration? This was unspeakably dangerous. There were people on the sidewalk, but not enough of them to hide behind.

And worst of all, to get back to the police station, I knew, Alex had to walk across the street and pass where I was. I couldn't be caught at another crime scene, not now, not now, I didn't have an excuse.

I gasped, inhaling a mouthful of snowflakes. I coughed as they turned to ice water in my mouth. The thick wooden newspaper stand that hid the entrance to the alleyway was a few feet away. I hid anxiously behind the right side of it, looking across the street to see where Alex was and decide what angle I needed to stand at to conceal myself from him. The owner of the newspaper stand, blessedly, didn't notice me. He was reading a magazine, turning the pages with lazy fingers. I breathed quickly in and out. My breath clouded the air.

Oh God.

It occurred to me briefly that maybe I should have just made a run for it, but it was too late for that now, wasn't it? But it was fine. I would be fine. I was always fine, and would always be fine. I looked carefully around the corner of the newspaper stand, searching for Alex.

He was crossing the street. And now he had reached my side of the street, and was turning toward me, and he was walking, and he was drawing closer. He looked around at everything around him, noticing everything, like he always did.

Oh God!

The stand would hide me for now. But when he came down the street and passed it, he would see me, standing suspiciously on the side of the stand where there were no magazines, a recently dead body in the alleyway to my right. I couldn't even slip around all the way to the other side of the stand to escape his eyes; it was crowded there, and the only space available was too close to the street. The cars were moving too fast to stop for me if I fell off the curb. I pulled my hood up around my chin and forehead and looked at my feet, as if that would help.

He was so close. Only ten feet away now.

There was a woman, I noticed suddenly, walking toward me, groceries balanced on the arm closest to the curb, closest to me, holding on to her son's hand with the other hand. Her son was a pretty little boy, cherubic, joyful looking, but his mouth was open and he was screaming deafeningly and pointing at something across the street that excited him. She was looking at him in the way only an exasperated mother can look at a child; intensely lovingly, with an undercurrent of irritation and resentment. She readjusted her groceries, a heavy bag filled to the brim with bread and sardines and cheese and apples—

Apples. Red and round. Yes, apples.

He would be here soon. My heartbeat quickened.

The woman was next to me and she was glaring at her son, and she didn't see me as I reached out and carefully, carefully, roughly jostled the shopping bag with my elbow as I pretended to get something out of the inside of my jacket.

"Hey!" the woman yelped, letting go of her child to grasp at her groceries as they cascaded out of the bag onto the pavement. Tomatoes exploded on impact, a sardine tin sustained a dented corner. And yes, the apples spilled too, red and fake-looking and lush, just like blood.

I mouthed indistinct words of apology, looking down so she couldn't see and remember my face, and she put her hands on her hips. She took one off to grab at her son, who was about to run off in some strange direction now that he was suddenly free.

I could pick out Alex's footsteps from the crowd now.

Still hidden behind the newspaper stand, I kneeled down, pulled my turtleneck sleeves up over my hands so I wouldn't leave fingerprints, and grabbed for her groceries, mumbling apologies up at her so my voice wouldn't be loud enough for Alex to recognize. She smelled like cheap perfume, and the hems of her black jeans were the frayed product of a bad tailoring job. I put her things back in the bag, which she had dropped next to my feet. Sardines, bananas, a package of vanilla yogurt.

"For God's sake," she yelled at her son, and rubbed her false eyelashes.

I put one apple in her bag. I made a big show of grabbing for a third behind her feet.

Alex was only a few feet away, and out of the corner of my I eye I could see he was still looking around, at the newspapers and the man selling them, at the sky, glancing almost uninterestedly at the moment I was having with this tired mother, and in seconds he would be on my side of the newspaper stand and he would be looking around and he would see me and even with my face staring at the pavement he would still recognize me and I swear to God my heartbeat was so loud that other people could hear it—

Alex came close. Closer, closer. As the woman yelled words I wasn't listening to, my hand found the third apple behind her ankles. I gripped it tight. My aim had to be perfect. I had to be perfect. I had to—

And he walked in front of me.

With a flick of my wrist, as the child screamed a shrill, high note, I released the apple, pretending to the mother that it was simply slipping accidentally out of my clumsy grasp. For a moment it wobbled because of its uneven shape and I didn't think it would make it to where I needed it to be, and I begged it inwardly, pleaded, to spin just right.

And it did.

It was perfect. The apple rolled tremulously over Alex's left foot as he was just about to walk into my line of sight and I was just about to come into his. I froze.

Alex looked down as he felt it pass over his feet, just brushing them slightly, and then with great speed rolled over and past them down the alley. He followed the red bouncing apple with curious eyes, and I bit my lip, anxiety alighting in me again after a brief moment of exaltation. Please, please. He had to notice. He had to notice the shadow of a body before he looked back to see who had thrown the apple and noticed me.

His head tilted slightly down toward me, knowing that some silly girl had accidentally let an apple slip away, instinctively wanting to see her face. But he was still half-way following the path of the apple, like I needed him to. And a breath caught in my throat; was I caught?

But then, like a miracle, the apple bounced down the alley and hit the poor crushed head of the dead man, and Alex, still halfway watching the apple, saw him with a jolt. And of course, then he was running down the alley, just like he was supposed to, feet whirling and breath steaming.

I slid my turtleneck sleeve back down onto my wrist. I watched as he shouted into the radio clipped to his collar, calling the rest of the police force. He stood over the body for a moment, just staring down, and then he began to pace. The woman nudged my shoulder roughly, wanting to know why I had stopped working. I put a box of cereal in the bag as her son groaned and moaned and fell to his knees dramatically and began to cry.

I knew Alex was thinking, and I knew he would realize soon that the body was still warm and that the murderer couldn't have gone far. He would begin searching soon. I had to leave before then. But quietly.

With machinelike efficiency, I finished putting the groceries back in the bag, and after a bit of shouting and grousing the mother and child went away.

I stood, narrowing my eyes, and looked around for my escape. It took me a moment to find it. But then there it was, a large group of twentysomethings moving down the sidewalk in an awkward clump. I could hear their voices from far away, and I studied them for a moment and then sighed, telling myself that I needed to be calm. The worst was over, anyway. Alex was occupied.

As the twentysomethings passed, I adjusted my hood again; I attached myself to the back of their pack so I wouldn't stand out from the crowd when the police looked at the video of people walking up and down the street. The group didn't notice me. As I walked away I looked down the alley at Alex one more time, at the pacing silhouette, and I had to feel sorry for him, because he was chasing me, and it was futile.

I stayed with the group for a few more blocks before separating and walking home alone.

◆ ◆ ◆

I found my mother in the living room again—it seemed to be becoming her place now—with a coffee-table book full of black-and-white photographs open in her lap. The sun came through the window and made the dust in the air glow as it lit on tables, couches, pillows, flowers, on my mother's thin shoulders. The Christmas tree in the corner of the room, strung with colorful lights, made everything sing with brightness. Slim and quiet, sinking down into the ivory couch cushions, my mother looked so muted, as if she existed only in pastel colors.

She sipped tea silently. For a moment I stood in the doorway, just watching her—then I spoke to let her know I was there.

"I'm home."

She looked over at me and smiled halfway, steam drifting across her face.

"Welcome back."

She was in a good mood today. Whatever it was that had made her that way, she spoke with a gentleness I hadn't heard for a long time. Her eyes were soft, and as she looked at me, I felt as if I were swimming in them—in their blue, their deepness, their knowledge.

Without thinking much about it, I crossed the room

and sat down on the couch next to her. I leaned over her shoulder to see what she was looking at. A photograph of a candle against a black background, the flame flickering quietly, lighting the picture with a serene glow.

Her eyes flicked from the photograph to me, back to the photograph again, and then they skimmed over my hands, folded in my lap.

"Oh," she said. She reached over to take my left hand into her right. As she touched it, I winced, and realized as she set it atop the photograph and turned it over that a purple bruise stretched over much of my lower palm.

She brushed her fingertips over the bruise, not hard enough to hurt. She didn't say anything.

"He gave me a little trouble," I murmured apologetically. She shook her head as if to say, *Don't apologize.* She really was gentle today—and fragile-feeling too, as if she were about to float away.

"Any other bruises?"

"A few, I think. They don't hurt. I'm fine."

"Any other complications?"

I was silent for a minute.

"Nothing that's dangerous."

She gripped my fingertips suddenly, a reflex. A reaction. "What happened?"

I leaned toward her and set my head against her shoulder.

"It's fine, it's not important," I breathed. I didn't want to explain, not now. She wouldn't be angry about it, because it didn't endanger either of us; but it would still worry her. And I didn't want her to worry.

I willed her to be silent, to just let me be, just for today. I imagined she would, when she was like this, pale, a fading shadow of the past. . . .

She reached around and settled one arm about my shoulders, the other around my waist. She closed her eyes. We set our heads in the creases between each other's necks and shoulders, a six-inch gap between our chests. I could feel her heartbeat radiating warmly out through her skin.

She held me like I was a child once again.

◆ ◇ ◆

That night there was precipitation. But it wasn't rain, and it wasn't snow, it was sleet, just angry sleet that pounded down, destroying. It melted the thin snow into muddy puddles and beat a ragged tattoo into the roof of my town house and kept me awake until just before the dawn, when the sleet finally abated and there was snow, light snow, snow like fog that brought some peace to the world again.

The story of the murder was on the morning news, with the scandalous tagline "The Perfect Killer Escapes from under the Noses of Police!" Somehow the story had gotten out, unfortunately. Everyone was talking about it, in whispers, in shouts, and every newspaper I passed had something about it on the very first page. Chelsea, in particular, was spooked. I went to lunch with Alex that day, and I was especially quiet. He talked twice as much to make up for my silence.

He was the one who should have been quiet, not me. He had more reason to be upset than me. He had lost the Perfect Killer again, after all, and he was being ridiculed in the papers for it. I was free and nameless, so far as the public was concerned.

But I was the one who barely said a word.

Chapter 20

Maggie ran in front of me, feet crunching through the thin, stiff sheet of snow with a sound like crinkling paper, a laugh on her lips. It was Thursday. Christmas was Sunday. Everything was winter.

"Bloody hell, I love snow," Maggie called, as enthusiastic as a small child.

"It's more like ice than snow—there's not enough of it," I said skeptically.

"No, there's enough," she replied, leaning over and gathering up a scarce handful of it in one pink glove. Without warning, she grinned and threw it at me. It landed on my shoulder, and a few icy drops of water splashed up my neck.

"*Hey*," I said with mock annoyance, smiling. "Stop that."

"What are you gonna do about it?" she teased. In reply, I picked up a handful of snow and threw it at her. I missed. The snow fell back onto the sidewalk with a small, pitiful hiss.

"Oh, that was awful." She giggled. "Can't you do better than that?"

"Hey—"

And suddenly we were throwing snow at each other in a flurry of cold, of sound.

After a while we grew tired of this and sat in the miserably small snow bank on the side of the road, the wetness of the snow seeping through our jeans. Neither of us really cared. We breathed deeply, smelling the scent of winter in the air. I laughed breathily.

"We're having a party on Christmas Eve. My extended family just decided they wanted one. They're a bit crazy," Maggie said.

"Okay."

"Do you want to come?"

I raised my eyebrows.

"Your mom can come too," Maggie added.

"That sounds fun," I said. "Actually, I'd love that."

"Really? Great," Maggie said happily. "It's at my house. I don't know the exact time yet, but I'll tell you when my crazy family figures it out."

"Cool."

"You weren't planning on doing anything else?"

"Nah, my mom and I were going to stay at home, just the two of us, because it turns out Alex has to work for most of Christmas because he's in hot water about the whole 'Perfect Killer escaping from underneath his nose' thing. And my dad's got business to deal with, so he's out of town. Going to a party sounds wonderful."

"Your dad really isn't coming home for Christmas?"

"No, he's not."

"Is he . . . I'm sorry if I'm prying, just tell me to stop if I am."

"Nah, it's okay. I don't mind," I said, shaking my head.

"Is he on bad terms with your mom or something?"

I shook my head again. I almost laughed. It was hard to be on bad terms with someone when you barely saw them—my mom and dad really weren't on any sort of terms at all. I felt a surge of bitterness and irritation. My mom might be almost neutral about him, but I wasn't. It angered me that he could be so emotionally distant from us both, so far away and empty. I couldn't understand it.

"They're on fine terms. He's just not really a *home* person, you know. It's not his thing."

"You don't mind?"

"Honestly, I nearly forget him sometimes." An image passed through my mind—nighttime on the sidewalk, two shadows coming home at the same time, seeing each other, barely saying a word, barely in the same place at the same time. He forgot me too.

I realized that I was good at that. Forgetting. Forgetting

Cherry, forgetting Dad, forgetting that I wasn't normal.

We fell into silence. We were near my house, which sat next to a small residential street a block from a main thoroughfare. A car passed quietly through. I rested my head on curled-up knees.

"Oh!" Maggie said.

I raised my head up and looked where she was looking, back toward the larger street a block down.

"Oh."

Down the street, waiting at a stoplight, was Dr. Marcell with groceries in her arms.

"Oh, it's so strange seeing teachers outside of school. I always feel like they don't have other lives, you know?" Maggie noted.

"Does she live around here? I've never seen her around here before."

Maggie shrugged. "How should I know?"

"That's so weird." I giggled.

Silently, I remembered how Dr. Marcell suspected me.

She stood still at the corner, her no-frills hair swinging in the faint wind like stubby feathers. I watched her curiously. Maggie did too. Casually, Dr. Marcell looked around, trying to find something to look at to pass the time until the light changed.

She saw us. She paused; I saw the recognition in her eyes, and I smiled and waved.

"Hi, Dr. Marcell!" Maggie shouted.

She was too far away to be heard without shouting and

she wasn't really fond of shouting, so Dr. Marcell just raised one of her hands in salute. She couldn't even really wave it, since she was holding groceries. Her arms shivered.

I wondered what she was thinking.

I wondered if, in some strange part of her, she knew, was certain, of what I was capable of.

I wondered if she knew what I was going to do.

The light turned and she walked away, across the street.

"Come on, let's go back to my house," I said with a smile, patting Maggie on the shoulder. "I'm cold."

As we walked along the icy sidewalks back to my house, I realized that Maggie was my best friend. It saddened me. Because she *was* my friend, though some things about her I did hate, and I had so many secrets I kept from her. She was my friend. And I hadn't had a friend in so long.

• ◆ •

It was late at night. Maggie was gone. My mom was still out—she had a dinner, one of her many, many dinners—but she would be back soon. I was tired, but I didn't feel like sleeping. I had just gotten off the phone with Alex. He sounded tired. I wasn't surprised. He was working overtime nowadays, struggling to retain at least some semblance of the leadership position he'd once had in the Perfect Killer case. It was slipping away from him in the wake of my narrow escape and the newly increased frequency of the murders. He was trying to retain his usual good humor, or at least a positive outlook, but he was having trouble.

"It's so frustrating," he had said, "that these people don't understand that I'm chasing a ghost. The Perfect Killer is a ghost, Kit. I'm never going to find him. He just walks through the streets killing people, and I can't do a damned thing about it. But no one else can either. Bringing in new leadership won't solve the problem. And this is my case. It's mine to solve or not solve. I know it inside out."

"But wouldn't some outside opinions help you?" I replied uncertainly, not even sure what I wanted in this situation.

"But they don't want new opinions, they want new leadership. This is *my* case. And I suppose they're listening—they're keeping me in charge, for now. But they're getting desperate. And they're just getting too anxious. They were anxious before, with the . . . teacup, you know, that whole thing, but now—I don't know what they're thinking, what they're going to do."

He sounded so stubborn—and for a moment, almost angry. But not quite. I wasn't sure Alex really knew what angry meant. I changed the topic, and we talked for a few more minutes about other things. Weather, Christmas, et cetera. We talked about how much snow we were getting, and how Harrods had wrapped Kit's gift for Maggie in that shade of pale-blue wrapping paper that matched the dress exactly, to an extent that it was almost eerie—and eventually his voice trailed off and he told me he had to sleep. I had been the one to hang up the telephone.

I flipped through my end-of-November letters one by one, sorting them, separating the requests I would grant from those I wouldn't—I'd been a bit haphazard with my choosing recently, and I figured it was probably best if I took the time to do things methodically, like usual. Yes, no, yes, yes, yes, no, no. One by one, forming two piles on the bed on either side of me.

Neat piles. Orderly. Safe.

My mind wandered back, far away toward that first day, that first late-summer day, nearly fall, that had begun things. I looked at my bedside table—it was there, beneath the drawer's false bottom, next to my latex gloves, the letter asking for Maggie's death. Michael's letter. It was waiting for her—and for me too. Our fates were bound together now, strangely and terribly.

Downstairs, I heard the door open. Briefly, I heard the sound of wind like a broken gas pipe and then the patter of footsteps. The door closed. My mom was home. I kept sorting the letters, one by one by one. I heard footsteps down the hallway and then footsteps up the stairs to her second-floor bedroom. Then I heard her pause as she realized my light was still on.

"Kit?"

I didn't reply immediately. I gave it a few seconds.

"Mom?"

"Why are you still awake?"

"It's not that late. It's only eleven. And it's vacation."

"Eleven? It's got to be later than that. Go to bed."

"Fine," I said. I didn't really mind. But it really was only eleven.

My mom started walking again. I got up off the bed.

"Mom?" I called again. She stopped walking.

"What is it?"

"I'm really sorry, but I won't be here Christmas Eve."

"What? But we always have Christmas Eve together. It's our thing." I was surprised to find that she actually sounded dejected. I felt sorry. But it couldn't be helped.

"I've got something I need to take care of," I replied. "I'm really sorry."

She hesitated. "Does it have to be that night?"

She knew what I was talking about just by the way I spoke. It was so obvious. She knew I was going to kill—and she was afraid. Afraid of something vague and unspeakable—and it was strange to recognize that in her voice. My mother, who had been so brave. My mother, the weak one, my mother the mountain, worn down by thunderstorms and mudslides and forest fires over time, broken down into something small and tame . . .

Somehow, it broke my heart.

Yes, it had to be Christmas Eve.

I couldn't explain in words that she would understand why I felt that it had to be Christmas Eve. Any other day would have worked just as well. But Christmas Eve felt like an important day to me, and Maggie's death had to feel important, and somehow the two seemed to go together.

"Yes, it has to be Christmas Eve," I said.

• ◆ •

In my dream Diana and I sat on a cliff top, our feet dangling over the edge. Both of us were silent. She stared out with vague anger in her eyes, and I watched her out of the corner of my eye, not daring to look exactly at her. She was beautiful, almost blindingly so.

There was a brisk wind that smelled faintly of cinnamon.

"Does it bother you?" she asked.

"What?"

"Does it bother you to not be me, sometimes?"

"I don't know what you mean. I'm always you."

"No, I'm always you, but you're not always me."

We were the same person; her words didn't make sense. But this was a dream, and it seemed, in the moment, to make sense to me. I nodded and stared down the sheer cliff face, down into the mist that obscured whatever lay at its base.

"It bothers me," I said.

She laughed and traced my line of sight.

"Do you know what's down there?" she asked, staring with me down into the murky darkness below.

"No. Do you?"

"It's madness."

She sounded sure, and I believed her. Our hair fluttered into our faces, and we pushed it out of our eyes with the same flick of our wrist. We were more alike than we seemed.

"Madness . . ." My voice trailed off miserably.

"We're both ready to fall," she said.

"We won't fall."

"We're both ready to fall," she repeated, more emphatically this time, as if she knew more than me, as if she were wiser.

"I won't fall," I murmured. She sighed. She knew I was a lost cause.

She laid a gentle hand on my shoulder and leaned toward me. Looking incredibly sad, she kissed my forehead like a mother, or a sister, and softly whispered, "Wake."

And then unexpectedly her face morphed into Michael's, and I did wake, and when I woke I was screaming and terrified, and Diana's face was nothing more than a dull memory from a vague dream.

◆ ◇ ◆

I stood near the window, near the stacks of old CDs in the sale bin, the ones they usually sold next to the cash register, the ones no one bought anymore because they were useless, of course. No one needed CDs anymore, not when everything was online. Behind me the grocery store bustled. It was Christmas Eve day tomorrow, and everyone was frantically shopping, trying to get the last pieces of their Christmas dinners before the things they needed went out of stock. I stood absently with my shopping basket slung over one arm, my jacket hanging over the other.

There was Cherry's CD, right there, on the top of the nearest stack. There she was, just on the front. Dressed in a long red gown with red lips and hair like a cloud around her face. She was fascinating, even in a photograph. Deliciously otherworldly. More like the woman who had convinced me not to kill her in a dressing room than the woman staring at gray coats in Harrods.

I was too hot. I put the CD back in the bin and put my shopping next to my feet so I could take my sweater off, strip down to my T-shirt.

"Kit?"

Oh, I knew that voice. I put on a smile, put my sweater on top of the oranges in my basket, and turned.

"Dr. Marcell."

"I didn't expect to see you here."

She was standing there with a few heavy-looking paper bags, looking almost confused, as if she couldn't imagine why I would ever need to buy groceries.

"I live right nearby," I said, gesturing uninterestedly in the general direction of my house.

"I figured. I saw you with Maggie."

"Oh, yes." I smiled. "That was funny."

"I live near here too," she offered, then hesitated, as if she was thinking twice about telling me. I nodded know-ingly, eyeing the wedding ring on her finger.

"With your husband?"

"Yes."

I looked pleasant, or at least did my best to look pleasant.

"That's nice," I said.

"Getting Christmas groceries?" she asked, eyeing the

oranges, tangerines, granola, chocolate, bread, and eggs in my basket. I giggled.

"Sort of. My mom bought a bunch of Christmas groceries—for the Christmas dinner itself—and forgot to buy anything else, so I'm stocking up on things to eat until then."

"Oh."

Both of us were quiet for a moment.

"It's wonderful how you're taking care of Maggie. I know Michael's death really affected her," Dr. Marcell said suddenly. It was unexpected. No one was talking about that anymore.

"Oh, thank you. It's only natural. She's my friend."

"You spend a lot of time with her."

"She's a good friend," I said carefully.

Dr. Marcell looked unsatisfied. I looked out the window. It was snowing again, soft and light, like breath in the air.

"The weather's nice," Dr. Marcell noted. I nodded.

"It's peaceful," I said.

It was. There was silence over everything. There was silence and tranquillity, like a cold lake, like a day without wind. The snow always did that. Muted everything, made it fade away somehow, as if everything was something less than real.

"Cold," she said. We laughed.

Another moment of complete silence as we both looked out the window.

"Why?" Dr. Marcell breathed.

"What?"

I don't think she had meant to say it out loud. "What?" she asked.

"You asked why."

"Oh, did I?"

"What did you mean?"

She halfway shrugged.

"I don't know." She shook her head, looked at me almost guiltily, almost suspiciously, hanging somewhere between the two emotions.

"What is it?" I asked.

"I think I was wondering why I can't trust you," she replied softly.

She had never said what we both knew in so many words. I had always felt and carried her silent suspicion like a burr—a constant reminder that I was, in fact, perpetually guilty—but having it so out in the open made it feel that much more real. It made me feel a bit more like Diana, a bit less like Kit. A bit more on edge, a bit less attached to the normal world around me. I took a few breaths before answering.

I smiled. "Sorry," I said, as if her distrust were something I could fix with an apology.

"I'm sorry too." And she was, really she was.

"For what it's worth, I've enjoyed your class."

"You've been a good student."

"Thanks."

"I'm so, so sorry."

"That's . . . good," I murmured absently, not really thinking.

I exhaled and smiled again and nodded at her and picked up my things.

"Have a nice Christmas," I said honestly.

"You too."

I dismissed myself, having nothing more to say. I walked away toward the cereal aisle.

Dr. Marcell's eyes followed me, always on me. I felt anxious. I felt like screaming. But everything around me was peaceful. I didn't want to disrupt the calm.

◆ ◇ ◆

I found my mother on the stairs past midnight. I was coming downstairs for water. Somehow I always seemed to need water near midnight. And so nearly every night I would make my way down the steep stairs, and usually I would be alone. Usually. But not tonight. Tonight my mother was sitting there on the stairs, one landing above the ground floor, underneath the black-framed photograph of the enraptured violinist, staring down at the red-green-yellow rug in the front hallway.

"Mom?" I asked faintly, seeing her there, pulling down on the hem of the overlarge T-shirt I wore to sleep because I was wearing nothing but underwear underneath. I hadn't expected to see anyone else awake.

"Kit," she replied, not turning to look at me, "sit down."

For a moment anger boiled up in me—who was she to tell me what to do? But it occurred to me that perhaps it had been more of a request than an order, and so, quietly, I sat down next to her. I folded my hands in my lap. She was sitting with her head leaning against the wall, and the stairs were narrow enough so that I could lean against the railing. I wondered absently how my father would get up the stairs when he came home—or down, maybe, I realized, if he was home already. I didn't really know. But then I remembered he was far away right now, on a trip, in America or somewhere like that, somewhere I had never been.

I looked at her hands. They hung over her knees, long and slim and graceful, just like the rest of her. They were fascinating hands. They meant so many things, those hands. They could do so many things.

Her sleek hair was mussed and wispy now, as if she had been sleeping but had woken up for some reason for the express purpose of waiting on the stairs for me.

"What do you want?" I asked gently.

"Just sit." She sighed. And in that moment, as she looked sidelong into my eyes, she sounded distinctly like a mother. Like the mother who had swept me up on Christmas and offered me to my father and comforted me when I began to cry. That mother. That long-ago woman.

So I did what she asked. I sat with her. We sat in silence for a very long time; it was a comfortable silence, the kind of silence where we didn't need words to fill the spaces, and even the ticking of the grandfather clock seemed almost too loud.

Eventually she spoke, her words slipping painfully through her lips like each one was taking something from her, like each word was making her vanish even more than before.

"I built this all myself," she said.

"Built what?" I replied, looking at her, not understanding. She was half dreaming; I could see by the look in her eyes. She was so tired.

"I built this house of cards."

"It's not a house of cards."

"It is, though, don't you see? A brilliant house of cards. A castle of cards. Constructed, contrived under my fingertips. It all belongs to me. It's beautiful, the way we live. My killings, and now yours—I taught myself everything I know, and taught you everything I learned. It's magnificent, what we can do. But it's like spun sugar. Our little world, our little game can be destroyed so easily, Kit. I didn't see that before."

I had to laugh.

"You sound like a poet," I told her.

It made her angry.

"*Listen* to me," she snapped. Now I was angry too.

"It will only fall apart if I'm careless. And I'm not careless. Not any longer," I replied, perhaps a bit harshly, but it was her fault that I was angry, wasn't it?

"That's not . . . that's not what I meant." She paused. "Tomorrow's Christmas Eve," she said.

"Yes."

"I'm living in a house of cards."

I took one of her hands and held it tightly; she closed her eyes.

"You should get some sleep," I advised. "You haven't slept, have you?"

She shook her head.

"I'm living in a house of cards," she said again.

"I promise I'll be careful. I won't ruin things, I swear. I'm a professional. I'll make things okay. You shouldn't worry. Trust me."

Confidence swelled in my chest suddenly. I was the Perfect Killer. I could do anything and more. I held her hand. The grandfather clock struck one. A car passed by outside; I heard the sound of its engine, like a growling animal under the silence of a midnight sky. My mother looked infinitely sad.

"Stay with me," she begged.

So I did. I stayed with her. It rained until three a.m., then stopped for an hour as water froze across the streets, and at about four in the morning, snow began to fall. I stayed with her until morning bloomed through the windows. We slept together, sitting on the stairs, our hands intertwined, the rhythm of our breaths synchronizing in sleep. She woke before me, and when I opened my eyes she was already gone.

Chapter 21

*C*hristmas Eve.

It was neither silent nor holy. The train roared with conversation and merriment, and I could feel tonight's latex gloves, safe in an interior pocket of my coat, pressing up against my chest. I didn't have Maggie's present with me; my hands were empty and cold. I didn't see the point in bringing it. She would never get the chance to open it, anyway.

I couldn't tell you if the train was mostly full or if it was empty, or whether it was cold or it was warm, or whether I sat alone or with someone else, because quite honestly I wasn't paying attention. I was near the door with my hands folded over my small purse in my lap, and I was thinking too intently to register much around me except for how many stops there were until I had to get off. You'd think I'd remember something as important as that train ride. But I didn't. I just didn't.

I was sad. I didn't think I would be sad. Logically I knew that she had to die. She had started a chain of events that sent me sliding. She had begun everything; she would end everything. I had to kill her in order to leave it all behind me. If I didn't, she might make me forget how I was, revert to how I had been before, when I had gone to meet Cherry.

I had taken Michael's challenge, and I couldn't turn away from it. It had to be that way. Unlike Maggie and so many others, I had a *purpose*. There were things that I was meant to do, had to do. There were rules. I made a decision and I killed; there were no exceptions, and that was just the way things worked. Maggie was no different from the rest, because I couldn't let her be, for the sake of my own sanity.

But even though I knew that much, the familiar lethargy of sadness settled over me. In the traitorous part of me that was still self-loathing, I didn't want Maggie to die.

But even though that corner of me hated the thought, I knew she had to.

Looking back on it, I realized she had been the root of everything.

She had been the catalyst to set things in motion. She had made me her friend and led me to be enemies with Michael. It was her fault that I had taken such a stand against him—without her influence, Michael and I could have been friends, or at least passive strangers. This relationship with Michael she had created for me had led me to murder. And that murder had led me to half madness.

It all began with her. She was to blame.

I was sure of it.

In every inch of me, down to my last molecule, in every thought, in every iota of my being, I was so sure.

With Cherry, before, I hadn't been sure, and that had been my downfall. I had been so uncertain. I wouldn't waver now, wouldn't waver, not even as Maggie breathed her last shuddering breath.

Michael's letter, cut and trimmed so it was small enough to fit, was folded in a heavy, ornate locket around my neck.

I felt like crying, but I couldn't.

Sometimes I ask myself, "What does it mean to be me?"

Whenever I ask the question, it just stares back at me. There is never any answer. Just a silence. What does it mean to be me? I don't know. Maybe that's just it. Maybe it doesn't mean anything. Maybe that's the answer. Maybe all I am is emptiness, is nothing.

As I sat on the train on the evening of December 24, all I felt like was nothing.

♦ ◊ ♦

When Maggie said "party," what she really meant was something more like "carnival." Her extended family must really have been fantastic to pull a party out of a hat like this.

It was visible and audible from blocks away. I walked from the train—a rather slow, cold, desolate walk—to her house. It was a bit out of the way, and the street was more open than most of London, with trees and alleys and patches of frosted grass between the town houses so they weren't just crunched up to one another. Much of the neighborhood was quiet, eating dinner or sitting around cozy indoor fires, but Maggie's house—midsize to large, white, and bland, just about as exciting as oatmeal—was lit up with Christmas lights like fireworks and filled with laughter. Its cheerfulness was almost intimidating. I stood outside it for a few minutes, just staring at it. I didn't quite want to go in. I had never been one for large crowds.

I took my phone out of my pocket, considered texting Maggie to meet me outside so I didn't have to brave the crowd alone. But then I put it back. I wasn't sure I wanted to have any permanent record of the fact that I had been talking to her. Not tonight at least.

I lingered on the sidewalk, watching figures pass by the window. Tall men, well-dressed women. All of them saying something, their mouths moving incessantly. It was strange. I had never imagined Maggie as a person who knew people like this.

The air chilled me. Faint wisps of snow and ice were tossed up from the sidewalk by the breeze, brushing my cheek, frosting my eyelashes. I didn't want to go inside. I hesitated. A deep feeling sank over me. Maggie would die. I choked on my breath. Maggie would die. I took a step away from the house. Maggie would die.

There was no use in delaying it.

I made myself walk forward. Up toward the house. The sound of voices and music grew louder as I grew closer. The muddled noises turned clearer—I could hear individual people now, and the sound of a trumpet and guitar, playing on the radio, within the noise. The sounds emerged into clarity. And closer, and closer.

And then I heard the sound of a door opening, and then Maggie's voice, behind a tall white fence that protruded from the side of the house, fencing off a small garden next to it.

"Come on, stupid dog," she said affectionately. I heard the patter of paws and the clinking of a dog collar as Maggie and the dog came out into the snow. I didn't know she had a dog. I changed course, away from the door and toward the gate, with a grin I forced onto my lips.

"Maggie!" I called.

"Kit, is that you?"

"Yeah, it's me."

"You made it!"

"I did."

"Is your mom here?"

"Nah, she couldn't make it, unfortunately."

"Oh, that's too bad."

"She's having dinner with some friends, so it's fine," I lied.

"Wait a second, I'll let you in," she said. I heard her walk over to the gate. After a few seconds she opened it slightly, just wide enough for me to get in without the dog escaping. I slid through the gap and into a small, quaint garden. The far end of it, covered in Astroturf, was apparently the dog's area. I watched the dog—a small, white, fluffy thing with legs so short you could hardly see them—walking around down there for a few distracted seconds, and then I turned back to Maggie.

"You've got quite a party here."

"Yeah, it is a bit big for such short notice," she said sheepishly. "But that's my family for you, I guess."

We were standing next to a window. The curtains were closed. Thick, dark curtains. The windows of the house next door were closed too, and we couldn't see any other windows on her house from where we stood.

I looked her in the eyes and forced myself to smile.

I think I had been wishing, in my heart of hearts, that it wouldn't work, that it wouldn't be perfect. But it was. My luck was too good. Nothing I could do about it.

No turning back now.

There was a small step in front of the door, which was hanging slightly ajar. I sat down, putting my head in my hands. I sighed.

"Something wrong?" Maggie asked, sitting down next to me.

"What?"

"You seem sort of unhappy."

"It's not the best day."

"Why? It's Christmas Eve, you should be happy."

A pang ran through my heart.

But it had to end.

"Christmas Eve," I mused.

"I love Christmas Eve. It's always so cheerful. With the presents and everything. Everybody's together, and everyone eats so much"—she giggled—"and feels sick after dinner since they eat so much."

I pulled up my knees and put my forehead against them so my hair rustled against my cheekbones. Inside, there was music. Faint, wafting music. I recognized the song. It was Cherry Rose's song, a new, slow song of hers that had been gaining popularity recently.

> *"Where have you gone,*
> *Where will you go,*
> *Where is your home,*
> *Tell me, can I know . . ."*

I imagined her singing it, red lips moving rhythmically, glistening, glittering in the stage light. I imagined her on a pedestal, with everyone watching her. A silhouette. Just a shadow in the dark.

"What would you do if you knew you were going to die?" I asked wearily, my voice muffled. I was speaking into my legs.

"What?" Maggie yelped. "Oh God, Kit, are you dying? Please say you're not dying."

I laughed, darkly amused.

"No, I'm not dying."

Not exactly.

> *"I want to hold you close,*
> *Hold you in my arms,*
> *But when you are here,*
> *You always do me harm. . . ."*

"I'm just having a weird day," I clarified. "I'm fine." Under my breath, I repeated, a second time, barely audible, "I'm fine. . . ."

There was an uncomfortable pause. Maggie was thinking.

She put a hand on my shoulders carefully. I shivered under her touch. I felt the patterns of her fingertips like a firebrand.

"We've been through a lot this past year, haven't we?" she said. I could feel her wistfulness. She exhaled slowly. She enjoyed our camaraderie, just like I did, our soft friendship.

"It's been a strange year," I agreed.

She laughed. "That's one way to put it."

"You've changed this year."

She shrugged. "I've grown. We all have to grow up sometime."

"Yeah."

"Are you sure you don't want to tell me what's wrong?"

"A few minutes. A few minutes, then I'll tell you."

"Okay." She rubbed my shoulder and let go.

"But really, what would you do? If you knew you were going to die?"

"Well, I already know I'm going to die. Everyone dies."

"I mean soon."

She laughed again. "But I'm not going to die soon."

I hated this part of her. The insipid, emotionless part of her. She didn't understand what I was asking.

Michael had seen this part of her as well, hadn't he? Hadn't he written about it?

She can't understand anything you want to tell her—she pretends to understand, but when you really need her to understand, she just runs away like nobody matters but her.

Sometimes it seemed like all Maggie knew how to do was run. In some ways, she had changed so much—in some ways, she hadn't changed at all.

"Never mind," I said.

The silence was heavy.

"Really, what's wrong?"

Snow covered everything beautifully. It dusted treetops. At the other end of the garden, the dog rolled in it.

> *"Your red-stained lips draw me to you—*
> *Your dark deep words, I know they're untrue—*
> *Your heart encircles mine*
> *And squeezes it tight*
> *I want to see a sign—"*

Snow over everything. Quiet. Deep. I had always liked snow. It always made things seem less real.

> *"But even with the dark and pain*
> *Even though things can never be the same,*
> *Yes, you know it's true—*
> *I still love you."*

I stood up and looked at the dog.

"Come on," I called. "Come on." With a yap, the dog came running. Maggie smiled as it ran around my legs. I reached down and petted it, and then I opened the door to let it inside. It went in happily, nails clicking against the hardwood floor. I closed the door again.

I stared at the white door. It needed new paint. It wasn't exactly worn, but it had a faded feeling to it, a tired feeling. Light leaked out from the window from my left, warm, making the white paint seem almost yellow.

I shivered.

It was cold.

Maggie was wearing a dress that wasn't warm enough for the weather. It was red, like blood, like Cherry's dress on the CD cover. She stood, her curly dark hair bouncing, a half smile on her lips.

"What are you doing?" she asked.

I stared at the door. I found the faint whorls of wood beneath the paint. I traced my eyes along each one, memorizing every line.

"Kit?"

I closed my eyes.

It was time.

I remembered the door, every inch. And then I made myself forget it, forget everything, and then I became someone else.

I breathed out. I smelled peppermint in the air.

Something *burned* through my skin, illuminating me from the inside out.

Just *burned*.

I opened my eyes.

"No," I said, "That's not my name."

"Yes it is," Maggie said, as if she knew everything, and took a step toward me.

I turned.

I would end this now.

"No," I said, "I'm not Kit."

She stared at me, unseeing.

I smiled.

And burned and burned and burned.

"I'm Diana," I said.

I'm Diana.

◆ ◇ ◆

I walked in the front door with a smile. My gloves were quietly buried in a corner of the neighbor's garden, washed out with their hose so none of my fingerprints would stick to the inside of the fingers if the police somehow found them. I had to go to the party; there was definitely surveillance footage of me coming here, somewhere along the way, and if I were caught on camera again, leaving so soon without joining the festivities, it would look incredibly suspicious. It was only natural that I would be at the party, anyway. Maggie was my friend, after all. There was nothing suspicious in it.

I couldn't go home. I couldn't just run. Running was too simple. Things were more complicated than that. I had to face the moment.

Right?

Oh, I didn't know. My thoughts were a blurred jumble.

I was stainless. My locket was empty.

I walked around the room casually, drinking ice water. They would find her eventually. It was only a matter of time.

I found a red armchair and sat down. I watched the people around me. They laughed, talked, moved.

A scream rang out.

I leaned back in the chair.

She was found.

◆ ◇ ◆

Oh God I can still feel it

The crushing, crunching, slicing, bleeding, death beneath my hands

Oh God, the hypnotism of it

The utter hypnotism, the merciless slaughter

The sickness and flattening weight of what I can do and what I have done—

Oh God I can taste it in my mouth, the thrill of the chase, the satisfaction of the kill, like a lion and a gazelle—

Oh God

The joy of it, the horrible joy, because I've fallen so far and I've let myself enjoy it, but I'm not supposed to enjoy it, I'm supposed to admire it from a distance, like a piece of art on a bookshelf but I can't

Because

Oh God

The paradise of death, that *crushing slicing burning* sensation

That beautiful sensation

I'm lost and I don't mind because I am so alive

Because I am a murderer

And I, Diana, enjoy the memory.

Chapter 22

We are all told from the very beginning that we are important. From the moment we can first understand words and perhaps even before then, we are continuously reassured that we have a place in things, that we have a part to play. The human race as a whole is a hopeful species. Of course there are exceptions. Some forgotten children, ones who slip through the cracks. And not everyone is told that they will be important in the same way. Not everyone will be a doctor, or a lawyer. Some people grow up believing that their importance is to love someone fully. Some people grow up believing that their importance is to be loved fully. Perhaps the reason my mailbox was always secret was that the people who visited it came to believe that keeping the secret was a piece of their importance. Maybe I was always given murders because they all thought that contributing to my legend was their importance. But we are all taught, in general, in some way, that someday our worth will be revealed. Someday we will be justified. Someday we will be free.

But the cold truth is that not everyone is meant to be important.

As we grow older, more and more people slip through the cracks, lose that hopefulness. In a way, losing hope and losing importance are the same thing. It is that youthful vibrance, that eternal longing and believing, that makes youth so important—if you grow old and lose that without finding another way to be important, you will slip away, fall into insignificance, like one sheet of paper. You may be useful, but you will never stand out from the crowd. You cannot look at a piece of paper and say, "I remember you." You never can.

I have had the privilege of being important. Or at least I have believed myself important. That's the trick, isn't it? Being able to tell when something is your imagination and being able to tell when something is truth. There is a fine line between them sometimes, a line you have to tread carefully, because there are monsters on either side. I have believed myself important. I have believed I had a greater place in things. I have held lives in my hands. But I still feel lost. Because I cannot know for *sure* that I was important. Perhaps in a hundred or a hundred and fifty years, if they still remember my name, I might be sure that I was important—but I plan to be long gone by then, so I will never know.

Perhaps it was all false justification. Perhaps I was simply fooling myself. Perhaps I was never anything more. Perhaps the people I killed had no meaning, and everything was for nothing. Perhaps I repeated the same things to myself over and over again until I convinced myself that they were true. Maybe I was never a higher power and murder was never the answer to the disconnectedness of the people, and maybe I was the one who was disconnected. Maybe I just needed an excuse to make things right, and my mom offered up such a tantalizing one and I just ate it up because I needed to.

But people still remember and even fear Jack the Ripper, don't they? More than a hundred years later, they still remember his name. Maybe they'll remember mine. The Perfect Killer. It really is a good name, I think. It has a ring to it.

But was it *worth* anything?

That's the hopelessness of it. The openness of it. The part of it I can never understand.

I am afraid of ambiguity and certainty and permanence and impermanence.

And so is everybody else.

Sometimes I imagine we're all like paper stars, folded up and gathered together, each of us convinced that we are glittering and celestial, each of us bent into a shape so we believe we're something we're not. If you gather up a thousand paper stars, you get a wish, they say. We're like that. Each of us is convinced we're special, but we are only worth anything when taken together.

I truly want to believe I'm special, and sometimes I can. But other times I feel like one of a thousand paper stars, careening through life, tumbling through reality, one in a thousand, one in ten thousand, just like the rest, like one sheet of paper, forgotten, insignificant.

♦ ◊ ♦

I sit in a police station—not the Chelsea station with the dog statue outside the door, but a station nearer to Maggie's murder. It is night. I'm in a waiting room. I'm on a plush green sofa with a few old pillows, waiting my turn. I was brought here three hours ago and told to stay; and so I stay.

Everything is silent. Outside the waiting room window, I can see the offices and hear the sound of the news on the television. Someone from somewhere has committed suicide, jumping off a bridge into the Thames. The police officers move through wordlessly. Some are in uniforms, some are in plainclothes, and all of them look halfway asleep.

Everything has faded now, the passion and the grief and everything else besides. I'm not Diana any longer. I'm Kit, and I'm alone. And so tired.

I'm still dressed up for the party, dressed up with nowhere to go. It's too hot in here. I've stripped off my jacket and my scarf, but I'm wearing long sleeves so I'm still hot. My hair is sweaty and pasted to the back of my neck. I'm bored. I watch the police officers moving back and forth, back and forth like ants. My eyes move rhythmically, and I try to keep myself from falling asleep.

I look for Alex. I don't see him now, but I know he's here. He's already visited the crime scene and come back. I saw him passing in front of the window a while ago, but he didn't see me when I waved to him. He had a harrowed look on his face. Naturally. I keep looking for him, because I have nothing better to do.

I hear the heating switch on. I breathe deeply as warm air floats through the air vent to my left.

I wait for my turn to be talked to.

Eventually the door creaks open. I smile pleasantly, but not too pleasantly. I smile like I'm scared, or sad. Alex walks in, scattered and unfocused, and there is no electricity in the air now—just dead silence. Across from me are two armchairs. Wordlessly, staring at the floor, Alex takes a seat in one of them. He rubs his eyes. The door falls shut behind him.

"God, Kit, you really have a knack for showing up at the wrong place at the wrong time," he says after a minute. He looks me in the eyes and sighs.

"Sorry," I say.

"It's not my problem, it's yours," he tells me. "A bunch of people think you're guilty now. *I* know it's ridiculous, but they don't. Even your philosophy teacher—what's her name—"

"Dr. Marcell," I offer.

"Even she's saying you're guilty. And a lot of people are starting to believe it. Even though you're—you. A teenage girl."

I don't say a word.

"Kit, are you listening?" he asks.

I nod. "Sorry."

He looks at me and realizes I might actually be suffering. He puts a hand on my forearm; the touch makes me shudder.

"Kit, are you okay?" he asks softly.

I shake my head. "No."

"She was your friend, wasn't she?"

"Yes."

"How do you feel?"

"Numb," I say blandly. "Just numb."

"Do you want something to drink, eat, anything?"

"No."

"You should have something."

"I don't want anything."

A series of faces flashes before my eyes. Mom, Cherry, Alex, Michael's mother, Dr. Marcell, even Louisa, the stupid secretary. The ones who are left.

There is a silence.

"Please keep talking. I don't like the quiet," I say.

Alex shrugs. "What about?"

"Anything."

He studies my face.

"You try so hard, Alex," I say distractedly.

Alex nods.

"I'm numb," I hear myself say. "I'm numb, I'm numb."

"Are you okay?" he asks again.

"No," I repeat. I need to fill the space with words. I talk quickly, barely recognizing what is coming out of my mouth as my own voice.

"They think I'm guilty?" I ask suddenly, even though we're talking about something else now. Uncomfortably, he nods.

"Some of them are really convinced."

"Will I go to jail?"

He shakes his head, but I see hesitation in the movement.

"They don't have any real evidence on you. They just have a bunch of circumstantial evidence right now, nothing else. You'll be fine."

I wonder absently what it would be like to be someone else. Anyone else.

"How's my mom?"

Alex shrugs. "She's having a hard time of it. She's worried about you."

"How so?"

"Oh, you know . . . crying a lot. Went over there earlier, just to make sure she was fine. She let me in but wouldn't talk to me. Just . . . sat in her bedroom and cried. She kept talking about cards, or something. Wasn't making much sense."

"I'm so sorry," I say vaguely.

"Are you apologizing to your mother?" Alex asks uncertainly.

"It doesn't matter," I reply.

Another pause.

"Was she nice?" Alex asks, taking his hand off my knee.

"Who, my mom?"

"No . . . Maggie."

I nod. "Very nice."

"I hate watching nice people die."

I laugh loudly and bitterly. The sound startles him.

"But that's your job, isn't it?"

He shrugs. "Well, sometimes mean people die, and that's not as bad."

I realize that I'm close to tears.

"I'm numb," I say again, quivering.

"Oh, Kit," he murmurs.

I'm numb.

I'm numb and I'm afraid.

I'm numb.

For a moment he looks distracted.

"What is it?" I ask.

"Nothing. I just keep thinking about that party, just keep running through it again and again. That image, the Christmas tree and the presents underneath it and the lights and the buffet and the empty cups on tables, all just deserted when the police evacuated the crime scene—I can't get it out of my head. I don't really know why. Maybe it's because it was just such a horrific place for a murder. And the fact that the murderer was probably a guest, or at least was posing as one—terrible. All those people, her family and everything, gathered together to watch her die."

"Alex, do *you* think I'm guilty?"

He shakes his head. "Of course not. You're just a kid, and that girl was your friend. You could never kill her. I'll make sure everyone else understands that too. There's no way on earth you could be a murderer. Holding you here is just stupid. They're holding you only because they don't have any decent leads."

He whispers the word "murderer" as if it is a curse.

"So what happens now?"

He sighs and leans down to put his head in his hands.

"I don't know, Kit, I really don't know."

I look around the room at the pale walls, at the long green sofa; the whole place feels empty. This room could be anywhere, and I feel like I'm in limbo, floating.

"I just can't stop thinking about it," Alex breathes.

"I don't like it here," I say lamely, like a child.

Alex sighs again, more heavily this time. He looks angry, but not at me. He's angry at the rest of the world, at the people who can't see the same good that he sees in me. I feel the sudden urge to reach out and touch him, to share strength with him, but I don't—halfway because I don't want to cross that boundary now, and halfway because I have no strength left to share.

"I know. I'm sorry." Alex shakes his head.

"How much longer do I have to stay? I'm tired. I want to go home," I whine.

I know I sound like a child, but I can't bring myself to care.

Slowly, like he's melting, Alex stands and looks down at me. "Wait here," he tells me, as if I have any other choice. He walks to the door and opens it with a long creak, looking out into the area outside, at the tired police officers passing back and forth. Then he shuts it and turns around, pressing his back against the wall.

"They haven't charged you with anything, and they don't have enough evidence to actually hold you, you know," Alex says quietly, guiltily. "Technically speaking, you can go. They *want* you to stay until they figure out what to do with you, of course . . . but you can just leave here, if you like. They'll probably call you back eventually for questioning. But you can go for now."

I stare up at him dully. "I'm guessing they didn't want you to actually tell me that."

He shakes his head and laughs drily. "No."

For a moment I say nothing. I listen to the muted sounds of footsteps and the television, and I focus on breathing.

"Thank you," I say eventually.

It takes all my energy to stand. When I manage it, I feel wavering and weak. Somehow I make my way to the door, and there I pause to look up at Alex, who is staring at the ceiling.

"Thank you," I breathe again, and he nods *you're welcome*. His eyes tell me that he is thinking intently about something else, and also that he is sad about something or other. He looks confused, but I don't think that confusion has anything to do with his belief in my innocence.

I am too tired to wonder about his thoughts, though perhaps I should.

On the way out of the police station, I remain in the shadows. I hunch my back and make myself small, digging my hands into my coat pockets even though my hands aren't cold. No one sees me. I am a chameleon, and as always, my luck keeps me safe.

I pause on the curb outside the building. It is snowing slightly, a light cold snow, floating down from the sky like ash. I reach out my hand to catch snowflakes on my fingertips, and they melt as they touch my skin. I look up to see if the stars are visible, but they aren't. They are hidden behind flat clouds and the glowing miasma of London's light pollution.

And then I look up into the windows of the police station to see if I can find Alex in one of them—and yes, there he is, three stories up, silhouetted in a window, pacing back and forth, staring at his feet. Poor Alex. I've twisted him around so much. I've played with his mind and his emotions, poor, poor Alex. I should never have spoken to him; the moment I first saw him, I should have run. I could have saved him so much pain. Now look at him. A perfect puppet. A plaything. An accessory to my will, letting me free from the police station, useful at last.

He's unusually anxious tonight, but I suppose it only makes sense. The snow falls. My breath forms clouds in the air in front of my face.

I begin to wonder what happens now—is it all over, will I be caught, can I be allowed to continue, can I even remain free, let alone continue killing, where will I go from here, where can I run from this lonely place—but I can't think about it. Thoughts in general escape me. I walk down the street in a haze.

I wonder uncertainly if this night is my last gasp of freedom. I feel as if it is the end of something. But no, I remember, Alex, Alex, useful Alex, he will keep me safe, won't he, because he believes in me. . . .

The streetlamps, pedestrians, and cars pass me, but I don't really see them. I can't form a real coherent thought until I board the train back to Chelsea, taking a seat near the window.

The train, now, is full of the odd ones, the ones who travel through the city near midnight. The stragglers, the drunken youths, the old men, the lonely people going home alone on Christmas Eve, or Christmas Day, whatever it is now. There is an old man across the aisle from me with hands covered in wrinkles like valleys. I watch those hands absently. I wonder what they mean.

And then everything shatters into emotion and comprehension.

It feels suddenly as if I have been punched in the chest.

I can't breathe. All the air is gone from my lungs and I am choking, doubled over, gasping for life. I touch my knees with my forehead. The man with wrinkled hands stands in alarm, takes a few steps toward me, asks me a question I don't register for a few seconds.

"Are you all right?"

It takes me a few more seconds to find the breath to answer. The train is still sitting at the station, hissing like an angry cat. The doors have been open for a long time, I think—but maybe they haven't, really. Time seems to be passing slowly, and everything feels stretched out.

"I'm fine," I reply weakly, even though I'm not. I continue gasping, and the man, uncertain as to what he should be doing, sits down again. Three rows in front of me, a drunk couple is paying no attention to my plight.

Eventually, I calm myself. I force myself to breathe normally. I sit up again and lean back against the seat.

Maggie is dead.

I don't know if minutes have passed, or seconds, or a fraction of a second. It feels like years.

I killed her.

"Happy Christmas," the old man says pathetically.

Maggie is never coming back. I'll never speak to her again.

Four weeks ago we ate ice cream by the Thames.

I told her she was loved.

"Happy Christmas to you," I reply.

The doors finally slide shut and the train moves on.

I think about London. Down here, in the underground,

things are dark, but I can imagine the world above. I can imagine the Christmas lights and lights from house windows and streetlights and lights from faraway planes and helicopters. Everything is light, is brilliance. Everything except for me. I am free, allowed to walk the streets of my city, by the Thames, across my Waterloo Bridge, if I want—but it isn't enough.

I killed Maggie Bauer.

Did she deserve to die?

Chapter 23

When I walk through the door of the polished white town house, my mother is waiting.

She isn't just standing, though; she waits in motion, in frenzied action. There are six suitcases in the front hallway; two of them are packed and closed, and the rest are open. She moves in and out of the kitchen and living room, carrying dishes and trinkets–vases, coffee-table books, quirky coffee mugs–and shoves them all into the bags anywhere they fit. She is wearing a sagging pink bathrobe over jeans and a white blouse, and no shoes. Her pale hair is crazed.

Her eyes are red, but she isn't crying any longer. She is steely, determined. She barely glances at me as I enter.

"We're lucky your father isn't here tonight. It makes

things much simpler. I've packed your bag. Help me pack the rest."

"What?" I reply numbly. "Why?"

She pauses to look at me in disbelief.

"We're running," she says, with an implied *of course*.

"Why?"

"You know why. It's because you went too far, Kit. Got too cocky."

"I–"

"You killed Maggie Bauer. I should have stopped you from going out tonight, I should have stopped you hunting her a long time ago, but I didn't. It was a stupid thing for me to do. Stupid, stupid. I don't know why I didn't–I was just far too passive. So you killed her, and we're not safe any longer. Living in a house of cards, didn't I tell you, living in a house of cards . . ."

Strangely, faced with danger and dire excitement, she looks more alive and beautiful than she has looked for years. Or perhaps it isn't so strange after all.

"Yes, but Alex–"

"Alex isn't a miracle worker. He can't keep you safe. Not now. You're obviously right in the center of these murders. Anyone can see it. Except him, apparently. Idiot."

She begins to run up the steep stairs, taking them two at a time, and I remember that her safety and freedom are on the line just as much as mine are. I run to the bottom of the stairs, fling myself halfway over the banister.

"We don't have to run. Alex *will* keep us safe, he will,

can't you see?! He's the one who let me out of the police station, Mom. He's looking out for me," I yell up at her. She just laughs.

"Stop thinking like a child," she yells back. "You can't always be safe. Sometimes, you just have to admit defeat."

"He's in charge of the investigation, and he really believes that I'm innocent. They don't have any evidence. Everything is just coincidence. They can't arrest me."

"He may be in charge, but he's not the only one working on the case, and he's only an honorary leader. He hasn't got any real authority, especially not lately. When push comes to shove, he can't help." She runs back down the stairs with a thick photo album in her hands and slips slightly on the last stair. I reach out my arms to catch her, but she doesn't need my help. She rebalances herself on her own.

"But he *can*, Mom. He *can*. Despite everything, people listen to him—he's just like that. They'll follow him."

My mom tosses the photo album into a nearby bag and grips my shoulder tightly.

"But you can't be sure," she hisses. "We can't stay here any longer, because we can't be sure of anything anymore."

She begins to zip up the bags. I still stand limply by the stairs, watching her work.

"Where will we go?"

"A car is coming to pick us up in ten minutes. We'll take a ferry to France—the train doesn't run on Christmas—and from there we'll go to—I don't know. We'll figure it out. We just can't stay here. We've really got to hurry, Kit—the boat leaves in two hours, and it'll take us at least an hour and a half to get to Dover. And there isn't another one for hours. Hours is too long. If we miss the boat, they'll realize we're gone and come for us."

"What about Dad?"

"What about him? He probably won't realize we've gone," she replies bitterly.

I hesitate.

I suddenly imagine him coming home to an empty house, opening the door, walking upstairs, going to his room, only hours later realizing that my mom and I are gone—only days later realizing that we are never returning. An anticlimactic end. Quiet, laced with silent loneliness.

I feel sorry for him. And it's odd to me that regretful sympathy is the emotion I leave him with, given all the anger I've felt toward him over the years. Or perhaps not so odd, once I start to think about it. After all, my anger always stemmed from the fact that I loved him, and the fact that he never seemed to love me the same way.

Before, when I talked to him on the phone, I felt as if I were saying something larger than the word good-bye. And now I realize what it was that I was truly saying—because I think I knew the truth, in some part of me, even then. I knew that I wouldn't see him again, not really. I might see him again as the Perfect Killer. But I would never see him again as simple Kit Ward, the girl he could have known and loved, his only daughter.

That afternoon on the phone, I didn't just say "good-bye."

I said, "Good-bye forever." I said, "I wish you well." I said, "I love you, despite everything, underneath it all."

"I don't want to go," I whimper to my mom. She whirls and looks up at me with scorn.

"Well, I don't want to go either. It's your fault we have to go. You're unstable, Kit, always have been. And you've never been a very good secret keeper."

Her words hurt me, and her scorn melts slowly into pity.

"I never should have begun this," she murmurs restlessly, and goes back to zipping up one of the bags, which is so full it looks as if it is about to explode. "Go upstairs and grab anything from your room that you want. There's a little room left in your bag. And get the letters. We'll burn them—they're dangerous."

For a moment I stare at her, trying to find a way out, but there is nothing. So I turn around and run up the stairs, past the beautiful photographs in their cold frames. Up to my scarlet-and-cream bedroom, where I tear open the dressers and the cabinets, looking for things I want to take with me. My mother has already packed up everything that was on top of my dressers and tables. I stuff the letters from the false bottom of the drawer into a backpack along with my box of too-small latex gloves, grab my makeup from the bathroom and a pair of shoes that my mother didn't take from the closet. And then I stand in the middle of the room and look around and realize that there is nothing more that I want.

My room is impersonal, empty. I have no reminders or memories. No souvenirs or ticket stubs. It is all utility.

For a moment, this makes me sad.

Downstairs, I know, my mom is moving around, grabbing objects and stuffing them into suitcases, banging through the house, but I am on the top floor and hear none of that. The air is silent. I breathe in the heavy scent of potpourri.

And then I turn and leave the room. I descend the stairs with an even rhythm, one foot after the other after the other like a drumbeat marching through my mind.

When I reach the bottom of the staircase, my mom is waiting impatiently with a box of matches. She grabs my things out of my arms, takes the letters out of my halfway-unzipped backpack, and shoves them into my hands with the matches.

"Put down your stuff, take the letters into the kitchen, and burn them," she says sharply. "Quickly. We haven't got forever."

I hesitate anyway. Her eyes narrow. She shoves me toward the kitchen door, and I stumble. "Quickly!" she snarls.

I scramble into the kitchen. I lose sight of her, but from the hallway I hear the sounds of the things I brought down from upstairs being frantically packed away. I lose track of what it is that I'm supposed to be doing for a half second; when I remember, I dash toward the cabinet.

I find a large metal bowl, slam it haphazardly down against the counter, and drop the letters inside. I try to light a match. My hands are shaking, and I break the first one. The second one lights, though, and I toss it into the bowl. It takes a moment for the match to begin its work.

And then the letters begin to burn.

It begins with the edges. They blacken and crumble inward, and flame licks away from them hot and orange-bright. The fire grows more quickly than I ever imagined it could. It is ravenous. In less than a minute, the letters become little more than ash.

For a moment, I am aware that my mother is standing in the kitchen doorway, watching, but then she turns away, as if she cannot bear to look.

I hear the loud crunching of car tires over thin ice on the street, just outside. It must be our car, come to sweep us away—a few minutes early, but oh well, it isn't as if I have anything to say good-bye to in this house.

I stare into the bowl, stare at the black ash simmering with embers of hungry flame, at the tendrils of smoke drifting upward. This was my life, I realize. These letters were my center, my purpose. And now they're gone. So quickly, so simply—just a spark, that was all it took. I can't see anything other than the flame, can't hear anything but the faint crackling of burning paper. This was my life, and now it's gone.

Eventually I turn away from the bowl and leave the fire alone. It'll just burn away by itself, anyway. I don't want to think about it anymore.

I feel distant, detached.

So detached that I don't notice Alex in the slightest until I step through the doorway into the hall and look toward the door.

Because there he is, plain as day, with his hands shoved into his pockets, tracking snow across the carpet, hair swept back from his face and slicked with melting snowflakes. The car outside must have been his.

His sudden appearance makes my heart beat quickly for reasons I cannot discern, or at least don't want to admit to myself. I wonder why he's here now, so soon after we spoke at the police station.

He looks at me quietly, and his dark eyes seem to be glowing from the inside out with some strange emotion that I can't identify. My mother has shoved the bags into the hall closet so he can't see them, and leans against the wall three feet to my left, probably staring at me as well. But I don't see her. I see only Alex.

"Hello," he says quietly.

"Hello," I reply. "Why are you here?"

"I've come to talk to you."

"Why? We've just talked," I ask listlessly.

"I just . . . I've got something important to say."

"What, have you come to confess your love to me or something?" I joke, and he laughs, but it's a pitiful, joyless noise.

The clock on the wall strikes one. I feel my mother's eyes on me, begging me to send him away. We need him to leave before the car arrives to pick us up and he starts asking questions as to why it's here so late at night, tonight of all nights.

"It's late," I say. "I'm tired. Can't this wait until tomorrow?"

"I–" He pauses uncomfortably. He doesn't know what to say. He really does want to talk to me right now. And I want to talk to him too. So badly. I want to say good-bye to him, even if he can't know I'm leaving forever, even if I can't so much as whisper the actual word "good-bye."

My mother's glare makes my skin prickle.

Headlights gleam from a distant street corner as a car arrives at a stop sign. This one absolutely *has* to be our car, my mother's and mine. Who else would be driving around here at this time of night on Christmas? Alex needs to leave, and now. And I know my mother would rather that I didn't go with him–but this is Alex, after all.

I don't think he'll go without me, anyway.

"All right," I murmur, giving in. "Let's go somewhere, let's walk. I need to clear my head, anyway. There's still a million things I can't stop thinking about."

He smiles slightly, not a happy smile, but a satisfied one.

"Really, can't this wait until tomorrow? It's one in the morning," my mother chimes in uneasily, looking skittish. Alex is hesitant.

"I'm sorry about the time, Mrs. Ward," he says, "but Kit and I have to talk."

My mother opens her mouth to say something more, but I shake my head to stop her.

"It's okay," I say softly. "He's my friend. Don't worry so much."

I know that my mother and I have to leave. I know that our car will pull up to the curb any minute now, ready to take us away, and I know we have to leave now if we are going to catch the ferry—but I can take a few minutes to talk with Alex for the very last time, surely I can have that much.

The car comes closer; we've got to leave now, or it'll arrive at the house before I have a chance to lead him away.

My mother looks like she's about to scream. I ignore her. She wants to pull me back and control me, but she can't. She never could. I walk toward Alex, who I know means me no harm. His presence is comforting, warm, secure.

He has given me my freedom. He will keep me safe.

"Thank you," he whispers, and I still can't decipher the emotion in his eyes.

The next few minutes are a blank. I remember nothing. I assume Alex and I walk out the front door and along the street, looking for a place to talk, and I assume the car pulls up to the house just as I lead Alex around the corner so he doesn't see it arrive, and I assume that after that, I just begin to follow his lead like a marionette—but I can't remember a thing. Not the sound of my footsteps or the colors of the Christmas lights, not the silent houses or the dark shadows of ice-frosted trees, not even the numb trusting peace that overtakes me as Alex and I walk together in silence.

Chapter 24

*T*he next thing I comprehend is the park.

Alex and I stand underneath a large oak tree in a place where the snow never touches the ground; the tree catches the snowflakes in its arms before they fall all the way down. The night is unfathomably deep. We are in a park I don't recognize on a street I've never seen, in a place where houses sleep soundly, peacefully expecting presents in the morning.

We are about five feet from each other, and both of us look up toward the cloudy sky between the bare branches of the oak. There is a small wooden bench to my right, his left, but neither of us moves to sit. Five feet off, a ragged snowman stands like a sentinel.

I am the first one to speak.

"It's good to see you. I know—I know we just saw each other, but it's good to see you again," I say, though I don't think that's a normal thing to be saying in this situation, whatever this situation is. He shuffles his feet absently for a second before replying.

"Good to see you too," he replies hesitantly, sadly.

"This has been a god-awful Christmas, really, hasn't it?" I say softly.

Alex looks so tired, and it's my fault.

Watching him, I almost want to cry. He looks like a wounded soldier, a part of a war too big for him. I want to walk toward him, take his hands, hold them tight. I want to soothe him without words. I want to turn my head upward, meet his eyes, press my forehead against his, and then—

No.

It can never be like that.

That's not how this story will end, no matter how much I wish it might. This story will finish with a finale that's not so fairy-tale.

"Yeah, god-awful," he mutters. There is too much space between us.

"Not one we'll forget anytime soon, I suppose."

He laughs wryly, and the sound surprises me.

"No," he says. "I don't think I'll ever forget it."

"Everything just seems sort of far away, doesn't it?" I murmur.

"Yes."

Alex stares at the ground, and I stare at him. And then for a moment his eyes flicker upward and meet mine, and my breath catches in my throat. The world around us vanishes. Hazel eyes stare into brown, brown into hazel. I can see nothing of his thoughts, and I wonder if he sees anything of mine. The air is sick with nervous silence. For a moment, it's as if time stands still just for the two of us.

Then he looks away again.

"It's terrible. It's all terrible. This whole business," I manage to say eventually.

"Yes, I can say with certainty that this has been the worst night of my entire life," he replies. He isn't bitter. He's just sad.

"Oh, surely you must have had some night sometime that was worse."

"No . . . this is it."

I laugh again, even though there still isn't anything funny.

"It'll get better. Things always get better. I'll help make things better."

He doesn't reply. I think he knows that I don't really believe what I'm saying.

If I can't have my fairy tale, it'd be nice if things could just stay like this, I think. I like things this way. And for an instant, I truly believe it can happen. And in his eyes, I can see the same emotion echoed. A hatred of change, a need for consistency and security.

And then I remember I don't have any time. I remember

the boat that I must catch in an hour and forty-five minutes, waiting at the dock with heat steaming against the windows, bright against the lapping darkness of the ocean.

"So, what did you want to talk about?" I ask.

He doesn't reply for a moment. He kicks a small pile of icy snow that makes a crunching noise as it sprays over the pavement. He looks as if he doesn't want to speak. I don't know why.

I think about how this silent peace in the air around us is only an illusion.

"I just kept thinking," Alex says softly, like he regrets it, beautiful, ancient, tired, eyes swirling with thought. I am silent, and he continues. "I just kept thinking about the house after the party."

Oh, so it's this again.

He's so earnest, so eager to do the right thing. Even now, in such a dark hour, he's still trying hopefully to solve whatever mystery he has imagined for himself, because he feels somehow that it is important. So this is why he wants me here—he wants to talk it out, he wants my advice and input. I am his confidante, his unbiased always friend. It only makes sense. My confusion clears.

"What about it?" I ask.

"I think I realized it, Kit. I realized what was wrong."

"And what's that?" I reply. I smile at him. He looks at me.

He doesn't smile back.

A pause.

A pause in which the world stands breathlessly still. The snow makes no noise, and no cars disturb the stillness of the air. Alex is motionless, and I don't breathe. He stares at me now, and there are so many things in his eyes I can't grasp.

He takes a step toward me.

"Ice blue," he says, as if he expects some sort of monumental reaction.

He doesn't get one. I say nothing, though I realize immediately what he's talking about.

I don't move, but beneath my skin I am suddenly chaotic.

I hadn't expected this sort of thing from him. I should have.

But no, this is okay. This is nothing. This is something I can talk my way out of. This is Alex who I'm dealing with, after all. My Alex.

"You know what I'm talking about, don't you?" he continues softly.

My expression reveals nothing.

"I don't have any clue."

It's a lie, of course.

"Blue. Ice blue. Blue wrapping paper, a box that fits a dress inside. Blue."

"I don't understand–"

He interrupts me in a voice frenzied with dismay and urgency.

"Your present for Maggie, Kit, it wasn't at the party. You

described what it looked like, you said it was wrapped in ice-blue wrapping paper, and there wasn't a present of that description anywhere at the party, not on the table with the rest of the guests' presents or under the tree with the presents from Maggie's family. It was nowhere. It just wasn't there."

He breathes heavily, and the world soaks in silence. His words make me feel as if I've just been punched in the chest.

"I forgot it at home, Alex," I say softly, reassuringly. "Why are you making such a big deal out of this? What's wrong?"

And for a moment he almost believes me. He almost believes that he is just like the rest, grasping at stupid straws. He *wants* to believe me, so badly. He studies my eyes, tries to find the honesty there. His gaze makes me uncomfortable.

And then he takes a step away and darkly whispers, "No."

I feel a deep irrational sense of betrayal.

Betrayal followed by fear.

"You don't forget things, Kit," he says. "No. You didn't forget. That's not like you. There was a reason you didn't bring it. And I'm afraid I know what it is."

He pauses and for a moment looks like he is breaking. The snowflakes brush the ground and disappear. Sudden painful cold permeates my heart.

He shudders and takes a deep, frenetic breath. His words blur together in a slurring half panic.

"You didn't bring the gift because there was no point,

and you never do anything that doesn't have a point. You didn't bring it because you knew she'd never get the chance to open it. It was unnecessary baggage."

And he's right, and there is no doubt in his eyes at all. He is made of steel.

I can't breathe.

No. This can't happen.

No.

He knows me far too well. He's finally put two and two together.

I am whirled into memory—

Once upon a time, worlds ago, I sat on the floor of the training room with my mother, slicked with sweat, content. Once upon a time I was a little girl. Once upon a time, on a sunny Tuesday afternoon, my mother hugged me and held me close, and I listened to the sound of her heartbeat. She told me she loved me. Later that evening she made me lemonade, and we had a picnic on the living room floor.

Once upon a time I loved wholeheartedly. Once upon a time I was more than a ghost, more than a wayward spirit. Once upon a time I was whole.

Once upon a time on a Tuesday afternoon, I lived.

But now the air is empty, and I think that moment occurred to me because it's simply just as far from the present moment as a moment can be. It's so, so far away from this desolate desert of a park, cold and empty under the orange-glowing streetlights—it exists in a seeming parallel universe where I never began any of this, in a universe where I live free.

The game has finished. It's all done.

Alex stares at me with something indescribable burning in his eyes.

I explode with emotion from the inside out.

I should have just stayed at home with my mother—I should have come up with a story about how tired I was, and I should have sent him away at any cost—I should have just run away with her when I had the chance—I never expected this. Not from him. Not from my Alex; I somehow imagined that we could go on forever in peace. But now the moment is here, and I should have gone with my mother, I should have just taken the ferry away from this place, so far away, because he won't keep me safe any longer, and I am running out of time, the boat will leave without us—he looks at me pleadingly—

"God, I'm right, aren't I?" he breathes.

My heart beats double time.

"No," I reply, but he doesn't believe me.

And I am a rat trapped in a cage. I want to run, but I can't.

No—there has to be a way out, there is always a way out—I close my eyes, trying to imagine that way into being. I live in desperation. I am halfway sleeping, halfway awake, caught in limbo, and I dream—

◆ ◇ ◆

I am standing at a fork in the road. Around me is a vast desolate desert. There is a signpost, but the signs are blank, and as far as the eye can see, both roads look exactly the same.

Diana is beside me at the crossroads. Silently, she holds my hand, and I feel her heartbeat echoing mine. It is a Tuesday afternoon.

"Have we fallen?" I ask blankly, remembering our previous conversation. She laughs. It is a child's question.

"We fell a long time ago," she tells me.

"Oh."

"Which way do you want to go?" she asks.

"What?"

"Which road do you want to take? It's your decision. I can't choose."

"They look exactly the same," I say helplessly.

"They do, don't they? But they're not, I swear."

"Do I have to pick one?"

"Yes, of course."

"Why can't you pick?"

"Because I'm not in charge. You are, when it comes down to it. I'm always you, but you're not always me."

"Which road do you want to take?"

"I'm not telling. You'll figure it out for yourself soon enough, I think."

"Why can't you tell me?"

"Because you have to pick for yourself. Those are the rules. That's the game."

Diana looks into the distance, steely-eyed.

"I don't want to play this game," I say.

"No one ever does," she replies.

◆ ◆ ◆

"You're the Perfect Killer, aren't you?"

I can't breathe.

My heart stops as Alex says those words, even though I knew they were coming, because him saying them is worse than anyone else saying them—so much worse, an exquisite and individual pain.

The last person on earth who believed me innocent is gone.

"No," I whisper. "No, I'm not."

"You *are*, though, aren't you? All this time. You're the Perfect Killer. It's why you wanted to be friends with me to begin with. It's why you could give me those little clues when we first met. It's why you got so upset that I was going to take that teacup. You tricked me the next time, somehow, when we went out to lunch, because you knew I wanted a DNA sample, right? All this time. All this time I kept defending you, and all this time you never deserved it."

This confrontation is so quintessentially Alex, I realize. He knows I'm a murderer, so he says it to my face. I don't know what he wants; I don't know what he hopes to gain. There are better ways to use this information than this. He could have brought a dozen men to arrest me on the spot—it would have been safer, smarter. There was probably justifiable legal cause for that somewhere, wasn't there? But he hadn't.

He looks at me helplessly.

He doesn't know what he wants either.

Regret, perhaps? Confession in the form of heartbroken apology? Maybe, perhaps, he wants to see me as Kit for as long as he can. And the moment he puts handcuffs on my wrists, he knows I will forever become the Perfect Killer in his eyes.

"How can you *say* that? I'm innocent. I'm only a teenage girl. You know that," I say. I hunch my shoulders over and put my hands in my pockets, trying to look small.

But even as I speak, Diana begins to simmer up within my chest.

"Kit, *don't lie to me!* Just admit it, just say it—"

He's on the verge of tears.

He *knows.*

All this time, everyone around him placed their suspicions on me, but he never believed it. But now that he has realized the truth on his own, realized it through his connection with me, he cannot be dissuaded.

I should have expected this. I should have known that I couldn't be safe from him forever. I should have remembered that he was the enemy.

I understand now what I didn't understand before. I understand that closeness cuts both ways. He has let me go from the police station and given me temporary freedom and a chance to run, but he has simultaneously become my downfall. Even if by some miracle we just go our separate ways here, simply, the moment he goes back to the station and looks at the case files, I am absolutely certain that he will be able to connect the Perfect Killer murders to me. He's clever that way, and he knows me too well. There is no escaping him.

I consider running anyway. My breaths come quickly. My legs tense, and I even begin to turn away toward the street before Alex realizes what I am doing and hisses, "Don't you *dare* run."

I freeze. Even now, I trust him enough to do as he says.

And I can't lie any longer.

I can't, I just can't.

No. I can. No. I can't do this, I can't, I can, I'm fine, no I'm not—I realize that I am shaking, I realize that I am angry and sad and weak and strong and I am a dichotomy of a human being and I am so far from whole and I can't think any longer and I feel like I am splintering into pieces—

And suddenly, like a snapping cord, I perceive everything with clear and utter rationality, without feeling. I see my two choices, the street signs of the two roads laid out before me. And I know that I must choose, and that I will be defined forever in the choosing.

One. I kill Alex. I run home and jump into the car I know my mother is already packing our bags into, and I take the ferry to France. I try to escape for a while longer, flee the country with my mother, while knowing that I have, by killing Alex, practically signed my own death sentence. One coincidental murder is unfortunate, two is an overly strange coincidence, but three is a pattern. I cannot hide forever, but I might be able to hide for a little while. They would hunt me down. I would have one more person's blood on my hands without a letter. A friend's blood, nonetheless. Some other police officer would catch me eventually and take the glory in Alex's place.

Two. I acknowledge what Alex already knows, let him arrest me and, probably, arrest my mother as well, in time. My father, of course, would be questioned but found innocent by ignorance. I surrender. I save myself more pain. I take the easy way out.

To kill or not to kill, that is the question. Either way, I lose.

The part of me that is Kit leans toward option two. I am unsteady on my feet.

But then Diana is there, raging toward option one, and I am suddenly feral.

I leap toward Alex. He is caught off-guard. I jam my shoulder into his sternum and knock him onto the pavement; he gasps as he hits the ground. And then I am upon him. I kneel halfway on his chest, swing my arm back so my hand brushes my forehead like Scarlett O'Hara—

But he yells and thrashes against me and flips me off him. I hit my back against the bench. I cry out and taste blood as it rises up in my mouth. Alex stands again and pulls a gun out from beneath his coat, eyes frantic; I scream and throw myself toward his calves, knocking him to the ground again.

I grasp for the gun, but he holds it away from me, trying

to get a good grip. And suddenly my hand is clasped over his, and we are both holding it.

"Let *go!*" he yells, but I don't listen.

I dig my nails into his hand and he pulls the trigger. The sound deafens me, but the bullet whizzes through empty air, harmless. I grip his hand firmly in mine and bash it against the ground, making him let go of the gun; the weapon skitters away over the pavement to a place far beyond our reach.

I claw at his skin, raking bloody gashes along his collarbone.

"How could you do it, Kit?" he cries out, and the sound echoes through me—*how how how how how?*

For a moment, I pin him to the ground, my knee grating against his sternum and my hands grinding his wrists against the pavement. I hover over his face, our noses almost touching, bleeding from my mouth.

"I'm not Kit," I hiss, "I'm Diana."

And he doesn't understand.

He struggles against me. I fight like my life is ending. We crash across the pavement, bruising ourselves, making ourselves bleed. He breaks my cheekbone. I break his arm. We paint the ground red. Neither of us feels any pain.

As the battle goes on, the eventual winner becomes clear. Every time we pause, I always have the advantage. He has brute strength, but I have years of skill and practice he can never hope to match. Every time we stop, I am hanging over him, or pinning him against something. He gradually tires, but strength still runs through me like an ocean current.

And eventually he just stops fighting.

We are settled against the base of the tall oak, crusted in blood and snow. I straddle his chest; I don't even touch his hands. He is weak and useless, and has no more strength to fight. So I just look down at him, and he cries at me.

Because he *is* crying. Slow, silent tears drift down his bloodied cheeks. Kit would understand those tears. But I'm not Kit. I'm Diana, and forever will be.

"How could you do this to me?" he sobs. "How could you just—just trick me, use me, and now—now, you're going to kill me, aren't you? I'll just become another piece in your game? How cold can you be? You can't get away with this again. You'll be caught this time. You know it too, don't you? The neighbors heard the gunshot. Look, all the lights are on. The police are coming here right now. They'll be here in a few minutes. There's nowhere to run."

Yes, they are coming for me. But Alex underestimates my prowess. If I end things, kill him quickly and run home now, my mother and I can still make it to the ferry before it leaves.

Maybe.

Time passes quickly. It's getting late. Things are becoming less certain, but maybe is still better than nothing. My mother is waiting for me, I know, standing anxiously with her arms crossed on the sidewalk, breath fogging the air. She won't leave without me, but if she waits too long, it may be too late. I have to return to her—I have to go home. I owe her that much.

I don't reply. I just stare into Alex's eyes. He stares back and shivers. The snow falls harder. I could kill him so easily, with a fist to the temple or a well-aimed punch to the nose, sending shards of his nasal bone up into his brain.

"I trusted you," he tells me. But no, he's wrong, he trusted Kit, and I am Diana.

And then for a flashing moment, I remember who he is. Alex. My Alex. Alex, so pure, so naive, so clever about the strangest things–Alex, who held me in his arms after Michael's murder, beautiful Alex, Alex who I have so terribly betrayed–Alex who I wanted, and even now, despite everything, in this terrible moment, continue to want–and it would be the easiest thing, wouldn't it, to lean toward him, to run my hands through his hair, to press my lips to his?

But no, I remind myself, looking into his eyes, seeing the way he has shattered, it's not easy. It's nowhere near easy. With things as they are, it's impossible.

What a pity it is that we've lived the lives we've lived.

And I remember the others, in a blinding blur. Henry Morrison, stupid Louisa, Dr. Marcell, Michael, Michael's mother, Maggie, Cherry Rose, my absent father, Maggie again, my halfway-defeated mother–who I realize I might never see again, at least not in the way it counts, depending on when the police get here. Escape is not guaranteed anymore, even if Alex dies.

Faces like ghosts. Faces I try to remember. Faces I try to anchor myself with. Faces I am forgetting, faces that are fading from me even as I try to cling to them.

Sitting atop Alex's chest, I bury my head in my hands and begin to cry.

I don't want to be Diana. I want to be Kit. I want the past.

I hear the far-off sound of sirens.

"Just kill me if you're going to do it. Get it over with," Alex pleads brokenheartedly, and he breaks my heart too. He will never forgive me. I can never forgive myself. There is no escape for me now, I know. Everything is over. I had my run. I was a murderer, a beautiful one, but I lived in a house of cards all my life—and now it's all coming back to punish me, and there is no escape.

I don't know if I'm Kit or Diana anymore. I hate Diana, but I don't know for sure if that's self-loathing.

I am standing at a fork in the road. Around me is a vast, desolate desert. There is a signpost, but the signs are blank, and as far as the eye can see, both roads look exactly the same.

I hold my hands out to Alex.

"Arrest me," I tell him. "I'm the Perfect Killer."

Acknowledgments

*F*irst of all, I would like to thank all the wonderful (my mom wanted me to use the word "incandescent" here) members of my family and extended family, who have supported me throughout this entire process; my parents' help was absolutely invaluable, and without them I'm pretty sure I would have had a heart attack or spontaneously combusted trying to manage everything. My brother and sister, too, were helpful in their own way. I'd like to thank them for encouraging me to get out of the house more and telling me that I need to get my driver's license instead of writing so much. (But seriously, they're great siblings.)

Another big thank-you goes out to the fabulous Alice Martell, who is tireless, enthusiastic, determined, and the best guide a teenage girl could ask for. I'd also like to say thank you to everyone at Katherine Tegen Books, especially Katherine herself, who is a wonderful person and editor, and, again, a great guide.

Thank you to anyone who has ever read this book in any form on its way to publication—this book would not have become what it is without your input.

Lastly, a very special thank-you goes to Bruce Vinokour, to whom I am completely indebted. Without him I would not be where I am today.